EVERYTHING DIES

Season One

T. W. MALPASS

Published by Sericia
© 2017 T. W. Malpass

ALL RIGHTS RESERVED. This book contains material protected under International and Federal Copyright Laws and Treaties. Any unauthorized reprint or use of this material is prohibited. No part of this book may be reproduced or transmitted in any form or by any means, electronic or mechanical, including photocopying, recording, or by any information storage and retrieval system without express written permission from the author / publisher. You can find news of upcoming titles by T.W. Malpass and sign up to the mailing list via
www.facebook.com/T.W.Malpass
Or
https://www.facebook.com/EverythingDiesSeries
Join him on Twitter: @TW_Malpass

This is a work of fiction. Names, characters, places and incidents are either products of the author's imagination or are used fictitiously. Any resemblance to actual events or locales or persons, living or dead, is entirely coincidental.

Cover Art: Michael Buxton
Technical Support: Guido Henkel

ISBN-13: 9781545560457
ISBN-10: 1545560455

Finite

Everything dies.

Even the maggots
and even the flies
that feed on the corpses
and chew out their eyes.

Everything dies.

Even volcanoes
that rumble and rise
to spew out their life fire
into the skies.

Everything dies.

Even your love
and that look of surprise.
Even blind passion,
that's fear in disguise.

Everything dies.

Excepting the hatred
and all of those lies;
like dark stars collapsing
to dust in the skies.

Everything dies.

Ian Futter.

Foreword

When I decided to write something in a more commercial sub-genre of horror, I spent a long time agonising over whether that should be zombie apocalyptic fiction. Not just because the market seems so saturated with it right now, but because of my own familiarity with the genre. My interest in zombies goes right back to the eighties, when it was much more of a niche.

About twenty years ago, I even attempted to write a series because I was so convinced that a world taken over by zombies would be compelling as an ongoing story. Not only did my idea come a little too soon, it became so mired in focussing on the mental illnesses developed by the survivors due to their isolation and the concept of sharing their world with walking corpses, it was virtually unreadable. It ended up being about a bunch of people who spent most of their time hidden away, slowly going insane and forgetting how to communicate with one another. Although that may be a more accurate depiction of the way in which humans would behave in that situation, believe me, it made for a mind-numbingly boring read.

Everything Dies is an all together different beast, and I don't mind telling you, it certainly does not reinvent the wheel when it comes to zombie fiction. In fact, it more or less sticks to the tried and trusted tropes of the genre, with a few notable exceptions. What I have tried to do is focus on creating interesting characters that you will care about or even love to hate, but their surroundings will probably act as a warm comfort blanket for avid fans of the reanimated dead.

I was also conscious that while this is indeed an ongoing series, many readers were getting a bit sick of the standard format. These books are written as a collection of episodes instead of traditional chapters. Each episode follows a particular arc and then ends with a hook into the next one – similar to a television show. Rather than the climax of the book ending on a cliff-hanger, it concludes in a way that should satisfy readers who wish to continue with the series and readers who don't. If you liked the book enough to finish it, but not enough to continue with subsequent entries, you hopefully won't feel as though you have completely wasted your time.

As always, thank you for joining me on this journey. I do hope you enjoy Everything Dies, and please share your thoughts on it with other readers – good or bad.

Stay classy, San Diego.

T.W. Malpass

Contents

Foreword	v
Episode One Homeland	1
Episode Two Teething Problems	55
Episode Three I Watched You Burn	85
Episode Four Rich Man's Burden	113
Episode Five Kill Switch	153
Episode Six The Breach	175
Episode Seven Bugs in a Jar	211
A Road Less Travelled	241
Episode Eight Frailty	249
About the Author	296

EPISODE ONE

Homeland

Chapter 1

Kristin Graham sat on the hill overlooking the east side of camp. She hugged herself as she felt the chill of early morning and wished she'd brought a jacket with her on her trip outside. She had to squint to watch the haze of the new day's sun creep over the rows of tents to her left – each roof emblazoned with the same logo: 'FEMA: U.S. DEPARTMENT OF HOMELAND SECURITY.'

The breeze caught a wisp of her blonde hair, blowing it across her face to expose the darker roots beneath. Three soldiers, leaving the confines of the barracks block, caught her eye. She focussed on the one striding out in front, heading towards the transit station. He was dressed in full combat uniform, but unlike the others, he wore a cap instead of a helmet. Kristin got to her feet and hurried down the hill in order to cut him off before he reached the heavily guarded gates of the transit.

When the officer peaked out from under the brim of his cap and saw her coming, he doubled his strides.

'Sergeant,' she called. 'Sergeant Banks.'

Banks turned to face her, his hands firmly clasped behind his back. 'Good morning to you too, Mrs. Graham.'

'If I didn't know better, I'd say you were trying to avoid me, Sergeant.'

'Now, why would I want to do that?'

Kristin squinted again, placing the edge of her hand over her brow to shield her eyes from the sunlight. 'Maybe because you still don't have an answer for me.'

Banks sighed. 'I've got an answer for you – it's just not the one you want to hear.'

She moved right up to him, purposely taking an extra step to breach his personal space. 'I just find it a little strange that we have hot running water, TV broadcasts, medical care, yet we have absolutely no contact with the outside world.'

'This is a contained unit, Ma'am. It's not connected to the main grid, and your TV ain't exactly cable. Besides, we have a SAT phone.'

'Good – you can let me use that.'

Banks shook his head, still enjoying their exchange. 'Military channels only.'

'Look, Sergeant. I know you're not a perennial hard-ass like Spears. You don't have to pretend to be for my benefit. My parents are two cities away, for Christ's sake.'

'Like I said, when it's safe to restore commercial communications, you will be the first of our residents to know.'

Kristin curled her lip in frustration and swivelled her hips to half-turn away from him.

Banks glanced impatiently to the transit gates. 'Your husband might get a real kick out of you being on his ass all the time, but I don't appreciate it so much. The rest of the folks in here are already gettin' whipped up over the food rationing. I haven't got time for another one of your court hearings, but when the lines are back up, you can make all the calls you want. You can even set the wheels in motion for whatever fancy human rights lawsuit you've got planned against the military for keeping you people oppressed and safe. Don't forget to mention the safe part, will you?'

'I don't forget things – occupational hazard.' Kristin stepped out of his space and started to walk away. 'I do enjoy our early morning chats.'

'I'll bet,' Banks said. 'Try not to obsess over it, Mrs. Graham. Enjoy the rest of the day with your family. At least you made it out of the infected zone together.'

Before he set off towards the transit again, she saw the sadness cast a fog over his eyes, and it made her feel a little guilty about their latest exchange.

She'd set him up as the antagonist from the moment she'd arrived. He was the mouthpiece for Major Spears, and all he'd given her so far was circumvention. Because of that, she'd never even considered that he might have a family somewhere too. She watched the guards open the armoured gate for him and imagined him sitting in his bunk after lights out, staring at a picture of his wife and children. It was the first time in all the time she had been there – almost three months – that she hadn't thought of him as just a brick wall she had to bang her head against every day.

The transit entrance clanged shut and Banks disappeared behind the steel bulk of the ATVS and transports. A fresh gust of wind kicked up the dust from the arid ground and Kristin blinked to stop it getting in her eyes. Although they were protected on all four sides by ten foot high perimeter fences and several guard towers, the camp always seemed so exposed in the morning, when most people were still asleep in their tents or containers. At least when the daily routines were in full swing and the kids were out playing, she could just about forget the horrors they had left behind in the infected zones, even if only for a moment at a time.

A patrolling soldier nodded in her direction as he walked by, prompting her to head back to the west side of the camp where the refugee accommodation was situated.

Chapter 2

Emily's head hung upside down from the edge of the sofa. The ends of her brown hair skimmed the floor, as she adjusted her eyes to the images on the TV set in the corner of the room. The middle-aged man sitting at the news desk reading the report was dressed in a pale grey suit. The colour of the suit was matched by the flecks in his hair; they reminded her of her daddy.

Reaching up to the sofa cushion, Emily fumbled around for the TV remote. She placed her hand on it and pointed it at the set and hit the volume button to increase the sound. She'd been upside down for so long that the blood had started to rush to her head, reddening her cute bubblegum cheeks. Due to the unusual position she'd adopted, she focussed on the top of the newsreader's head.

'President Palmer has pledged to release an unprecedented disaster relief fund to help the country rebuild its damaged infrastructure, it was reported today. This appropriation will allow FEMA to respond to any necessary challenges and aid a rapid recovery, according to a White House spokesman.' The report then cut to some pre-recorded footage of an aerial shot from a helicopter. It captured an incident unfolding on a road surrounded by woodland. At least twenty armed soldiers were positioned behind two armoured vehicles, pointing their rifles at the line of trees. At the bottom of the screen, the news ticker read 'Bend, Oregon'. The soldiers seemed to be readying themselves for something, and the same news reporter started to talk over the footage again. *'Elsewhere, National Guard teams have joined the clean-up operation to isolate and eliminate the outbreak within each confirmed infected zone.'*

Emily sighed, struggling to swallow on account of being upside down. 'This TV is so boring,' she said. 'All they ever do is repeat the same stuff.'

Vincent Graham glanced up from the sidebar in the kitchen at the back of their open plan container. 'That's just the news for you, honey,' he said, taking a meagre amount of butter and doing his best to spread it over one slice of toast. He placed the toast on a plate and carried it to his daughter. When he saw her tiny feet poking above the back of the sofa, he gave one of her ankles a tap. 'Sit up. Your breakfast's ready.'

She did as he asked and flipped herself the right way up to sit back on the sofa next to her stuffed rabbit toy, its left ear folded over itself like it had been badly chewed on. The young girl took one look at the toast, barely moistened by a knob of butter, and screwed up her nose. 'Dry toast again? Why can't I have Fruit Loops for a change?'

'As soon as the roads are clear and new shipments can get through,' Vincent said.

Emily looked up at him, rubbing the thighs of her purple onesie. Adopting a matter-of-fact tone, she asked 'are the monsters blocking them again?'

He wanted to reassure her, but no matter how hard he tried to smile, he couldn't. 'I'm afraid so.'

Emily turned her attention back to the news report. The soldiers' targets had already begun to emerge from the woodland. There were seven of them in total – each one ambling slowly, but with deliberate intent towards the armoured vehicles. *'General Reiser confirmed that the operation is moving forward with great success and stressed that the military response would remain proportionate,'* the reporter said. On his last word, the soldiers opened fire, tearing into the bodies of the amblers. Some fell immediately. The others took the bullets and kept on coming.

'I told you not to watch this stuff, Emmy. It will give you nightmares,' Vincent said. He grabbed the remote from the couch and switched the TV to the blank image of an external channel.

Emily shrugged her shoulders, gnawing away at the corner of her toasted slice of bread. 'It's OK, Daddy – I don't dream anymore.'

Vincent stared down at her for a moment. She didn't realise he was watching her, and he was glad about it. He feared the look in his eyes would make her feel anything but secure. 'I'll put on some cartoons for you instead.' He walked over to a pile of DVDs next to the TV stand. 'Which one?' he asked.

'Erm, you choose,' Emily said.

Vincent selected the case at the top of the pile and waved it in her direction. 'What about Dora the Explorer?'

She shook her head. 'Nah. I've seen it about fifteen times.'

'You've seen all of them about fifteen times.'

Emily threw herself back into the sofa cushion and giggled. 'Then get me a new one.'

Vincent smiled as he removed the Dora the Explorer disc from its case and slid it into the DVD player, built onto the side of the TV. 'It's funny. You never complained about watching them on repeat when we were at home.'

The girl laughed again, flashing both rows of her tiny teeth. There was a gap in the middle of the lower set where one had fallen out. She put her arms around her stuffed bunny and hugged him close as the opening titles of her cartoon began.

Before Vincent could return to the kitchen to tidy up, Emily put the piece of toast in her mouth and tugged at it. It caused her to wince sharply and she dropped it onto her plate, reaching up to the back of her right cheek. 'Ouch,' she said, almost bursting into tears.

'Your tooth again?' Vincent said.

She nodded, her bottom lip protruding.

'How much does it hurt on a scale of one to ten?'

'Seven,' she murmured.

'Seven doesn't sound too good. Daddy will get you another painkiller once you've finished your breakfast. Try to chew on the other side of your mouth for now.'

They both turned as they heard the rattle of the container's flimsy front door. Kristin stepped inside, still chilled by the early morning breeze.

'Hey. You didn't wake me,' Vincent said.

'You looked so peaceful. I didn't want to disturb you,' she replied.

'Hey, Mommy!'

When her daughter peered over the top of the sofa, Kristin instantly noticed the way she was frowning and how her cheeks were drooping. 'Hi, sweetie. What's wrong?'

Emily responded by pointing to the side of her mouth.

'That wisdom tooth is giving her some trouble,' Vincent said.

'When are we going be able to get her to a dentist, Vincent?'

Vincent walked over to his wife. 'It said on the bulletin that the military are really pushing them back now.'

'It has been saying the same thing on the news for the past two weeks, but nothing ever changes,' Kristin said.

'Before you go off, remember what I said. Try to focus on the fact that we're safe and together.'

'It's a bit late for that,' she said, taking off her jacket.

'Christ, you haven't been venting at Banks again, have you?'

'Somebody has to. We're cut off from the rest of the world with no new information. They rarely have the medical supplies people need, and then there's the rations.'

'The supply route will be cleared soon. You'll see,' Vincent said.

'Spears should appoint you as their official spokesman. You sound more convinced than they do.' Kristin threw her jacket over a chair and headed for the other rooms.

'Where are you going?'

'To take a shower,' she said.

'Fine. No problem.' Vincent stood in the middle of the room, deep in thought. Then he smiled and winked at Emily when he realised she was watching him. 'You're missing the best bit.' He gestured towards the cartoon playing on the TV.

Chapter 3

When Kristin opened her eyes it was gone three in the morning. Her mouth was dry. A hot chemical taste stained the back of her throat, like she'd been chewing on tyre rubber. She rolled over and felt around the mattress where Vincent should have been. The gentle whimper coming from the other room told her where he was. She crawled out of bed and reached for her night robe.

Vincent paced up and down on the synthetic fur rug in the living space, Emily pressed against his chest. Her butterball cheeks were damp with tears, but she still managed to smile when she saw Kristin wander in, rubbing the sleep from her eyes.

'Oh, sweetie.' Kristin brushed Emily's fringe away to touch the skin on her forehead. Her temperature was high. Not quite at the level of a fever, but she could barely keep her eyes open, let alone speak. 'How long have you been up with her?'

'Just over an hour,' Vincent whispered.

'Why didn't you wake me?'

'It's fine, honestly. I gave her another painkiller, but I don't think it worked too well. The fact she's so tired is the only thing that's helping,' Vincent said.

'If that bitch at the medicentre stonewalls us again, I swear to God I'll flip her upside down and shake her until something stronger falls out,' Kristin said.

'I'll see to it first thing in the morning.'

'Are you sure I can't do anything?'

Vincent smiled at her as he gently rocked their daughter to sleep. 'I got this.'

Kristin leaned in, planting a lingering kiss on his lips. 'I'm just going to...'

'Get some fresh air?'

Kristin's grin separated her lips and she kissed him again.

Vincent flicked his head to tell her to get going.

She wandered back into the bedroom to fetch her pack of cigarettes, then ventured outside. As soon as she'd sat down on the middle one of the steps leading up to their door, she struck up her lighter and pulled hard on her smoke. Placing her head between her knees, she held her breath, only rising to blow out the fumes when they started to tickle her throat.

The spotlights on the north fence gave a strange glow to the trees in the woodland beyond. Their tops swayed angelically. Everything on the outside seemed quiet – peaceful. It was hard to imagine that some kind of horrible death could be waiting for them there. She noticed the body of a guard shifting about in the right-hand tower close to the back exit, but when she examined the tower to the left side, it was empty.

The noise coming towards her almost caused her to drop her cigarette – the sound of feet dragging through the dirt. She relaxed as she recognised the familiar combat fatigues that could be seen on people all over the camp. This soldier wasn't walking in the usual rigid way. His body hung loose, like he didn't give a shit. Instead of being down by his side, his rifle was resting on his shoulder. He saw Kristin and altered his direction so he would pass by her on his patrol.

As he approached, she realised her legs were slightly apart and pulled her robe over her knees. 'You scared me,' she said.

The private's expression was sullen, his face squashed into his tightly strapped helmet. 'No one outside after nine, Ma'am.'

'I'm sitting on the step of my trailer.'

The soldier took two more paces forward, sliding the gun into both hands, pointing it at the floor in front of her. 'You gonna make me repeat myself?'

Kristin straightened up, finding it hard to believe what she'd just heard. There were so many things she could say – wanted to say, but she bit her tongue. Taking one more drag on her cigarette, she flicked it at the soldier's feet, so the embers bounced across the toes of his boots, and marched back inside the container.

Vincent and Emily were absent from the living space. She walked over to the table where they ate their meals and slumped into one of the chairs. A collection of Emily's crayon drawings were scattered over the table top. Kristin picked one and held it up to the light. As soon as she examined it she burst into tears, burying her face in her hands. She tried to cry quietly, but in the confined space the sound carried.

Vincent crept in from Emily's bedroom and sat in the chair next to her. 'What is it?' he said.

'I saw this picture and realised I'd gotten so caught up in this place, I'd forgotten about Tugger,' she sobbed.

'Good ol' boy,' Vincent said.

'We left him out there all alone.'

'The border patrol would have shot us if we'd tried to force him through the checkpoint. You can't blame yourself.' Vincent grabbed her by the hand. 'Maybe he made it to the woods. You know how much he used to love the woods. Or maybe someone else, another family, picked him up and took him elsewhere.'

Kristin shook her head. 'That asshole guard. He could see how much it tore Emily apart and he couldn't turn a blind eye, even when everything had gone to hell.'

'He was just a boy, Kris. A scared boy following orders.'

'Like I needed another reason to hate the military.' She rubbed angrily at her sore eyes and then slammed the flat of her hand on the table. 'What the hell are we doing here, Vincent?'

'Taking a breath? Trying to hang on to what's left?'

'What is left?'

Vincent gazed at her longingly. 'We are.' He kissed her forearm and she responded by running her hands through his dark, greying hair.

Chapter 4

The next morning, Emily was the only one who looked remotely ready to start the day. Both Vincent and Kristin had grey smudges beneath their eyes and hang dog expressions.

Vincent brushed against his wife on his way out. 'I'll see you soon.' He led Emily by the hand from the container block, heading to the northeast corner of the camp where the medical centre stood.

It was gone eight a.m., so the areas open to the refugees were starting to fill with people, mainly children running around and playing on their bikes and scooters. Once Emily had stopped waving back to her, Kristin took a stroll south towards the transit and military barracks. Before she could get clear of the containers, a thick-set man with thinning brown hair clamped his eyes on her. He quickened his pace to catch her up, struggling to run in his open-toed sandals.

'Hey, Graham,' he shouted.

She recognised him on account of his shorts and footwear. His family were staying in one of the containers a few doors away from theirs. He had a gut that hung lower than the seam of his shirt, and he always seemed to be pouring with sweat. She noticed that his ankles were swollen to twice their normal size, hence the sandals. 'You goin' down to the barracks again?' he said.

'It's Kyle, isn't it? I'm not sure why it's any of your business what I do with my day.'

'It might be when what you're doin' affects the rest of us,' Kyle said.

'Excuse me?'

He waddled up to her, pulling a dirty handkerchief from his front pocket to wipe the perspiration away from his forehead. 'Human rights lawyers. Making money by defending some diaper-head across the other side of the world against patriots who spilled blood for this country.'

'Wow. You come up with that all by yourself?'

'I ain't the only one who is sick of your bullshit.'

'My bullshit, as you so eloquently call it, is about trying to make things better for all of us here. Don't you think we deserve a little more transparency? I don't see anyone else asking the questions,' Kristin said.

Kyle put his handkerchief away, even though his face was still as shiny with sweat as always. 'I know most folks are just grateful to have a roof over their heads. I know those soldiers have lost men keepin' us safe. I know if you keep pushin', they might decide not to try so hard next time they go out to clear the roads of infected.'

Kristin stood her ground. She'd dealt with plenty of Kyles before, especially in her profession, and she wasn't about to be intimidated. 'I don't think you've thought this through. The soldiers need those supplies too. You think they'd starve themselves over a petty dispute? You know, I'm sure I read somewhere that a lack of nutrition can lead to intense paranoia.'

'Well ain't that nice?' Kyle stepped up to her, so close Kristin almost gagged from the pungency of his body odour. 'You may think you're somethin' special on the outside, but behind these fences, you're just another mouth to feed – a big fuckin' mouth that needs to learn when to stay shut.'

'Might wanna step back there, sailor.' The female voice came from behind Kristin. She turned to see a black woman fixing a steely glare upon Kyle.

'Why don't you mind your own? I don't know you, lady,' Kyle said.

The woman seemed unperturbed by his comment. 'Unless you want to get acquainted with me a little better, I suggest you take your anger someplace else.'

Kyle took a second to ponder her advice, and noted how much her stare burnt right through him. He then sneered at them both and pointed an accusing finger at Kristin. 'This camp don't need another Erin Brockovich. We just need some food in our bellies.'

The black woman looked him up and down and settled on his bulging gut. 'Some of us could go longer than others.'

Kyle puckered his lips to respond, but thought better of it and stormed back towards the container block.

As Kristin opened her mouth to speak, the woman cut her off. 'I get it. You didn't need anyone running to your rescue. I just get a kick out of pissing on morons like that.'

Kristin smiled and held out her hand. 'I'm Kristin.'

'Raine. Raine Miller.' She shook her hand, but avoided eye contact. Kristin thought she looked like she was dressed for a building site. Her loose-fitting combat pants were strapped tight at their bottoms with work boots. Her over-sized knitted sweat shirt had a round, open neck, revealing the straps of the black vest underneath and her firmly sculpted deltoid muscles.

'I don't think I've seen you around before,' Kristin said.

'I've seen you,' Raine replied.

'That right?'

'Some of what that asshole said wasn't far off the mark, y'know. A bunch of Oorahs cooped up in a powder keg like this aren't gonna take too kindly to a woman calling bullshit on them.'

'You think I'm wrong doing what I'm doing?'

'Didn't say that. Just might be a smarter way of going about it,' Raine said.

Kristin was surprised by her new acquaintance – in a good way. They had spent the best part of three months in the camp and she could already tell this woman was by far the most interesting person she'd met there. 'Will you walk with me?' she said.

Raine shrugged. 'I was heading in that direction anyway.'

As they got closer to the barracks, the numbers of kids running around diminished. The soldiers would often discourage them from getting too close to their quarters. In the beginning, they had been much more responsive to the refugees, but lately Kristin had observed a significant change in their behaviour in the last couple of weeks in particular.

'Are you here with your family?' Kristin asked.

Raine shook her head. 'No family. I'm over there.' She glanced to the rows of tents on their left.

'I have a husband and an eight-year-old daughter. We managed to get out together.'

'I don't envy you then,' Raine said.

'Why?'

'Because it's hard enough to look out for yourself in this mess, without having to worry about other people.'

'That's an interesting way of looking at things.'

'Or a realistic one.'

Kristin gazed into the dark chasms of her eyes. The intensity burning there was what had attracted her to the no-nonsense woman in the first place, but there was something broken there as well. Kristin wasn't sure if she wanted to know its origin. 'So, are you going to show me a better approach to getting answers?'

Raine looked up to the perimeter fence at the front of the camp, just past the transit. 'That guard tower – tell me what you see.'

Kristin examined it, and the outline of the figure inside. 'I see an armed lookout.'

Raine adjusted her focus to the tower on the other side of the transit. 'What about the next tower?'

'It looks empty.'

'That's because it is. If you walk around the entire camp, you'll notice that every other guard post is empty too, but that's only been the case for the past two weeks. Before that, every post was manned around the clock.'

'Maybe the surrounding areas are more secure than they used to be. They said they had made headway clearing the roads.'

'Maybe,' Raine said. 'Or maybe there just aren't enough soldiers to go round anymore.'

'There have been more going out to open the supply route.'

'That's what they say, but don't you think they'd be coming back by now, or at least be on rotation?'

'They're abandoning us?' Kristin said.

'Either that or they're in a much bigger shit storm out there than they're letting on.'

Kristin scanned the outskirts of the barracks to try and distinguish if the amount of men on show had lessened. 'Sounds like you trust them less than I do.'

'I don't trust anyone when they're armed to the teeth, stressed out and low on food. Besides, it's not just the military we should be worrying about,' Raine said. 'For the most part, we have no idea who we've been trapped with in here. When strangers are forced into close proximity, it's inevitable their lives will collide in some way.' She turned to a section of fence adjacent to a container that had been converted into a makeshift school for the younger kids. Sitting against it was a young man in a black hooded top. The hood was pulled up over his head, but his lips were still visible. He was cross-legged and rocking back and forth, and appeared to be chanting something under his breath, picking up handfuls of dirt and watching it slip through his fingers as he did so. 'Don't know about you, but I don't want to have their lives crashing into mine.'

Raine's words and the sight of the strange young man sent a chill through Kristin's body. The disturbing thought was closely followed by the distant sound of an engine.

'There.' Raine pointed to the road leading to the front entrance of the camp. The vehicle travelled at speed, kicking up dust as it headed towards them.

Chapter 5

Vincent finally reached the front of the line in the medical tent. The stiff-looking woman behind the counter seemed as unapproachable as could be – clad head-to-toe in combat fatigues like their other guardians. He'd never seen her before, and he was certain that spelt trouble.

Before he stepped up to the counter, he glanced behind him to the entrance. Emily stood just outside. She was pushing the limits of his instruction to stay close by, but that was Emily. For the time being she was relatively free of pain. However, even at that distance, Vincent could see the swelling forming on her right cheek. She stared at the ground in front of her, kicking at one of the tent pegs with her tiny red boots.

'Are you with us, sir?'

Vincent turned back to the counter and was greeted by the stony expression of the female soldier. 'Yes. It's my daughter. She has an abscess under one of her molars. We've tried her with painkillers, but it just isn't going to settle. Ideally, the tooth needs to come out. Of course, I understand you can't do that right now, so I was hoping you had some antibiotics to fight the infection in the meantime.'

'I'm afraid that's not possible. We're down to the bare minimum here as it is,' the woman said.

'Look, I know how it is, but this is the third time the tooth has flared up and it's absolute torture for a child of her age.'

'I appreciate your situation, sir, but we don't have the resources to deal with it at this time.'

Vincent let out a despairing breath and drew the flat of his hand over his hair. 'Can you at least give me some stronger painkillers?'

'Nothing that would be manageable for a little girl. Try combining Paracetamol and Ibuprofen.'

'We've already tried that and it barely makes a dent. She needs proper medical attention. If the abscess bursts and she swallows the pus, she could go into toxic shock.' Vincent noticed the uncomfortable shift in the woman's stance and then laughed ironically. 'Jesus. You aren't even a doctor, are you?'

The woman straightened up again and looked from under the bill of her cap at him. 'I'm a qualified chemist.'

'That's just great. When's Doc Sanders coming back?'

The woman paused for thought. 'Doctor Sanders was killed during an operation in one of the infected zones over a week ago.'

'He's dead? Why wasn't there an announcement?' Vincent said.

'Lots of our personnel have died during this conflict, and we are not obligated to notify the public every time it happens.'

'You at least have a duty of care if it directly impacts us.'

The woman sniffed and attempted to rein in the frustration that she clearly felt. 'We have everything under control. Once the roads are clear, we have a backup doctor and a dentist standing by.'

Vincent shook his head in disbelief and ran both hands through his silver-flecked hair. 'You seem to have a lot riding on clearing these roads.'

'Points of access are crucial during any conflict, sir. Now, I can give you some more of the medication you already have, but unless you want me to go into your daughter's mouth myself with nothing more than a pair of pliers and good intentions, I suggest you sit tight and let us do our jobs.'

He resisted the temptation of saying what he really wanted to say, instead turning his back on the medical counter all together. He soon forgot about the less than hospitable substitute doctor when he caught sight of the man bending down at the entrance of the tent, deep in conversation with Emily.

Vincent rushed over and took her by her arm. 'Emily, I thought I told you to stay inside where I could see you?'

'I was just talking, Daddy,' Emily said, frowning.

The young man stood up and beamed at him. He couldn't have been any older than eighteen, but he towered over Vincent. He'd clearly been exercising. Moisture had soaked into his grey sweat shirt, creating a large ring around his neck and armpits. His eyes were a piercing emerald blue, his skin fresh and healthy. He was good-looking in the classical sense. The kind of student who would date the head cheerleader at school. 'You have any luck?' he asked.

'Huh?' Vincent replied.

'Emily was just telling me about her tooth.'

Vincent relaxed from his paternal reflex and smiled. 'Oh, I got the same answer we get for everything around here.' He offered his hand to the boy. 'Vincent Graham.'

'Adam Willard. Pleased to meet you, sir.' Adam shook it and Vincent was surprised by the strength of his grip.

'I don't think I've seen you around West Block before.'

'I'm staying just around the corner in one of the tents. It's where they put the singles.'

'Your family?'

Adam struggled to maintain his smile at the question. 'My folks – they were visiting my uncle in Montana when things started to escalate. I've not heard from them since.'

'I'm so sorry to hear that.'

Adam shrugged. 'It's OK, Mr. Graham. There's a good chance they made it to the camp in Helena.'

'Yeah, I'm sure they did.' Vincent felt an instant connection to the kid. He couldn't imagine what it must be like for a teenager to be separated from their parents during the crisis. 'How have you found it around here so far?'

'It's OK. Could be worse, right? Most people keep themselves to themselves, and I understand that. They are just looking out for their families. I tend to keep myself busy by going for runs.'

'Keeping fit's not a bad idea.' Vincent put his hand on Emily's head and pulled her close.

Adam looked down at her and the swelling around her cheek. 'Listen, Mr. Graham. I'm on my way back to my tent. If you'll take a walk with me, I think I might have something you will appreciate.'

It wasn't like he had anything more to say to the stiff in the medical station, and the young man's offer intrigued him. 'Sure. Lead the way,' he said.

Vincent and Emily followed their new friend to a collection of tents close to the children's recreation area.

'Hold on one sec.' Adam ducked inside the flaps of his tent and emerged a moment later, clutching something in his right hand. He moved up close to Vincent and forced the object into his grasp.

Vincent glanced down at the brown-coloured bottle and read the label. 'Amoxicillin? Where did you get these?'

'I was studying at Minnesota State, and I had a bad case of bronchitis just before everything went to hell. You know how it is in school – every kid goes home and then arrives at the start of a new term to spread their germs. Anyway, I had a further course prescribed because I couldn't shift the damn thing. They happened to be in my backpack when I was relocated to the camp. I figured I'd keep it quiet. Never know when they will come in handy. I guess it's a good job I bumped into Emily today.'

'Adam, this is... I don't know how to thank you,' Vincent said.

'It's nothin'. Just remember to say hi when you see me around.'

'We will. Won't we, Emily?'

'Sure thing,' Emily said, with a grin.

'See?' Adam said. 'She's feeling better already.'

'So you were studying at Minnesota State?' Vincent asked.

'That's right, sir. Even got selected for the Mavericks.'

'I had... have a brother who taught history there. Frank Graham.'

'I remember him. Never had any classes with him, but he seemed like a good guy. He sure loves basketball.'

Hearing someone talk about his big brother again cast a warm feeling over Vincent. He missed Frank more than anyone. 'He sure does.'

Their conversation was cut short when they noticed most of the refugees around them were heading towards the south end of the facility. Vincent peered over the tops of the tents to the main entrance. A large truck had pulled up outside, and a crowd had already gathered by the transit gates. They were being forced back by a detail of soldiers. 'What the hell is going on down there?'

'Beats me. Let's go check it out,' Adam said.

Chapter 6

Kristin and Raine allowed the ravenous crowd to flow past them. Raine glared sideways at the people who bumped her shoulders on their way to the transit gates.

The sizeable truck that had approached from the main access road had turned around before being ushered inside the facility, and was now waiting to roll into the refugee zone.

'This is gonna get messy,' Raine said.

Kristin acknowledged her with a look, closing her hands into fists to brace herself for an even greater surge of bodies. The gates began to open and eight soldiers marched out in tight formation, forcing the baying rabble of old and young back the way they had come. One male refugee tried to break through the line. He was swiftly knocked to the ground by the butt of a rifle.

As soon as the armed guards had created enough space, the truck started crawling through in reverse. The refugees reached out their arms to touch the vehicle, even though they were too far away.

'It's best we hang back. See what kind of mayhem breaks out first,' Raine said.

'I'm not going to argue with you,' Kristin replied.

By the time the truck had fully emerged from the transit station, the crowd was surrounding it on both sides, still being held off by the military. The canvas at the back was pushed aside to reveal more soldiers inside the main compartment. One of them held up his hands to try and quieten the shouting and pleading. 'Folks, please. If we can all stay calm, we can do this much easier. There's absolutely no need to push and shove each other. There's enough for everyone. Whether you're in the front row or right at the back, you will all get a package.'

Raine smirked at his announcement. 'Watch this,' she said.

No sooner had the man started handing out packages, when another huge swell of desperate bodies slammed against the sides of the truck. The soldiers on the outside fought hard to hold the line. One fell to the ground and was immediately hauled to his feet by his colleagues. Just as it seemed the rioters would punch their way through, the burliest looking member of the unit lost his patience and fired off a single rifle round into the air. The majority of the crowd scurried back, some falling and getting their legs tangled in the process.

The spokesman in the truck cursed under his breath and addressed the refugees. 'Are we finished? Now, let's try this again in an organised fashion.'

This time there was at least some semblance of civil behaviour. The soldiers were able to hand the packages down without a major incident.

'Kind of hard to tell the difference, isn't it?' Raine said.

'From what?' Kristin said.

'Between them and those things out there.' Raine gestured towards the perimeter fence.

'Can't say I'd know. I've not seen one of them, except on TV.'

'Then you're lucky, or maybe not.'

Kristin wasn't exactly sure what she meant by that, but it didn't sit well with her, and she had a feeling it wasn't supposed to.

Amongst the stragglers watching from the back with them, Raine noticed the man in the hoodie who she'd pointed out to Kristin earlier. His hood was still pulled up, but the end of his nose and chin protruded from the shadows. His skin looked pale, his chin darkened by dense stubble. Although his top was baggy, Raine could tell his frame beneath it was painfully thin.

He wasn't rocking or chanting anymore, but he was just as jittery as before, tapping both hands against his thighs and bouncing up and down on the balls of his skate shoes.

The man in the truck had held true to his word. The calmer the refugees were, the faster they obtained their packages and dispersed. The soldiers even accommodated those who asked for extra rations for loved ones who weren't present. Just as the private had said, there was more than enough to go around.

Before long, Kristin and Raine found themselves at the front, inches from the back of the truck. Kristin gazed over to the barracks. A man was standing on the roof of the large container, overseeing the disposition of food supplies. She recognised him as Sergeant Banks. When Banks noticed her, he promptly turned his back and walked away. She was certain he would take great pleasure in telling her that she should have listened to him in the first place instead of causing unrest. That was for another day though. Right now, the only thing that mattered was getting supplies to feed her family – for the next week at least.

'Ma'am,' one of the soldiers in the truck said, handing her a pack.

'Oh, thank you,' Kristin said. 'I'm here with my daughter and husband.'

'Two more for you then.' The private collected two extra and passed them down.

'I'll wait for you,' Kristin said to Raine as she moved away from the depleted congregation.

Before Raine could get to the front, she saw the young guy in the hoodie reach up for his supplies. As soon as he had gripped the package he froze, staring at the soldier who was in the process of handing it over; it was as if he'd pulled a gun and aimed it at his face. He seemed older than his years because he was so gaunt. His deathly-pale complexion only accentuated the sense of heroin chic. Even out of the shadows, the dark patches around his eyes were thick and ingrained.

'Sir, is there a problem?' the soldier said.

He didn't say a word; his eyes were fixed in terror.

'You feeling OK?'

All of a sudden, he came to his senses, snatching the pack to his chest. 'Yes. I'm fine.'

Only three stuttered words, but enough for Raine to establish that he wasn't a native – British, possibly.

He realised that Raine had joined the soldier in scrutinising his behaviour and turned tail, staggering off in the direction of the prayer room. Raine watched him leave, and eventually he cast a nervous glance back at her.

By the time she'd collected her pack and found Kristin, she'd been joined by Vincent, Emily and their new friend Adam.

'Raine, this is my husband Vincent and my daughter, Emily.'

Raine dipped her head towards Vincent and looked down to Emily. The little girl clung to her father's shirt-sleeve.

'Raine has been looking out for me during the scramble for resources,' Kristen joked.

'Yeah, rather you than me by the sounds of it,' Vincent said. He smiled at Raine, hoping for some recognition, but the woman's thoughts were elsewhere.

'Oh, and this is a new friend of Emily's,' Kristin said, pointing to Adam. 'I can't thank you enough for what you've done for her.'

'It's no problem, Mrs. Graham. It was a lucky coincidence that I had what she needed,' Adam said.

'Please – call me Kristin.'

'Don't bother,' Vincent said laughing. 'I've tried telling him and he insists on calling me Mr. Graham.'

'Force of habit,' Adam said. He peered over to the truck and the dwindling numbers of people there. 'Well, I better get my food, I guess.'

'You go for it,' Vincent said.

'See ya.' Adam wasted no time in jogging over to get his rations.

Kristin, relieved that they were finally getting what they needed, squeezed her husband's hand. 'Shall we head back?'

'Sure,' Vincent said.

'Raine, will you walk back with us?'

'Nah, you go. I'll catch up with you later.' Raine's attention was still focussed on the east side of camp.

'OK. You're welcome to drop by any time.'

'I might just do that.' With that, Raine strolled off, clearly distracted.

In jest, Vincent curled his lips to pull a face. 'You certainly make some interesting friends, honey.'

'Shut up,' Kristin said, slapping his broad chest. 'She's nice – in a distant sort of way.'

'I think she's mean,' Emily piped up confidently.

'Why do you say that, Em? Vincent said.

'She looks at people funny.'

'Can't argue with you there, but it doesn't always mean something bad. It could be that she's just shy or guarded when she meets someone new.'

'What's "guarded?"'

'When you get older, it can change the way you approach new people,' Vincent said.

'When I'm guarded, I don't stare at people like that,' Emily said.

'But you, my little bundle of joy, don't have the withering burden of experience. Now let's get you back so you can take your medicine.'

Emily screwed up her face, as if she could already taste the pill in her mouth. 'It really doesn't hurt at all anymore.'

'I'll bet it doesn't,' he said. Vincent and Kristin shared a smile and escorted their daughter back to the container.

Chapter 7

Vincent watched Emily gobble up the last few crumbs of her cookie and set the beaker of water on her knee. She rolled one half of a tablet between her fingers.

'Don't be such a drama queen. It's not that bad,' Vincent said.

'My throat's too small,' Emily whined.

'It's not too small. Emily – it's not. Just don't think about it. Put it on the back of your tongue, throw your head right back and drink.'

Emily frowned at him as if the tooth, the pill and them being at the camp were all his fault. She then popped the pill in her mouth and took a gulp of water. She shut her eyes tight, her cheeks expanding like a bull-frog. At one point, it seemed that the tablet would come flying out and the water with it. Finally, she gained the courage to swallow; after a couple of seconds of clawing at her throat, the discomfort wasn't quite as bad as she'd expected.

Vincent pretended to look shocked. 'Guess what? You're not choking.'

Emily shook her head in disapproval of his mockery. 'If I do start, you'll be the first to know about it.'

They both heard Kristin giggling in the background. She held the back of her hand up to her mouth, a carving knife dangling loosely in her grasp. She stood in the kitchen area, preparing a meal from one of the ration packs.

Vincent caught a whiff of what she was chopping. 'Wow. What is that?'

'Smell good?' she asked.

'Yes, ma'am.'

Kristin smiled and examined their much needed supplies. 'We've got peppers, onions, a clove of garlic, cheese, powdered eggs. Only cured meat, I'm afraid, but once I've mixed it in with the other stuff, you'll never know the difference.'

Vincent stared across at her, his arms folded. 'Have I ever told you how much I love you?'

Kristin made a face as she tried to fight the vapours of freshly chopped onion. 'All the time, but I could stand to hear it again.'

'Woah, Mommy's getting a big head,' he said, looking to Emily, who hadn't taken her eyes off the TV screen since swallowing her medication.

'Perhaps she needs some of Adam's pills,' she said.

Vincent and Kristin dissolved into laughter and shared a long look. It suddenly dawned on them they'd been caught up in a moment where they'd forgotten about their situation – about what lay outside the fences of the camp, waiting.

Kristin gazed down at the vibrant colours that littered the chopping board. It was amazing to see real food again. 'I wish I'd cooked more at home. I used to love it, but when I got home from work most days...'

'Most evenings,' Vincent said.

'I was always so tapped out. At least I was useful then. I feel more like a fifth wheel around here.'

Vincent made his way over to the kitchen and leaned over the breakfast bar. 'Crazy talk. I need you. Emily needs you.'

She brushed away the grey flecks of hair that she found so attractive from his forehead and lowered her voice. 'You two would do fine without me.'

'Stop,' Vincent said.

'You don't understand – it gives me comfort to know that.'

He sighed. 'Fine. Be comforted, but just know, we're not letting you go anywhere.' He stretched across to kiss her, almost losing his balance in the process. 'I know one person who seems to cope well on her own.'

'Who?' Kristin said.

'Your new friend.'

'Don't be cruel. She's just...' she searched her mind for the right word.

'Intense?'

'Intense is a good description.'

'I am the writer,' Vincent said.

'Well, I like her.'

'Invite her over for dinner then.'

'You think I should?' Kristen said.

'Why not? There's enough to go around.'

'Oh, not this again,' Emily said, cursing at the television.

Vincent waddled comically into the living quarters. 'What is it, honey?'

'The stupid news.'

'A little tip for you, Emmy. You stop turning the stupid news on, you stop having to watch it.' He collected the remote from the arm of the sofa and pointed it at the set to turn it off. Before he hit the red button, he noticed something curious about the broadcast – something familiar. A sentence from the news reporter he'd heard before.

The aerial shot of the woodland road in Bend, Oregon flashed up on the screen, showing soldiers poised behind their vehicles for the oncoming attack. The reporter's words rang true again. They seemed to play in slow motion in Vincent's head. *'Elsewhere, teams of the National Guard have joined the cleanup operation to isolate and eliminate the outbreak within each recognised infected zone.'*

'It's the same thing,' Vincent said under his breath.

'You say something?' Kristin called from the kitchen.

Emily's grin exposed each one of her delicate teeth. 'I told you so, Daddy.'

'The news report – It's the same as yesterday,' he said.

'So? That's not unusual – it wasn't, even before the outbreak,' Kristin replied.

'No. I know, but this whole news feed...'

'What about it?' Kristin put the knife down on the chopping board, disturbed by his unease.

'Everything about this, right down to the words the reporter is saying; it's exactly the same broadcast as yesterday.'

Chapter 8

The young man in the hoodie came to a stop between a row of tents and the shower block, just out of sight of the guard towers on the back fence. Raine had managed to follow him without being detected and was now hiding behind the edge of a shower container.

The man scouted in every direction for witnesses. The majority of refugees had already retired to their accommodation to prepare what would be their first decent meal in weeks. He never noticed Raine lurking around the corner and proceeded to fall to his knees in the dirt. He placed the grey, unopened package next to him and rolled up his sleeves. The dirt was loose and easy to cast aside. Using both hands, he dug a hole, burrowing away like a frightened rabbit until it was at least a foot deep. Once he'd attempted another scan of the area, he grabbed the package and shoved it in its fresh grave, filling it in with the pile of dirt and trying to press it flat.

When he was satisfied with how it looked, he jumped to his feet, rubbed his dirty hands on the front of his pants, and started to stroll back towards the centre of camp. He didn't get far. Raine startled him by jumping out from behind the shower block. She grabbed him by the front of his hoodie and threw his slight frame up against the wall of the container.

'What the hell was that?' she demanded through gritted teeth.

'What was what?' It was clear to Raine now that he had an English accent.

'Unless you're one strange-looking squirrel, you're not coming back for that later.'

Recovered from the initial ambush, he stared at her with a sense of calm. 'I guess I just don't like chicken and rice.'

'You never even opened it. What do you know?' Raine lifted him away from the container and slammed his back into it again.

The man half-smiled. 'The same as you. I've seen you watching them. If this had happened a week ago, we wouldn't still be having this conversation: a guard would have been here already, asking you why you are bullying me.'

'You haven't answered my question. Why bury the food?'

'You tell me?'

Raine paused for thought, coming to the conclusion she might have already guessed. 'It's poisoned?'

'She shoots, she scores,' the man said.

'Bullshit.' Raine scowled and the man looked down at her own pack, which was tucked into the front of her combat pants.

'Feel free to sample the military cuisine. I hear the pecan and chocolate chip cookies are just to die for.'

Raine pushed him aside and started to walk away. 'Don't stray too far. I'll be back for you.'

'Where are you going?' the man said, straightening his clothes.

'To stop someone making a mistake.'

'You're going to spread our little secret?'

She ignored him and carried on.

'You might want to rethink that.' He unintentionally raised his voice, then glanced nervously behind him to ensure he hadn't alerted their protectors. He took one step forward, as if he intended to follow her, but instead slipped both hands inside his pockets, lowered his head, and skulked off in the opposite direction.

Chapter 9

Vincent was washing the pans in the basin as Kristin served up the first hot meal they'd had in almost two weeks. 'Leave them,' she said. 'Eat before it goes cold.' She picked a slice of green pepper from one of the plates and crunched into it.

Emily sat at the dining table expectantly, knife and fork already held upright. Kristin saw how grateful she looked and smiled. 'Vincent, if you don't sit down soon, I think she'll finish yours too.'

The family jumped in unison as the door to their container burst open and Raine forced her way inside.

'What the hell are you doing?' Vincent said, shielding his daughter.

Raine ignored him and pointed to Kristin's food. 'Have you eaten any of that yet?'

'Raine, what's going on?'

'Have you!'

'What? No, I had a couple of mouthfuls while I was preparing it,' Kristin said.

'Then go into the bathroom and make yourself puke.'

'Huh?'

'Stick your fingers down your throat. Right now!'

Vincent moved towards their intruder. 'Get out of here, you maniac. You're scaring my daughter. You're scaring us.'

Emily sat rigid in her seat, her eyes fixed on Raine.

'She should be scared,' Raine said. She then spied the small plate littered with cookie crumbs on the arm of the sofa. 'What's that?'

'Emily had something to eat before her pill,' Kristin said.

'From the package?'

'No. Will you please tell us what's going on?'

'The new food is poisoned.'

'By whom?' Vincent said, about ready to drag her to the barracks to report her.

'The same people who gave it to us.'

'The military? Spears? Don't be ridiculous,' he said.

'Are you willing to take the chance that I'm lying?'

'I'm going to take the chance that you're crazy. Didn't I tell you, Kris? Even I never suspected this. You need help. Now get out before I throw you out,' Vincent said.

Kristin stared into Raine's eyes. The intensity burning behind them did not look like madness to her. She pushed past her husband and rushed into the bathroom.

Vincent stood within touching distance of Raine. They remained silent, listening to Kristin heave up the unsubstantial contents of her stomach. She emerged a few minutes later, a little paler and wiping the sticky remnants from her lips.

Confused, Vincent looked to his wife for reassurance. 'Kris, wha—'

'I'm fine,' she snapped. 'So we'll hear you out, but you better start making sense or we'll march you out of here and you'll be arrested for trespassing.'

'You go into those barracks and you'll never come out again,' Raine said. 'I have someone in the camp – a source. I don't know how he knows, but he knows.'

Vincent rolled his eyes. 'That's it?'

'No, that's not it.'

'Why are we even entertaining this, Kris? You barely know this person.'

'The number of soldiers in this camp is decreasing by the day. They are leaving in fours and fives in the middle of the night and not coming back. There aren't even enough to regularly man all the guard posts anymore,'

Raine said, looking at Kristin. 'Don't you think it's strange that they have supposedly cleared the roads in order to get all this food to us, and yet not a single unit has returned?'

'They're probably regrouping at the army base in Johnston,' Vincent said.

'If the base in Johnston is still standing, they'll be fortifying it for the long haul; they won't be coming back here.'

Vincent threw a hand up in a dismissive gesture. 'More guess-work?'

'What about the TV, Vincent?' Kristin said. 'What you said about the broadcasts repeating themselves?'

Raine nodded. 'They've been recycling the same shit on that fake news channel for weeks. They wanted us to think they had everything under control, so that everyone would be compliant and unsuspicious for just long enough.'

'So that's it then,' Vincent said. 'All of those kids out there, who probably have family in camp just like this one, have decided they're going to arbitrarily exterminate the very people they were assigned to protect?'

'Only the officers and a few trusted men will know. Once it's done and no one comes out of their trailers and tents in the morning, the others will have no choice but to fall in line. It's gone too far now. When it comes to the bigger picture, we're just collateral damage. Those young men and women will have to accept it if they want to survive,' Raine replied.

'Daddy?' said Emily, who had almost been forgotten since Raine's unceremonious entrance, looking to her father for reassurance.

'It's OK, sweetie. Just sit tight. We're only talking to the lady,' Vincent said.

'Say you're right and they do intend to do what you claim, what do we do about it?' Kristin said.

'If our illustrious sergeant gets wind that we know, he'll immediately separate us from the rest of the population. We need to lie low here until nightfall. I know which area of the fence we have the best chance of escaping through without being seen. It'll be much easier now most of the guards are gone. They won't have a big presence outside tonight because they'll want everyone to feel at ease.'

'You want us to make a run for it – out there with no protection?' Vincent said.

'Have you been listening to anything I've said? Most of the refugees are filling their bellies right now. They're already dead; they just don't know it yet.' Raine began to back away in the direction of the door. 'I suggest you pack some supplies – essentials only, nothing that will slow you down. I'm going to get some of my own things together and collect my source in the process. Then we wait until lights out before we make our move.'

'What makes you think we won't just walk right across the camp and report you as soon as you leave?' Vincent asked.

'I don't know. Maybe because you aren't as dumb as you look?' Raine said. She left, closing the door behind her.

Vincent and Kristin both let out their breath and held each other close. 'What do you make of all this?' Vincent asked.

'I think it sounds insane, but we have everything to lose if she's right and we ignore it. We should see how it plays out, meet this source of hers,' Kristin said.

'I can believe that Banks would lie to us about what's really going on out there – but to slaughter us like cattle?'

Kristin shook her head. 'I don't know why, but I trust her.'

During their embrace, something dawned on Vincent and he broke away. 'Can you look after Emily for a minute? There's something I need to do.'

'Sure, but what are you talking about?'

Vincent made for the door. 'If that woman's right, she's not the only person who's done us a great favour today. If it's not too late, I'd like to return it.' He glanced back to Emily, who seemed about to burst into tears. 'Be brave for Mommy. I'll be back before you know it.'

'OK, Daddy,' she replied softly.

Chapter 10

Vincent hastened towards the tents on the other side of the camp. He was more aware of the patrolling guards than ever. With each step, his paranoia intensified. Of course the guards didn't know; how could they?

Fortunately, he was able to find Adam's tent from memory by retracing his steps from the medical station. He made sure the coast was clear before ducking through the canvas opening. It was dark inside, and it was hard for him to see if anything was moving. 'Adam?' he whispered.

'Mr. Graham?' Startled by the voice coming from outside, Vincent tried to stand up and banged his head against the tent's frame in the process. Adam was still wearing his sweat-shirt and jogging pants.

'Adam. Have you eaten from your pack yet?'

'No. I didn't finish my run earlier, so I decided to go for another one. Why?'

'We can't talk about it here, but I need you to trust me.'

'Sure, Mr. Graham. Whatever you say,' Adam said.

'Good. Do you have a bag inside?'

'A bag? Yeah.'

'Go pack some essentials and I'll wait for you out here.'

Adam's eyes narrowed. 'Pack my essentials?'

'I thought you agreed whatever I said?'

'I did, but I don't—'

'Adam, please. I'm trying to help you.'

Adam saw the sincerity in his eyes. 'I'll just be a second.'

Once he'd emerged with his backpack, they hurried to the container block without saying a word. Kristin waited for them at the door and embraced Vincent as soon as he stepped inside. 'Did you see her?' she said.

'No, I didn't.'

Emily scampered from the living area into her father's arms. 'See, I told you I'd be right back,' Vincent said.

'Erm, I don't mean to press, Mr. Graham, but would you mind telling me what all this is about?' Adam was still standing by the door nervously, with his backpack over his shoulder.

Vincent ushered Emily into their living quarters before addressing the teenager. 'You might want to take a seat for this, son.' He proceeded to talk and Adam listened, occasionally glancing at Kristin to see if she had also been taken in by this elaborate conspiracy theory. He told him about the depleting guard detail, the claims they had sent the camp's only doctor into a dangerous area to be killed, the looped news feed broadcasting events that had probably happened months before, and most crucially, the plan to poison them using the much sought-after food packages.

Adam sat in silence, doing his best to take it all in. His healthy glow had faded to a sickly shade of grey when he looked Vincent in the eye again.

'I can't say as I've noticed any of those things. The soldiers have never been anything but nice to me. I don't wanna believe it – don't wanna even consider it... but I can tell you folks believe it, and what do I know after all? Before all this, I just thought about grades and playing ball. If you say this is the right call, Mr. Graham, then I'll do what you think is best.'

Vincent smiled at the boy in order to mask his own self-doubt. Adam was placing his trust in him. If it turned out to be wrong, and this whole thing was some paranoid delusion cooked up by their intense new acquaintance, then he would never forgive himself for bringing such a sweet kid into unnecessary danger.

There was a gentle tap on the door before it opened. Raine stepped inside, holding a drawstring bag that looked virtually empty. Someone else followed close behind her, head bowed. Kristin immediately recognised the black hoodie and the young man's shifting stance. 'This is your source? The guy who you said you wanted to avoid?'

'Your source?' the man said, flipping back his hood to reveal his gaunt face. 'Gosh, this is exciting. I sound like Deep Throat or something.'

The Grahams looked at each other in disbelief at his flippancy.

'His name's Ethan,' Raine said. 'He may be a little odd, but I doubt we'd all be here if it weren't for him.'

'I don't think you give yourself enough credit. You were spying on me, remember?' Ethan said, before losing interest in the adults and starting to smile at Emily. 'Hello there. What do they call you?'

'Emily,' she said, smiling back.

'I'd prefer it if you didn't speak to my daughter,' Kristin said.

'I agree,' Vincent added.

Ethan held up his hands and backed away. 'Fair enough. Your home, your rules and all that.'

'Who's the kid?' Raine said staring at Adam, who seemed a little more than intimidated by her.

'This is Adam,' Vincent said. 'He's—'

'My friend,' Emily said.

Her interruption seemed to disarm Raine and she relaxed her rigid posture. 'I hope this is it. The more people who know, the more dangerous it becomes. There's already gonna be quite a procession to get to the back fence.'

'How exactly are we going to get there without being seen?' Vincent said.

Raine leaned back to rest her muscular butt against the breakfast bar. 'I've been mapping the guard rotations for the past few days. If we move at nine thirty, I know exactly the route to take to avoid detection.'

'You were planning to leave before you found out about the food?' Kristin asked.

'I told you. I don't like being caged – especially with people I don't know.'

'Amen to that,' Ethan said.

'Your plan only gets us to the fence. How do we get to the other side?' Vincent said.

Raine jumped down from the breakfast bar and loosened the top of her bag. She reached in and pulled out a pair of wire cutters. 'I stole them from one of the engineers.'

'I don't know about anyone else, but I feel safer already,' Ethan said.

They sat in silence for a moment as the enormity of what they were about to attempt started to sink in.

'So I guess we just have to wait until it's time?' Kristin said.

'Does anyone have a pack of playing cards?' Adam said.

'I have some,' Emily declared excitedly. She raced to her room and returned with a deck of cards in their own box. She threw them on the dining table, spreading them over its surface. The backs of each one were illustrated with images depicting classic nursery rhymes like Humpty Dumpty and Jack and Jill.

'Wow. These are great,' Adam said.

'Maybe we can play Go Fish.'

'That sounds swell, Emily.'

'Well, golly gee willikers,' Ethan said under his breath. Raine, Vincent and Kristin all glared at him accusingly. He stopped sniggering, put his back against the wall and slid to the floor, then folded his arms like a scolded child.

'Who else wants to play?' Emily said.

Raine ignored her. Instead, she moved over to the window and peered through a gap in the blinds across to the east end of the camp.

'Mommy and Daddy will sit this one out, honey,' Kristin said.

Adam smiled and shrugged his shoulders. 'Looks like it's just us.'

'We can play with two. We just have to remember to deal seven cards each,' Emily said.

Kristin and Vincent felt like going to the bedroom for a lie down, but as happy as Emily was playing endless rounds of Go Fish with her new friend, they worried about leaving her on her own with a room full of strangers.

Ethan had fallen asleep on the hard floor, wrapping his arms around himself like a toddler. Raine stayed at the window, noting every single person who walked within eye-shot of the container.

Eventually the Graham's moved to the sofa to rest. Kristin laid her head on her husband's shoulder. She thought about reaching for the remote, and then remembered all she would see would be events that had been and gone. Cold reality gripped her all at once. The truth was they had no idea what the world had become since they'd entered the camp, or if anything remained of their old lives.

Chapter 11

Kristin felt something nudging her arm, and she began to stir. She winced at the tight knot in her neck as she lifted her clammy body away from Vincent's.

Raine stood over both of them, staring. Her skin seemed darker in the low lights of the container. 'It's time,' she whispered.

Kristin's vision crawled back into focus. The blinds on the windows were closed, but she could sense night was upon them. Her next instinct was to twist around on the sofa to look at the dining table. Emily wasn't there.

Before she had time to panic, Adam appeared next to Raine. 'I put her to bed, Mrs. Graham. She put herself to bed actually,' he said.

'She's been sleeping soundly – just like you,' Raine added.

'I'm sorry. I didn't mean to doze off. We were up most of last night because of Emily's tooth.' Kristin rubbed the sleep from her eyes.

'She did mention that it had started to ache before she fell asleep. I knew where the pills were, but I didn't dare give her any: I had no idea when you'd given her her last dose.'

'It's OK, Adam. Thank you.'

'If it's that bad, it needs to be dealt with. We can't have it being a problem once we get out there,' Raine said.

'Don't worry. We won't slow you down,' Kristin said. 'And it kind of sounds like you'll leave us behind if we do, anyway.'

'I didn't say that.'

All the talking and moving around finally roused Vincent from his curled up position on the sofa. Kristin left him stretching, getting up and walking to Emily's bedroom. The little girl was lying on her stomach. She must have pushed the sheets to the bottom of the mattress because they had wrapped themselves around one of her calves.

Kristin sat down beside her and placed her hand on the small of her back, relieved when she felt it rising as her lungs inflated. She touched her forehead to check her temperature. The skin contact caused Emily to flinch but she didn't wake. She felt warm – warm enough to be running a slight fever. She wanted to kiss her, but she didn't want to disturb her again. Kristin knew she needed to get up soon. She just looked so peaceful where she was.

Vincent appeared at the doorway holding half of a painkiller and half an Amoxicillin, as well as a glass of water to wash them both down. He didn't say anything at first; he just wanted to watch Kristin watching Emily. 'I'll do it,' he whispered. 'I'll wake her.'

Kristin forced out a weary smile and got up, touching his chest as she passed by him. Raine was waiting to greet her in the living quarters. 'Time to get your stuff together.

We move in ten minutes,' she said.

Kristin collected the two bags she'd packed before Raine had returned with Ethan. She'd followed her instructions and left out everything considered non-essential.

Raine stayed by the door and waited for everyone to gather up behind her. Kristin first, then Vincent cradling a still-sleepy Emily in his arms, with Adam and Ethan bringing up the rear. She stared at each one of them in turn as she spoke. 'We travel single file and you follow my instructions. If I signal to wait, you wait. If I tell you to run, you haul ass. No questions, no hesitation. We take a straight route to the tents and approach the fence from the northeast. There's a blind spot for the currently occupied towers between the rec area and the water pump. That's our way out. Once I open that door, no talking – not one word.'

'Are you absolutely certain about this?' Vincent said.

'Anyone feels like backing out, by all means stay behind. You can watch the news replays until the soldiers break in here in the morning to put a bullet in your head. Or you could sample their fine cuisine.' And that was the end of the discussion. Whatever misgivings they had, they were all going to do it.

Raine glanced down at her watch. 'Out of the ten guard towers, six are manned right now. There are also four soldiers patrolling the grounds. In one minute, our route to the east side of the fence should be clear – we will be able to go unhindered.'

Those 60 seconds seemed to go on forever, but eventually Raine yanked the door open and jumped down. Crouching, she hugged the outer wall of the container and peeked around the corner. The guard patrolling the perimeter of the west fence had his back to them. She waved the rest of the group down to her.

They followed closely, across the exposed divide between the container block and the tents, eventually ducking behind the wall of the showers. The camp was shrouded in darkness. Only the lights from the barracks and the roaming spot lamps mounted on the watchtowers cut through the blackness.

Amidst the deathly silence, they heard the distant crunching boots of the foot patrols near the transit station coming from the south. Raine got down on her hands and knees and began to crawl, pointing to indicate that everyone should do the same.

Vincent struggled to support Emily's weight underneath him while trying to move using one arm.

Before they had reached the halfway mark of the tent block, Raine raised her hand. They stopped and held their positions, still on all fours. Another set of footsteps could now be clearly heard. These were heading directly north through the centre of the camp. Raine looked back and saw a single man strolling, as bold as brass, towards the front gates. Tall and wiry, he was wearing a tattered cap and had a hiking pack over his shoulder.

One of the foot patrols spotted him almost immediately and ran over to confront him. 'Past curfew, sir. Where do you think you're going?' The soldier opened his palm to form a stop sign.

It didn't deter him. The wiry man kept on going, forcing the private to raise his rifle. 'Are you deaf or just stupid? I said stop.' The soldier's shout alerted another guard close by, who started jogging over to the commotion. They also caught the attention of one of the towers near the entrance. Its spotlight beam turned towards them like a roving eye.

Raine instructed the group to eat the dirt and they got as low as they could.

'Look, I don't want any trouble.' The wiry man spoke in a calm, deep southern accent. 'I just want outta here.'

'Get back to your tent, sir. You can discuss this in the morning with the CO,' the soldier replied.

'All I'm doin' is exercisin' my right as a citizen of this country.'

The group could see the wiry man was hiding something behind his back. The glow from the spotlight revealed a small hatchet. He narrowed his eyes as he stared the young soldier down. 'Best let me through, boy, and open the goddamn gate.'

A third guard approached from the container block, and three more emerged from the barracks and headed to the scene.

Raine was about to signal to make their move when Adam stood up and wandered out into the open, his hands in the air. Vincent attempted to grab hold of him, but it was too late. Another tower spotlight on the back fence zeroed in on him and the soldier running from the containers aimed his weapon at the boy.

'Hey, listen. We-we. Please don't shoot.'

The soldier gazed beyond him and immediately noticed the others crouched near the tents. 'You there. On your feet. Out where we can see you.'

They had no choice. Raine rose quicker than the others and stormed into the light, giving Adam a glare that made him feel more terrified of her than he did of the soldiers.

The appearance of the refugees distracted the private watching over the wiry man, providing him with a window of opportunity. He whipped his hatchet out from behind his back, but the private managed to block his first swing with his rifle. He then struck the man in the chest, knocking him to the ground. 'Stay down, asshole, or I will shoot you in the face,' he said, sticking the gun barrel against his pointed nose.

By the time the guards from the barracks had reached them, they had got all the escapees lined up, their hands behind their heads – all except for Vincent.

'Put her down and get your hands up now!' one of the soldiers demanded.

Vincent continued to cling to Emily, who shielded her eyes from the harsh lights, shaking and sobbing. 'She won't let go of me. Can't you see she's terrified?'

'I said—'

'Stand down, private. He's not going anywhere.' The voice came from an officer who had rushed from the barracks with an armed escort. He looked straight into Kristin's eyes and they immediately recognised each other. 'You!' Banks said. 'I guess you've already realised that you're never going to make that phone call.'

'You're a lying bastard,' Kristin said.

'Lying is sometimes part of following orders, Mrs. Graham.'

The lights and the raised voices had inevitably disturbed some of the residents close by, and a number of them were now starting to exit their tents and containers.

Banks noticed this and signalled to the patrol guards. 'Get them back inside.'

As his men ushered them back the way they came, Kristin saw one refugee double up in pain, clutching his stomach when he climbed the steps to his container.

Banks cast his eyes over the rest of the group, and his gaze settled on Raine. She glared back at him, her lip curled in a snarl. He raised his eyebrows and smiled at her, looking almost impressed by her resilience. 'Let's go,' he said.

'Go where?' the wiry man replied.

'Where you were heading.'

Bank's two escorts shoved the group on and led them to the gate situated at the back of the facility. Banks unhooked a set of keys from his belt and used one to release the bolt. They marched across the marshland into the forest of black ash trees that surrounded camp.

'I don't want to go in here, Daddy.' Emily wrapped both arms around Vincent's neck so tight, he found it hard to breathe.

'I'm sorry, sweetheart, but we have to.'

'Please, Daddy. Please.'

He didn't just sympathise with her, he empathised. Even with the threat of what Banks might do looming over them, it was nothing compared to the unknown threat which might be lurking within the dark vegetation. The musty scent of damp clay and oil hit his palate and made him feel sick. It wasn't just the smell of the woods that turned his stomach: something had been rotting in there for a long time. Every ash tree exhibiting the slightest deformity could be mistaken for a twisted creature hiding in half-shadow. The ground beneath their feet seemed to give a little more with each step. The ambience of the place threatened to close in and overpower them. Yes, Vincent acutely understood why his daughter was afraid of this oppressive place.

He quickened his pace to reach the front, where he found Banks ploughing on through the undergrowth like a man possessed. 'Sergeant, whatever you're thinking about doing, please leave her out of it. She's just a little girl. She didn't choose to try and escape,' he said.

Banks looked back dismissively. 'What do you think I should do with her?'

'Take her with you – wherever you're going.'

Banks laughed in disbelief. 'You'd entrust your daughter to a bunch of leathernecks with PTSD, fighting for resources?'

'I'd do anything if it meant her staying alive.'

'I wonder if you've really thought that statement through enough. "Anything" is a strong word, which enables all sorts of possibilities.'

'So that's it? You're just going to execute us out here?' Adam's voice faltered as he spoke. The young man tried to hold back his tears, shaking so much he found it difficult to put one foot in front of the other.

'You're gonna die anyway,' Banks replied.

'We didn't eat the last meal you prepared for us,' Raine said.

'Doesn't matter.'

'Why couldn't you just let everyone in the camp go and take their chances on the outside?' Vincent said. 'Better yet, put guns in their hands to help you fight back.'

Banks slowed down for the first time since they'd entered the woods. 'I thought you people were smart enough to work it out on your own. There is no fighting back. There's nothing left to fight for. Not anymore. If we'd opened up the camp, it would have meant just another five hundred people dying and rising up against us. Humans are much easier to eliminate in large groups than those things are.'

'So a nationwide genocide is the solution?' Vincent said.

'We lied to you about the other camps like we lied to you about everything else. There are only nine left in total.'

'In the state?'

'In the country.'

Bank's comment stopped the entire group in their tracks, but they were immediately forced to move again by the poised rifles of the two guards walking behind them.

'What are you saying?' Vincent asked.

'I've already told you. You just don't want to hear it. It's lost, Graham – the whole shit-show. The infection did break out in San Fran. We didn't lie to you about that, but it spread too fast for us to prepare ourselves for what we needed to do. Sending your troops out to kill some Arabs is one thing – getting them to turn their weapons on their family, friends and neighbours is another. The fuckers multiplied like a nest of roaches. As soon as one piece of infrastructure came down, its weight brought the rest with it. Fort Pennalworth was overrun weeks ago. We've only just taken it back, and that's where Major Spears has relocated the entire unit to until he decides his next suicidal move. Oh yeah, that crazy son-of-a-bitch thinks we can actually take the world back.' Banks said. 'Those creatures, they gather – form herds. We've never been able to work out why, but when they do, they migrate towards the nearest coastline. It's almost like they're being pulled in by the tide. We've been monitoring their movements, trying to redirect them. Even engaged some of the smaller groups. It cost us.' His eyes began to water with dread. 'We came across one last week – larger than any we've encountered before. Thousands of those rotten pieces of shit. It's been heading straight for the camp and it hasn't changed course. It'll be there by tomorrow night. We plan to leave by the morning.'

'And the folks back there?' said the wiry-looking southerner.

'There won't be anyone around to protest. The food rations were laced with a slow release toxin. If anyone's still alive in the morning, they'll be incapacitated. When the herd rolls through, it will flatten it. What we've done to the refugees is a mercy. There is no refuge any longer.'

Kristin shook her head as she processed the implications of the military's plan. The children, the families that had been living around her. 'Jesus Christ. You actually believe that, don't you?'

'Yes, Ma'am, I do.'

He led them onwards for another few minutes until they reached a clearing where their feet sank up to their ankles, soaking through their shoes and socks. The soldiers pushed them up front and raised their rifles.

The group huddled together, counting each second they had left. Vincent made Emily turn away from the gun barrels and held her tight, reaching out for Kristin's hand.

Raine stood rigid, her hands balled into fists, ready to make a dive for the soldier closest to her.

Ethan remained hunched over with his hands in the pockets of his hoodie. An ironic and broken smile shaped his lips.

'Sergeant, listen. You don't have to do this,' Adam pleaded. 'There's a child here. We could just keep going. Your major need never know.'

'Don't you grovel to them, kid,' the wiry man said. He snorted, hawking up as much phlegm to the back of his throat as he could, and then spat a ball of mucus at the feet of their captors. 'Go fuck yourselves – twice.'

The two privates tightened their stance and took aim, fingers poised over their triggers, awaiting their orders. The group averted their eyes – all except Raine and the wiry man.

'Stand down,' Banks said.

Both men looked at him in bemusement. 'Sergeant?'

'You heard what I said.'

'But Major Spears...'

'Major Spears won't find out – will he, Private?'

'No, sir.' The soldiers relaxed and lowered their weapons, and their potential victims breathed a collective sigh of relief.

'Finally found your humanity beneath all that conditioning, Sergeant?' Ethan said.

'No change of heart. This is why I brought you out here. I follow the major's fucked-up orders, but I'm no murderer. It made me sick to my stomach to give the order to hand out those food packs.'

'So what happens now?' Kristin said.

'You carry on heading that way.' Banks pointed further into the dense and twisted vines and trees. 'Once you're on the other side of the tree line, if you trek across the fields for about half a mile, you'll come to an old sawmill. We used to use it for storing supplies. Past that point, I can't predict what you might run into.' Banks turned to the soldier on his left. 'Private Skully – your sidearm.'

'Sir?'

'Give it to me, now.'

Skully drew his pistol and handed it over. Banks approached Raine and held it out to her. 'You seem like someone who would know how to handle this.'

Raine scowled at him, refusing to take the gun. Kristin stepped forward and accepted it instead.

Banks pointed to the side of the Beretta. 'That's the safety. It holds fifteen rounds. Make every one count.'

'Thank you,' she replied.

'You might not be grateful for long,' Banks said. 'Haynes, give Jethro here his hatchet back.' He gestured towards the wiry man, and the other soldier walked over to him and offered him the double-edged tool.

The wiry man snatched it from him. 'The name's Jake, asshole,' he said.

'Now get going. You should reach the sawmill in an hour.' Banks watched the rag tag group head off and disappear into the maze of black ash.

'What the hell was that, Sergeant?' Skully said.

'A bargaining chip,' Banks said, continuing to stare into the shadows of the woods. 'Maybe it will turn down the temperature in Hell a little for when we get there.'

Chapter 12

'It's been longer than an hour,' Kristin said. There was no sign of the trees around them thinning out. The gentle chirp of crickets and grasshoppers reached their ears and the smell of rotten vegetation made them feel queasy.

'Here. Let me take her.' Vincent held out his arms to take Emily's limp body from Adam. He was grateful the boy had offered to take shifts carrying her, but he wanted her close again.

Kristin couldn't let the feeling of unease go. Every patch of woodland looked identical to the last; it was like they were walking on a treadmill of revolving scenery. 'We're going in circles.'

'You're wrong, lady. I've been marking the trees,' Jake, the wiry man, said. 'We're going exactly where we're meant to.'

Jake's tall silhouette reminded Raine of a wooden marionette. His nose protruded from his face, complemented in its strangeness by his elongated neck. 'I'd feel rude if I forgot to thank you for blowing our cover at the camp,' she said.

'You'd have never made it out anyhow,' Jake said.

'What the hell were you doing back there?'

'Article Twelve.'

'What?'

'Everyone lawfully within the territory of a state shall, within that territory, have the right to liberty of movement and freedom to choose his residence. I was just exercising my God-given right.'

'God didn't write the constitution. Besides, none of that matters now.'

Jake chewed on his bottom lip and frowned at Raine, before spitting another wad of mucus into the swampy ground. 'Firstly, the founding fathers made those laws, and they were ordained by the man upstairs. Secondly, there's nothing that matters more right now than Article Twelve.'

'Oh, you're one of those,' Ethan said, struggling to keep up the healthy pace Jake had set.

'If you mean I'm a patriot – guilty as charged. And before you start, I don't need some wet-nosed Brit lecturing me on definitions. I know full well I'm surrounded by liberals here. If it wasn't for you assholes, we wouldn't be in this mess in the first place.'

'How you figure that?' Raine said.

'Always thinkin' science has the answers. Taking the attitude that if it can be done, it should. This is one experiment that worked out real well for us, didn't it?'

'Got even a single shred of evidence this was man-made, chief?' Ethan said.

'Why you think it started in Egypt? They were testing some weaponised virus out there and it got out of control like it always does. Only this time the Band Aid they tried to stick on it just wasn't big enough – not nearly big enough.'

Raine and Ethan glanced at each other in disbelief. 'You sure you haven't been bitten there, chief? Perhaps you're running a fever?'

'I'm sure, and the name ain't chief either. It's Jake Masterson. Most folks call me Salty.'

'Of course they do,' Ethan said. Even in the moonlight, the colour of Salty's angry orange hair sprouting from beneath his cap couldn't be tamed.

'This is all very fascinating, but it doesn't help us find a way out of here,' Kristin said.

'We're almost there. Trust me, I know my way around a forest,' Salty said. 'I was a conservationist before all this.'

'Isn't that just a fancy term for gardener?' Raine said.

Salty gulped hard and turned to face up to her. 'Y'know, I've had just about enough of the jive you're talkin''

'The jive I'm talkin'?' She knew what he meant – why he chose that specific word. The round neck of her sweater left most of her shoulders exposed, and as she flexed, her trapezius muscles popped beneath her skin.

'Both of you shut up a minute,' Kristin said. 'Listen.'

It didn't sound like much of anything at first – just the movement of a small animal or a rotten tree branch falling. Then it got louder; it sounded like it was being made by something heavy. Moans started to accompany the noises. The group zeroed in on its location; it was coming from the direction in which they were heading. They all took a few steps back. Vincent shifted to the back, pressing Emily's face into his chest.

'Is it the monsters, Daddy?'

'Yes, I think so. Don't worry. I'll protect you.'

The creature broke through into the clearing from behind a shrub. Its chest was concave, the bare bones protruding. A huge hole gaped beneath where its guts used to be. The putrid stench that oozed from the corpse almost made them choke. Its lips had receded over its gums long ago, exposing two brown rows of splintered teeth. Its eyes were sunken into their sockets, the black of its pupils replaced by a sickly grey fog. It lurched forward, clearly ravenously hungry, reaching out for them with its shredded arms of hanging flesh and tissue.

EPISODE TWO

Teething Problems

Chapter 1

'Back up!' Salty pushed his hand out behind him at the rest of the group and raised his hatchet. The creature kept coming. It had once been a man, but it was something else now. It possessed a hunger that it never had in life, and it wanted them for the empty space where its stomach used to be. It gnashed its brown teeth as it closed in.

Salty braced himself for the impact of metal on skull-bone, but before he could swing, a second creature shambled from the darkness and gripped Raine by her shoulders. She spun around to avoid its bite, crying out as her back slammed into a nearby tree trunk.

Distracted by the new attack, Salty turned his head. By the time he'd refocused on his target, it was too close for him to strike. He put his hands on the dead flesh and forced it away. When he tried to retreat he felt the denim tighten on the arm of his jacket. It had managed to get hold of him.

The others gasped, trying to process the danger they were in. A third corpse took them by surprise – this time from behind. The tibia of its right leg was broken and splintered fragments jutted from the exit wound. It struggled to maintain its balance, but that didn't stop it from heading straight for Emily as she clung to her father.

Vincent saw what its intention was and had no choice but to let go of Emily. She landed awkwardly at his feet and began to wail. The creature grabbed a handful of his shirt in its spindly fingers, almost taking some of his skin with it. Vincent pushed back, and there was a crisp snapping sound as its already fractured bone broke into two parts. All of its weight shifted forward and they both toppled over in the wet earth.

Kristin drew the Beretta and pointed it at the creature as it recovered from the fall and began to crawl towards her stranded daughter. Emily sat up and fixed her terrified gaze on the monster. It gargled its own coagulated blood as it edged closer. Less than five yards away, Kristin took aim at its head and tried to squeeze the trigger. It wouldn't budge. She rotated her wrist and saw the safety lever still locked in place.

The reanimated body reached for Emily's foot and the little girl shut her eyes in the hope that it would transport her somewhere else – somewhere safe. Adam raced over and scooped her up just before the creature could get to her leg.

Kristin released the safety, lined it up in her sights and fired. She hadn't prepared for the recoil and the shot missed its intended target, kicking up the ground inches from Vincent's back. He rolled over and covered his head. Attracted by the noise of the blast, the crawler twisted and dragged itself in the direction of Kristin.

Raine continued to fight her attacker. She used all the leverage she could, but with her back right against the tree, she couldn't force the creature off her or lift her legs to kick out. It opened its rotten jaws and snapped at her neck like a turtle.

Ethan had backed right up from the mayhem and tangled bodies, watching it unfold at a safe distance. There were so many people in danger; he couldn't decide which one he should help first. What he really wanted to do was run and never look back. He looked frantically about him for inspiration and spied a broken branch. Picking it up, he ran up behind the creature that had Raine pinned, and smashed the branch over its head.

To his dismay, it disintegrated on impact without causing so much as a blemish to the creature's flaking skull – the wood was rotten to its core. Maybe the thing realised that Ethan was easy prey – maybe it smelled his fear. It let Raine go and ambled after him instead. Raine slid down to the base of the tree, fighting to catch her breath.

Kristin trained the Beretta on the crawler again. It was now almost upon her so she couldn't miss, and this time she was ready for the kick. As the bullet struck, its face caved in. Its body fell limply to the ground. She immediately ran to her husband and helped him up.

Ethan attempted to flee from his pursuer, but the ground suddenly started to slope down in front of him and he slipped into a ditch, landing on his back. The creature followed him in and grasped for his flat sneakers. He kicked out with both feet, hyperventilating as he sank further into the mud. He didn't have the power in his legs to fend off its advances. It gained enough traction to crawl on top of him, eyeing up the flesh on one of his thighs. As it opened its shredded jaw it froze before it could sink its teeth. Its eyes rolled to the back of its head and it released its grip on his pants. Ethan couldn't comprehend what had happened until Salty put his foot on the corpse to extract the hatchet buried in the back of its shattered skull.

Salty adjusted the brim of his cap and stared down at him with an air of disappointment. 'Are you gonna lay in the dirt all night there, Twilight?'

Ethan, still shaking from his ordeal, took the man's hand and struggled to his feet. Once he saw the state of the others, he realised that he wasn't the only one. Raine still sat at the base of the tree, panting. The dark skin of her chest glistened, her sweat pooling in the indent at the bottom of her neck.

Vincent took Emily back from Adam and Kristin joined them in a family embrace. 'You saved her,' Vincent said.

'Just picked her up is all,' Adam replied.

'Thank you,' Kristin said.

'You're welcome, Mrs. Graham.'

Unlike the others, Salty seemed relatively unfazed by the ordeal. He surveyed the gruesome scene, checking first that the creature Kristin had shot was out of commission, and then he strolled back to where the first one had grappled with him. Its severed head lay next to its body, still animated, staring up at him with its soulless, grey-tinged eyes. It groaned with the same desire to feed as it had before its amputation.

Salty brought the hatchet blade down onto its face, almost splitting the thing in two. What was left of its brain escaped and soaked into the marshland. Everyone else turned away in disgust at the popping sound it made, as if the blow had relieved a trapped air pocket. 'I take it by all the pansy-assing around that none of you have had to do that before?'

They all shook their heads except Raine, who just glared at him from against the tree.

'Well, you better get used to it,' Salty said, picking up his bag. 'Otherwise, ya'll been better off eatin' Uncle Sam's mercy meal.' He set off again into the trees, leaving the others to recover and collect their things.

Chapter 2

Salty boldly made a path through the undergrowth, knocking away any twigs and plants with his hatchet. The trees began to thin out and eventually they saw fields and the distant shape of a building. It was a pale night, casting a blue haze over the relatively untouched world around them.

The tall southerner stopped at the edge of the tree line, placing his hands on his hips. There were walking corpses in the fields – at least twenty in sight.

Kristin came up behind him, holding the Beretta like it didn't belong to her. 'We should have listened to you,' she said.

Salty continued to gaze into the field. 'Yeah, looks can often be deceiving, darlin'.'

His response was condescending, but she let it slide. 'Thanks for getting us this far.' She stretched out her arm and held the gun right under his nose.

He took one look at it and adjusted his stare back to the danger in front of them. 'You should keep it. You've had a crash course in its use now. Besides, by my reckonin' you're gonna need it more than I will.'

Kristin tucked the Beretta into her jeans. He was right again. It dawned on her that being smart now meant fighting to keep it, not looking to give it away.

The others hung back, delving into their bags to get some water to clean the sweat and dirt from their skin. Raine came face-to-face with Ethan for the first time since their skirmish with the dead. 'Not so tough after all then, huh?' he said.

She narrowed her eyes at his self-satisfied tone. 'As soon as we find a safe place, you and I are going to have a conversation, and you'll be doing most of the talking.'

Ethan took a moment to consider her less than veiled threat and gave her an enthusiastic salute before turning his back to put his bottled water into his shoulder bag.

'Daddy, my tooth's getting really sore.' Emily looked up at her father, barely able to keep her eyes open. Strands of her thick hair stuck up in every direction like a bird's nest, but running a brush through it wasn't a concern for Vincent. The side of her face had started to swell again. This time it seemed twice the size as before.

'We're gonna be stopping in a little while, sweetie. You can have something to eat and then it will be time for your pills.'

'I don't like them.'

'But they'll make you feel a whole lot better, and you can sleep. We all can.' He ran his hand over her forehead, pretending to move some stray hairs from her vision, but he was really checking to see if she had a fever.

'Hey, kid. Get over here,' Salty said.

Adam glanced around and then pointed to himself. 'Me?'

'Yeah, you.'

Adam made his way to the edge of the field.

'I want you to double back into the woods and look for any branches you can find. Not the rotten crap – the sturdy ones we can use as weapons.'

'Erm, OK.'

'Don't stray too far past the tree line, and keep your eyes peeled for any more of those things wandering around back there. You see one, you come and tell me. No being a hero.'

'Right. I mean, yes, sir,' Adam said.

'Don't call me that. I'm not one of your teachers. Salty or Jake will do just fine.'

Adam nodded sheepishly and set off into the woods.

Salty snorted and spat on the ground before he addressed the rest of the group. 'OK, listen up. We're gonna head across those fields to the mill.

There's a few of the dead in sight, and there'll be more when we get closer. They're pretty spread out, so it won't be too tricky to get around 'em. They're as slow as they are dumb. Stay on your toes and they will go hungry.'

Vincent gathered Emily up again and kissed her. 'We just need to make the walk over this field and we can take shelter,' he said.

'Are there cows?' Emily asked.

'What?'

'In the field. Are there cows?'

'I'm not sure, honey. I can't see any.' All Vincent could see were the round-shouldered silhouettes of the dead. If there were cows in the field, they were most likely lying on their sides with their guts open to the night air.

He bent his knees to collect his bag, but Kristin picked it up before he could get there. She slung it over her free shoulder. 'You have enough to deal with, and I have this.' She lifted her shirt to flash the handle of her pistol. 'Just concentrate on getting her across.' The couple turned as they heard the snapping of twigs coming from the trees. Adam emerged carrying two reasonably straight branches under his arm.

Salty pointed to Raine. 'I need you up front with me.' He then looked at Kristin. 'Don't pull the trigger unless you have no choice. The sound will draw the rest in on us, and there might be military patrols nearby.'

Adam approached them, looking pleased with himself. Raine took one of the branches and bounced it on her hands to assess its weight.

'You keep the other one, kid, and take the rear.' Salty then gestured over to Ethan who had sat on the ground away from the others. 'Twilight can stay back there with you. If things get wild, I don't like the idea of him mething out anywhere near me.'

Everyone got in line and readied themselves for the short but potentially dangerous journey. 'There seems like a lot of them,' Kristin said as she examined the expanse of land and the amount of corpses drawn to the sawmill itself.

'They move like old folks. As long as you keep up with me, we'll avoid them easy enough. It's whether there's any waitin' for us inside that we should worry about,' Salty said.

Adam made his way over to Ethan and the man removed his hood to greet him. 'Erm, we're going to make a play for the sawmill. Jake would like you to bring up the rear with me.'

'Seeing as we're bringing up the rear, it would be a pleasure... Adam, isn't it?'

'That's right.' The innuendo went straight over Adam's head. He offered his hand to help Ethan up.

'It's OK, Adam; I've got this.' Ethan got to his feet and staggered a couple of steps to the right before regaining his balance.

'Jeez, are you alright?'

Ethan rubbed frantically at his eyes. 'I'm fine. I just went a little lightheaded. It's low blood sugar or something.'

'You think you can make it to the mill?'

'Absolutely. Make sure you don't mistake me for one of those things and club me with your big stick.'

'Don't you worry about that,' Adam said.

'Let's do this then.' Ethan picked up his bag and wandered to the others.

Salty led the group at walking pace at first, and then broke into a light jog. The dead close by seemed oblivious to them, not breaking their endless march. As they approached the sawmill, they saw another, smaller building peeked out from behind it. The mill was open-plan; there were two ramps positioned on either end, leading up to the twin saw and workshop. Three roamers were currently inside of it, bumping around against the abandoned machinery and drying yard.

Salty immediately veered away towards the second building. When they were half way there, Kristin felt the earth give way under her left foot. It got caught in a gopher hole and when she tried to run on, she twisted it. Already off-balance, the weight of the two backpacks sent her crashing to the ground. She screamed, alerting Vincent. He turned around and went back for her, watching his own step to make sure he didn't take a tumble with Emily in his arms.

Kristin shook herself and sat up. She flexed her ankle once she'd pulled it free, and pain instantly shot up her leg muscles.

'Kristin?' Vincent said. 'Emily, you're gonna have to go down so I can help Mommy.'

The little girl shook her head and clung tighter to her dad, wrapping her legs around his midriff.

'I've got her, Mr. Graham.' Adam handed his branch to Ethan and ran over to aid Kristin. He grabbed one of her bags, and Vincent scooped up the other one. Kristin winced as Adam helped to support her weight.

'It's my ankle,' she said. 'I think it's sprained.'

'Can you walk with my help?' Adam said.

'Just about, I think.'

'Erm,' Ethan said, drawing their attention to the dead that were nearby. The commotion from the fall had piqued their interest and several of them had changed course and were now stumbling towards the nearest source of food.

'Come on, let's go,' Salty said, waving them on. He and Raine had opened up a gap between the others in order to reach the second building, and they needed to catch up fast.

Vincent carried on with Emily, keeping a close eye on Kristin and Adam, who were struggling on the best they could. Ethan brought up the rear on his own, holding the branch out in front of him like it was a poisonous snake.

As Salty had feared, the double doors to the barn building were secured by a latch and bolt. He raised his hatchet and began to hack at the wood that the latch was screwed to.

Raine braced herself for the two rotting wanderers, who were attracted by the sound of the splintering wood and the clanging of metal on metal.

The creature closest to them was making for the back of the line. It used to be a woman, and she still didn't seem particularly old on account of her cropped shirt and hot pants. The shorts had once been bright pink, but had since become caked in dirt and blood. Her blonde hair drooped forward, covering her face. A large clump was missing at the front. It looked like it had been torn out, right down to her inflamed scalp.

Salty looked up from the lock and noticed it was almost upon them. 'Deal with it,' he said.

Kristin pulled the Beretta and brought it up to her eye. Adam pushed her arm away before she could pull the trigger.

'Remember what he said, Mrs. Graham.'

Ethan fought against his instinct to take flight. He closed his eyes, trying to psych himself up to swing, to deliver the killer blow to the creature's head. As he stepped towards it, he saw the metal feet from the wood chipper jutting out from the ground directly behind the creature, so he rotated the branch, wielding it like a spear and pushing it out in front of him to jab his slobbering attacker in the chest. He forced it back. A second prod sent it toppling over the frame of the chipper and onto its back.

The creature groaned as it tried to get up, but it lacked the coordination to reach its feet again, and just flailed about in the dirt instead. Ethan smiled in relief and stepped back in line.

Before the other rotters could reach them, the latch and bolt finally separated from the shattered wood and the doors swung open. Salty held them just long enough to bundle everyone inside, then slammed them shut. There were two brackets on the inside. Raine gave up her branch, jamming it in between. Even though the dead immediately pressed themselves up against the doors, it was going to take at least forty to break it down.

The survivors tried to forget about the dead outside and faced the darkness of their hiding place. A small window on the first floor allowed a moderate amount of moonlight to seep in. While others listened intently for signs of movement, Kristin unzipped her bag and fumbled around until her fingers ran over what felt like three candles and a matchbook. Still hopping to keep the weight off her injured ankle, she passed a candle to Adam and Salty and lit the other herself.

As far as she could see, they were alone. The first floor was relatively bare. At the far end were what looked like a set of cupboards and an office desk and chair.

Salty struck a match to light his candle and moved towards the wooden staircase situated near the room's centre.

'I'm gonna see if it's clear up there,' he whispered. 'If it is, we should bed down. Those goons outside are less likely to wander off if we stay down here.'

'Be careful,' Kristin said.

She heard Emily sobbing next to her. Vincent stroked her hair and whispered a calming, 'Shh, shh' in her ear.

'It's OK, sweetie,' Kristin said, squeezing one of her delicate arms.

'Her abscess is getting worse,' Vincent said.

'How many antibiotics do we have left?'

'Seven. Breaking them in half makes fourteen. Twice a day, that's a week's worth,' he said.

One of the dead outside slammed hard against the doors, causing them to buckle slightly. The impact shoved Vincent forward. Emily squealed and he held her head, forcing her to look at him. 'Don't worry. They know we're in here, but they can't get in. We're safe right now.'

'Will they go away?' Emily said.

'If we're really, really quiet.' As soon as she heard that, she immediately stopped sobbing and rubbed the tears from her eyes. One side of her face had swelled to such an extent that she looked like she'd been physically abused.

The floorboards creaked above them, and Salty came halfway down the stairs. 'It's clear. Come up.'

Adam and Raine helped Kristin climb the steps and set her down on a dirty mattress in the corner. It had sheets and a pillow, and there was even a TV opposite. Raine explored the other side of the room by candlelight. The smell she was inhaling was unmistakable – stale urine. At first, she thought someone had pissed over the wall, but then she discovered a bathroom cubicle. It had all of the necessary plumbing, but it no longer worked and had been used several times. There was also a basin fixed to the wall. The scorched ceramic surface inside had turned black, as if something giving off intense heat had been left to burn there. A bar of soap riddled with pubic hairs sat on the flat edge at the back of it.

'Hopefully, those things will have moved on by sun up. Then we search for a ride and get the hell outta Dodge,' Salty said.

'And go where?' Raine said.

'I might know a place,' Salty replied. 'Somewhere safe.'

'Where's that exactly?'

He removed his cap, revealing thin layers of wispy red hair at the front and sides of his pale head. 'No offence, ma'am, but I'd rather keep that to myself for now.'

'Fair enough.' Raine set her pack down a good way away from the stinking cubicle, put her back against the wall and slid down to sit on her butt.

Salty examined the rest of the barn conversion's second floor and then made for the stairs again. As he passed Ethan, the young man removed his hoodie and laid it down on the floor to cushion himself. Salty stood and stared at him, examining every inch of his face.

'Can I help you?' Ethan said, looking puzzled.

Salty took another moment to regard him. 'Don't I know you from some place?' he said. "Cause I'm startin' to think that I do.'

Ethan shrugged. 'I don't know. Do you know me from some place?'

Salty shook his head and put his baseball cap back on. 'I guess not.'

'OK!' Ethan replied.

Salty wandered over to the mattress, where Vincent was trying to get Emily off to sleep. 'I know this ain't the best time to be bringing this up, but we gonna have to deal with that tooth – and sooner rather than later.'

'What do you mean by "deal with it"?' Kristin said.

'Well, if that critter stays where it is, your daughter could have much more to worry about than a bad toothache,' he said. 'The infection has already spread to her jaw by the looks of the swelling. If it gets into her neck or brain, we could be lookin' at septicaemia or even meningitis. Now, I don't know whether you've taken a look around this place, but we don't exactly have the kind of equipment to treat something like that, and it would certainly be more than the immune system of a little girl low on food and water could cope with.'

'OK, you've made your point. We'll deal with it,' Vincent said. 'Just let her get some rest first.'

'Soon as it's light and we can see what we're doin'.'

Vincent nodded, cupping a hand on Emily's forehead to check her temperature again.

'I'm gonna take a look-see downstairs. Might be something we can use.' Salty held his candle out to aid his descent down the dark steps to the ground floor, careful not to make any noise that would alert the creatures lurking on the other side of the doors.

Kristin watched Raine closely. Her black skin blended in with the shadows. She tilted her head back against the wall, staring off into space. Kristin rose from the mattress, elevating her injured leg as she did so.

'Where are you going?' Vincent said.

'To talk to Raine. I won't be long.'

'You should rest.'

'You're right; I should.' Kristin stood up and hobbled across the room. She smiled at Raine, but she got a glare in return. Kristin could almost see the rage burning behind her eyes. 'Mind if I sit? I'm not too fancy on my feet right now.'

Raine granted permission by glancing down to the empty space next to her.

Kristin winced as she slid down the wall, then adjusted her position until her leg was as comfortable as was possible. 'Are you alright?'

'Why wouldn't I be?' Raine snapped.

'Easy – I thought we were on the same side back at camp. If it weren't for you, those soldiers would be loading our bodies into a mass grave.'

'You're optimistic. We'd be lucky if they just torched us.'

'You suspected, didn't you? Even before Ethan?'

'I know how they operate,' Raine said.

Kristin glanced over to Ethan. He was wringing his hands as he muttered something indiscernible under his breath. 'So what's his story?' she asked.

'Not sure yet, but I'm going to find out,' Raine said.

'What about this Salty guy? Can he be trusted?'

'I told you, I don't trust anyone,' Raine said. 'It's the only way to be sure.' The harsh lines of her features seemed to soften when she realised what she'd said. 'No offence.'

'Don't worry about it. I know how things are now.' Kristin felt a sharp surge of pain through her ankle and gasped.

'We should take a look at that.'

'I'm fine, really.'

Raine's stare intensified again. 'You don't look fine. Let me look.'

⋏

Salty shifted his weight backwards as he crept up to the cupboard door, half-expecting something to burst out of it and grab him by the throat. He snatched at the handles and flipped the doors wide, pushing the candle flame towards the darkened shelves. A collection of cables weaved between large machine batteries like colourful electric eels. The rest of the contents consisted of machine parts – some he recognised, some he didn't.

He closed the cupboard and tip-toed over to the office desk, where he noticed a dark red stain that had soaked deep into the cushion attached to the back of the chair. He sifted through the files on top of the desk, but there was nothing of interest in them. They were full of accounts, employee details, and an accident report book. When he turned his attention to the draw underneath the desk top, it wouldn't slide open. There was a small keyhole in the middle of it, but no key in sight.

Salty had no desire to go fumbling around in the dark for it, so he snatched at the drawer's handle… and again. On the second attempt it shot open, rattling the legs of the desk against the hard floor. He held his breath and heard a murmur outside. It was the right pitch to be female. A thud on the wall next to him indicated that the creature had collided with the exterior. He froze and listened as its dragging footsteps moved to the other end of the building.

The candle flame revealed that the items inside the drawer weren't worth the risk. A few pens and pencils, some paperclips, a ball of string and a carton of salt were all that was on offer.

⋏

As Raine slid her shoe from her injured foot, Kristin had to grit her teeth just to stop herself from crying out. She peeled her sock away from her ankle and pressed her thumb into the badly swollen flesh. 'It's not great,' Raine said. 'You could do with staying off it for at least a week.'

'Too bad we don't even have twelve hours.'

'That's one thing me and the new guy agree on. It's a safe haven for now, but it could quickly turn into a death trap if we overstay our welcome. I'm not comfortable with how close we are to the military patrols.'

'Preaching to the converted on that score,' Kristen said.

'Just as well I've got a roll of bandages in my pack.'

'Really?'

'I brought the essentials.' As promised, Raine retrieved a roll of thick white gauze from her bag.

'Always prepared, huh?'

'Not always, but it's probably better than some of the shit you packed,' Raine said.

Kristin giggled, and then remembered where they were. 'Thank you.' She saw the hint of a smile curl the woman's lips.

Kristin watched her husband getting Emily off to sleep while Raine started to wrap her ankle. He leaned over her, singing something to her in a whisper. Emily sung along too. Kristin recognised it as the tune from her daughter's favourite cartoon. The child gazed up at Vincent in wonder. 'We didn't have her until late in life because Vince and I only found each other eleven years ago. Both divorcees, but Em was the first child for both of us. I used to worry – y'know, about carrying in my forties, all the risks involved with that. He kept telling me it would be OK. He'd wanted kids for the longest time. I knew it, even though he never said it. Just look at how he is with her. She worships the ground he walks on.'

'Does that make you jealous?' Raine said, tugging on the slack of the bandage.

'I don't know whether you've noticed, but I'm not exactly cut out to be a mom. I guess I just wasn't born that way.'

'Doesn't mean you love your daughter any less.'

'No, but I sometimes wish I could be more like him.'

Raine stopped the bandaging as a question crossed her mind, one she couldn't help but ask. 'Even now?'

Kristin looked away from her family, as if snatched from a wonderful dream. 'No. Not now.'

They heard the creak of Salty's steps on the staircase. He appeared clutching the spoils of his search to his chest. 'Looks like they're thinning out down there. They'll be all but gone by mornin',' he said. 'But until then, we need to keep watch. The windows up here give us pretty much a panoramic view. We can keep an eye on the door from the top of the stairs.'

'I'll take first watch,' Raine said. 'I'll just finish up on her ankle.'

'Fine by me,' Salty said. He walked over to his backpack near the basin and settled down. 'Wake me in a couple of hours and I'll take over.'

Raine wrapped the gauze one more time and tied it off. 'There. Should give you a little more support.'

'That's great.'

'It will have to do. Go on. Try and get some sleep with your family. I'll wake you if anything happens.'

Chapter 3

Emily blinked before she opened her eyes. Her parents were lying next to her; both of them were still. Her face hurt a little and her cheek felt puffier than ever. The shadows on the dusty second floor seemed to close in on her the more she concentrated on them. A figure was moving around near the window, and Emily's first thought was to shake her father awake so he could hold her and tell her not to be scared.

Instead, she hesitated, watching from the mattress as the figure stepped into the light. It was Raine, making sure the coast was clear. Salty lay curled up in a ball under the basin, snoring like he didn't have a care in the world.

Emily sat up and looked around. Ethan was still in the same position, his back against the wall. His eyes were open but didn't seem to be focussing on anything in particular. 'Hey,' she whispered.

He snapped out of his trance, startled by her voice. 'Hey! You scared me.'

'Sorry. I didn't mean to.'

'That's OK. How's your tooth?'

'It still hurts. My daddy says if I keep taking the pills, my face will go down eventually and then it won't hurt so much.'

'A wise man, your daddy,' Ethan said.

'Don't you want to go to sleep?'

Ethan pushed his fingers through the curls in his hair to scratch his scalp. 'Sleeping's not really my thing.'

'Everyone needs to sleep, silly.'

'Me, not so much anymore.'

Emily's eyes widened with a thought. 'Are you scared the monsters might get you if you close your eyes?'

'Something like that.'

'Do you know why they're here?'

'There have always been monsters, Emily. They just weren't so obvious before.'

A voice suddenly interjected from across the room. 'I-I don't think Mr. Graham would want you to be doing this.' It was Adam. He'd been listening the whole time.

'Chill out, Kobe. We're just talking,' Ethan said.

'I think you should listen to his advice,' Raine added from her spot by the window.

'When I used to get scared at night sometimes, or I had a bad dream, my daddy would tell me there were no such things as monsters,' Emily said.

Ethan turned back to face her. 'You have to understand something about your dad. When he told you that, he was doing it to protect you from what the world is – for as long as he could. But it's better now because the monsters don't pretend to be something they're not. Makes it easier to see them when they come for you... and they will come for you, Emily.'

'Hey, hey! Stop!' Vincent said, sitting up with a start.

'I told him already, Mr. Graham,' Adam said.

Ethan smirked and frowned at Adam at the same time. 'Do you still think you're on the honour system or something?'

'Lie down and go back to sleep.' Vincent forced Emily to flip over and face away from Ethan. He then leaned over her to stare him down. 'You don't speak to my daughter again. You don't speak to her, you don't touch her, you don't even look in her direction. Do as I ask and we'll get along just fine. You got that?'

Ethan reached up and gave him a lazy salute. 'Aye aye, Captain.'

Vincent broke his stare and lay back down to nurse his daughter to sleep again.

Chapter 4

When Vincent woke, the daylight was starting to break through the windows. The guard rotation had changed and Salty was now on duty. Everyone else, including Ethan, was asleep.

Vincent heard Emily cough like she was choking and he quickly got her into a sitting position. 'What's wrong, honey?'

He found it hard to understand her because she hardly opened her mouth when she spoke. 'Nasty taste.'

'Get her to spit it out,' Salty said.

Vincent pulled her off the mattress and got her to lean forward. 'It's OK. Let it go.'

Emily did as he asked, and a clear, slimy pus mixed with blood, like a disgusting kind of treacle drooled from her lips and splashed onto the hardwood.

'Daddy?' She started to sob, confused and frightened by the mess she'd made.

'The abscess burst, alright,' Salty said. 'Don't worry, kid. It's a good thing.'

'He's right, Emmy. Just as well you didn't swallow it,' Vincent said as he stroked her hair.

'Will it be all better now?' she asked.

'It should have relieved some pressure for sure,' Salty said.

'Does your face feel any better?' Vincent said.

'I think so.'

Vincent reached over to grab a bottle of water, accidentally nudging Kristin in the process. He handed the bottle to Emily. 'It will take the taste away and clean out your mouth,' he said.

As she drank, he noticed that Salty was assembling a small fire in the centre of the room using pieces of paper and broken bits of wood.

Kristin sat up and saw him at work. 'What are you doing?'

Instead of answering her, Salty looked at Vincent. 'Can I have a word with you in private?'

Vincent kissed his wife and handed Emily over. 'Can you watch her please? Her abscess just burst.'

'Oh, Emily. Are you ok?' Kristin gave her a hug while the child continued to sip from the bottle.

'It doesn't hurt so much now,' she said.

Vincent got up and walked over to Salty. 'What is it?'

'I'm gonna warm up some water and add salt to it. If she gargles with it, it will stop her wound from getting infected.'

'What wound?'

'The place I know of is at least a day's drive from here – that's if we find a vehicle. Even when we get there, there's no tellin' if we'll ever find more antibiotics. Your daughter feels better now, but unless we remove that tooth, the abscess could always come back.'

'You're suggesting we remove it here – right now?'

'Ideally, you'd want the swelling to go down first, but I can't guarantee we're gonna get this chance again.'

Vincent thought about it for a moment and shook his head. 'I can't do that to her.'

'It ain't just about her. If she's sick when we're on the road, she could be a danger to us all.'

As much as he fought to admit it, Salty was right. If he refused and it played out that way, he would be responsible for it. 'How do you plan to do it?'

'You're gonna want to give her one of those painkillers first.'

Chapter 5

Emily sat rigid and shivering in Vincent's arms, gripping his hand for dear life. Salty slid the ream of string carefully through his fingers. He then pulled it taut so it tugged on Emily's infected tooth.

The little girl flinched and started to hyperventilate, digging her fingernails into her father's skin. 'It's OK, Emily: it's already loose. You'll hardly even feel it,' Vincent said. He was just glad she was facing away from him, so she couldn't see the uncertainty written all over his face.

Kristin stood with Raine. She wanted to say something to comfort her daughter, but couldn't think of a single word.

Adam had taken a walk downstairs, having decided he'd rather not be around when it happened.

Ethan sat in silence with his hood up and his head between his knees.

Salty wrapped the other end of the string around the handle of the open door to the bathroom cubicle, turning up his pointed nose when he smelled the cloud of stale urine coming from inside.

'This is how they always used to do it back in my day, kid. Dentists were expensive. They weren't for people in my neighbourhood.' He laid his hand on the door. 'Make sure you keep your mouth open, otherwise you could lose more than one.'

On hearing his warning, Emily overcompensated, opening her mouth like she was letting out a silent scream, still shaking wildly.

'No need to fret, little darlin'. The beauty of losing your first teeth is there's new ones ready to grow back in their place... I'm gonna give you a five-count and then I'll do it, OK?'

Emily nodded and shut her eyes tight.

'One... two... thr.' Before Salty had finished the countdown, he slammed the door shut, and with a twang of the string, the molar flew from her mouth and bounced over to where Salty was standing, leaving a thin trail of blood and saliva in its wake.

Vincent made her lean forward immediately. First, he passed her a bottle of water to swill her mouth out. Then he gave her the warm salt water that salty had made to help clean the wound. Once she was done gargling, she spat the now-frothy pink liquid onto the floor.

'You tricked me,' she said, catching her breath.

'Hurts less when you least expect it.'

She frowned at him all the same.

'Did it hurt that much?'

Emily thought about it. 'Not much, I guess.'

'There you go then. Now you keep swilling that salt water and it should heal up nicely.'

'OK,' Emily said. 'Thank you, Salty Jake.'

'You're welcome, Missy.' A brief smile broke across his face, softening his usually harsh features.

'Thank you,' Vincent said sincerely.

Salty's solemn look soon returned to him. 'You can thank me by getting ready to haul ass. We've already wasted part of the mornin'.'

The group gathered their things shortly after and then headed out. The dead had scattered again, so they were able to slip away unnoticed. Salty led them west. They travelled through over a mile of open fields. Occasionally, they came across a few ragged-looking figures stumbling along in the distance, but they never got close enough that they needed to engage them.

Adam continued to take turns with Vincent to carry Emily whenever he got tired. Raine did her best to support Kristin's weight so she didn't put too much pressure on her ankle.

Ethan kept to himself, as always, and listened to his iPod beneath his hood.

Salty insisted they were getting closer to the road, but in order to get there, they had to pass through a plot of cornfields. They entered with a great deal of caution. Eight-foot-tall stalks of green and golden brown rose up around them in every direction, above them the burnt-orange clouds of the breaking dawn.

Every rustle or flap of a bird's wings in the midst of the crops brought fresh concern, but Salty ploughed on ahead, sometimes slashing away with his hatchet to remove any obstructions.

'We have no idea what we're walking into,' Vincent said.

'We're heading for the road,' Salty said, never looking back. 'Why don't you put the kid up on your shoulders? She might be able to tell us somethin'.'

Vincent hesitated. Salty noticed.

'I doubt there are any snipers waiting to take a pop at her, but whatever,' Salty said.

'I'd like to, Daddy,' Emily said. She smiled up at him. The swelling on her cheek was already starting to reduce.

Salty gurned with satisfaction. 'Well OK then. Tell us what you see.'

'I will.'

Vincent hoisted her up and placed her on his back. She shuffled forward to get comfortable and straddled his neck.

Kristin almost fell over several times trying to navigate the uneven ground of the tilled earth. Finally, Raine made her stop and shouted to the front. 'We need to stop for a while. She has to rest.'

'Negative. We ain't stoppin' till we reach the road,' Salty said.

'I see something.' Emily pointed excitedly to the north.

'What is it?' Salty said.

'Errm, a truck!'

'You sure?'

'Yes. It's a big green truck.'

'It movin'?'

'No, it's standing still.'

'OK, darlin'. You keep pointing at it and we'll follow.' Salty dropped back so he could let Emily guide them.

Kristin ignored the throbbing pain in her ankle and pushed on too.

'Tell us if you see any people, Emily,' Salty said.

'Aye aye, Captain,' she replied.

Vincent was about to laugh at her remark, but then he remembered who had used it on the previous night. He looked behind him and couldn't tell whether Ethan was smiling beneath his hood.

'Daddy?' Emily tugged on his ears, causing him to face the right way again, so she could watch the static truck.

Every now and again, Salty would have to adjust their direction based on Emily's body language, keeping their voices down to a whisper.

After a while, Salty asked 'Are we close now, darlin'?'

'Pretty close,' she whispered back.

'OK, Vincent. Take her down.'

Vincent lifted her from his shoulders and sat her down.

'Raine, you come on ahead with me. We'll check it out – make sure there are no surprises. Everyone else stays put until I give the signal,' Salty said.

'Here. I won't take no for an answer this time.' Kristin pushed the Beretta into Raine's hand. She closed her fingers around its handle and followed Salty into the corn.

Once Salty shifted the last stalks aside, they emerged onto a road, about thirty yards behind the vehicle. He took one step back and peered around the swaying corn to get a better view. Just as Emily had said, it was a big green truck – a military cargo transport to be exact – extremely similar to those housed at the refugee camp.

He felt a tap on his arm and Raine handed him the gun, a look of dread on her face. Salty examined her haunted expression with interest.

She turned her gaze from his and released the weapon.

'Hang back and make sure I don't get blindsided.' Holding his hatchet in one hand and the Beretta in the other, he crept up to the back of the truck. He slammed into the steel of the tailgate and lifted the canvas sheet to peek inside. The bed of the vehicle was empty. He moved around to the driver's side and edged closer to the cab, eyes fixed on the glass of the side-view mirror.

He ducked underneath the open window, and then popped up, wielding the gun. He almost squeezed the trigger when he noticed the soldier sitting at the wheel. The young man was still, his head resting back against the seat. His skin was bleached white and his brown hair soaked through with sweat. The name on his fatigues read 'Hollister'.

'Raine, get your ass up here.'

Hollister suddenly lurched forward and let out a spluttered breath. Salty jumped back and raised his gun again. The soldier sat back after his coughing fit. His eyes roamed around the interior of the cabin before he noticed that he had company. 'Who the hell are you?' he said, trying to focus on Salty.

'Seems to me – I should be asking the questions. Seeing as I'm the one with the gun on you,' Salty said. 'Where did you come from and are you alone?'

Hollister let out a weary laugh. 'Just down the road a ways.'

Raine arrived at the driver's window and locked eyes on the soldier. 'He bit?'

Hollister responded by reaching across his body and tugging open his shirt. A shallow bite mark on the top of his shoulder was oozing with blood and clearly infected. He let go of his shirt and slumped back into place. 'We were on a recon in Westport; we got swarmed. Only half of us made it out. When we got back to base, I knew Spears would have someone put me down, so I stole this and got the hell outta there.'

Raine noticed the man's neck pulsating as he struggled to breathe. He threw up a hand to wipe the cold sweat from his brow, but his movements were so uncoordinated that he hit himself in the face and then gave up on the idea.

'Now I think about it, I don't know why I ran exactly. I guess I just wanted to keep going for as long as I could.'

'You said Spears. Are you from Fort Pennalworth?' Raine said.

'That's right. How did you know?'

'We escaped from the FEMA camp.'

Hollister instantly looked wearier. 'Then you know. What we did.'

Raine nodded.

'I'm sorry.' Hollister's voice broke as his emotions bubbled over. 'Seein' as I'm heading straight to hell, none of that forgiveness shit matters now, right?'

'That depends.'

'On what?'

'On whether it matters to you.'

Raine's remark seemed to stem the flow of his tears and he smiled. 'The Major is gonna send men to look for me. He doesn't give a damn about me. He just wants his truck back. You better take it and leave.'

'And you?' Raine said.

Hollister glanced over to the medical kit next to an assault rifle that was propped butt first against the footwell and the inside of the passenger door. 'Do me a favour, would you? Give me a shot out of there for the pain? My bones feel like they are on fire.'

Raine rushed around the front of the cabin to access the passenger seat. She flipped the latches on the kit and opened it.

'They're in the—'

Before Hollister could finish, she'd already located the drugs amongst the trauma bandages, tourniquets, surgery tools and Kirlex Gauze. She picked out the vials of morphine between the Narcan and Epinephrine and quickly loaded one into the auto-injecting pen nearby.

Salty watched her closely through the opposite window as she held the soldier's leg firmly and then brought the pen down into the flesh of his thigh.

Hollister sighed and started to breathe a little more slowly, taking the sweet relief into his bloodstream. 'Nice. That's better. Now give me a hand getting out of here.'

Salty opened the driver's door and put an arm across his back and the other underneath his legs. Raine came back to help him carry Hollister to the side of the road.

'Set me down over there in the sun.' He directed them to a spot free from the shade of the corn so he could bask in the early morning light. When the light hit his face, he looked even sicker. His eyes were clouded by ruptured veins.

Raine crouched down next to him and opened out her hand. In her palm were the remaining vials of morphine and their delivery device. But Hollister shook his head. 'Keep 'em. By the time this shot wears off, I'll be gone anyway.'

Salty looked down on him, still holding his hatchet and the Beretta. 'Sure you don't want us to take care of you?' he asked.

'Nah, I've got this.' He reached down and placed his hand on the handle of his holstered sidearm. 'Besides, I haven't decided which way I want it to go yet. I've been thinkin' maybe I wanna see what it's like to come back.'

'Why?' Raine said.

Hollister thought carefully before he answered. 'Because I wanna know what happened to my mom, to my sister.' Right then, his voice changed, became dual. One voice was his own, but the other was something else – something distorted and monstrous. It bled through into every other word he uttered. 'Did they remember when they were gone? Did they think of me? Maybe I'll find out. Maybe I won't. You better go now.'

Raine wasn't sure whether he had noticed the change in his own voice or not, but it was clear he knew his end was close at hand.

Salty strode to the edge of the corn and called to the others. 'Hey. We need to move. Hustle up.'

'There are more of you?' Hollister said.

'A few,' Raine said.

The others arrived shortly after they were summoned, Kristin lingering behind, using Adam as her latest crutch. They were startled by what they found on the road; all of them gathered around the fallen soldier.

'What happened?' Vincent said.

In his feverish state, Hollister spied Emily holding onto her father's hand. She stared at him with the intense curiosity of a child. Hollister smiled. He tried to raise his arm from the ground so he could wave, but could only wiggle his bloodied fingers.

'Just get your family in the back of the truck, and we'll bring you up to speed once we get movin',' Salty said.

'What about him?' Adam asked, pointing to Hollister.

'He's been bitten,' Raine said.

Each of them passed by the soldier on their way to the back of the vehicle. Vincent got in first, and Adam lifted Emily up to him, then he helped Kristin hop on board before climbing in himself. He held out his hand to Ethan, but he ignored it and struggled to pull himself inside. They sat on the raised blocks on either side and gazed at one another like prisoners of war being transported to an undisclosed location.

Salty got behind the wheel and started the truck's engine. Raine hung back with Hollister. 'Thank you,' she said.

'I didn't really have a whole lot of choice, so don't thank me. If I hadn't gotten my dumb ass bit, I'd probably be helping Spears hunt people like you down. I'm worse than those dead bastards out there.' The monstrous voice had all but taken over his own. It growled low – distended.

'No, you're not,' Raine said.

She closed her eyes for a moment, hoping he'd be dead when she opened them. She turned her back on him and walked around to the passenger side of the cabin. As soon as she entered, Salty pulled away, leaving a trail of tailpipe fumes to drift over Hollister's shivering body.

Salty squinted at the fuel gauge. 'We've got half a tank of gas left.'

'Will it get us where we're going?' Raine said.

'If we don't get blown to shit first.'

'Spears may be looking for his truck, but it makes better camouflage than a civilian vehicle.'

'Small mercies, huh?' Salty said.

'Yeah, right.' Raine felt the barrel of the assault rifle pressing against her leg. She gazed out of the window and saw a group of five roamers in the adjacent field. They seemed to know where they were heading, all together. Shambling, swinging limbs, occasionally staring up into the cruel rays of the new day.

Episode Three

I Watched You Burn

Chapter 1

O.B. tried to take in another deep breath, but the stale air inside the station wagon just didn't cut it. He felt like he constantly had a pair of hands around his throat and the heat of the other bodies wasn't helping. Sweat seeped from between the ample folds of fat on his belly, further darkening the black fibres of his T-shirt. Even his wrists were moist beneath his silver-studded leather bracelets, and his spiked, blue-tinted hair was starting to flop in the humidity. He reached for his soda can in the cup holder, swilling the last dregs around inside it before knocking it back. It felt warm and sickly as it went down and didn't do anything to quench his violent thirst. 'Please, can we just open one window, Mama?'

Paula Gonzalez looked at him accusingly from the driver's seat. The woman was so large, she could only just manage to squeeze behind the wheel without being crushed, her summer dress clinging to her fat like floral body paint. 'How many times, Oswald. I don't want anything getting in here. Think about your sisters for a change.'

O.B. twisted awkwardly so he could view the passengers in the back. He could already hear his youngest sibling, Renata, loud and clear. She'd been screaming and kicking her legs in her car seat for the past twenty minutes. His teenage sister, Jazmin, sat beside her, but was far too interested in her cellphone to take any notice. She frantically jabbed the touch screen display with her index finger, hoping for a miracle: network service. Sara, his middle sister, sat with her legs open, a big bag of cheese poofs resting between them, happy as a clam. Her face and the front of her shirt were smeared in orange dust from her snack. Behind them all was their cousin, Bruno. He was gazing at O.B. in desperation, trapped between the screaming baby and their barking golden retriever.

Right then, O.B. had an idea. It surprised him that enough oxygen was getting to his brain to allow him to have one. 'What about Colonel?' he said.

'What about him?' Paula replied, glaring over the frame of her chain-linked glasses.

'I read that if a dog is stuck in a hot car, they can die from a fit or a heart attack in less than fifteen minutes.'

'Where did you hear that?'

'It's true, Mrs. Gonzalez.' Bruno piped up. 'They can't sweat like we do, so they overheat real easy.'

Paula paused for thought. She'd gotten so used to her constant body odour that she rarely noticed it, but even she was aware of how ripe the car had become. 'OK,' she said. 'Open one of the back windows for the Colonel, *por favor*, but just that one, so my *chico* can get some air.'

'Thanks, Mama,' O.B. said.

'I wasn't talking about you.'

The dog barked again, reminding him where he stood in his mother's chain of consideration.

Bruno rubbed the top of his head and leaned over the seat to gaze over Jazmin's shoulder, as she continued to angrily prod her phone screen. 'Y'know you're wasting your time, right? It said on the news before we left that the cell towers were down, from the East Coast to New Mexico.'

Jazmin felt his hot breath on her neck and immediately rolled her eyes. 'I know one cell tower that needs to come down. Mama? Bruno is staring down my top again,' she said.

'Quit it, Bruno. That's your cousin,' Paula shouted.

'I wasn't. She's a liar,' Bruno said, slumping back into his seat.

The argument forced a smile from O.B., but his screaming baby sister and the oppressive heat of the car quickly wiped it away again.

Sara suddenly stopped gobbling her cheese poofs and grabbed Jazmin's cellphone, smudging the orange dust from her fingers all over its screen.

'Goddamn it, Sara. You little retard,' Jazmin said.

Paula shifted her body to look behind her, rocking the car's suspension. '*Mi corazon*! What did you call your sister?'

'She cheesed the front of my cell!'

'I just wanted to play one of the games,' Sara said. 'You're only trying to text your boyfriend anyway.'

'Shut your mouth,' Jazmin said, her dark eyes bulging as though they were about to pop.

'Jazmin is too young for boyfriends,' Paula said.

Sara smirked and delved back into her bag of cheesy poofs, unable to keep her mouth shut for long. 'So who was the boy that came over last time she babysat for us?'

Jazmin wanted to reach over and smack her in the mouth, but she figured she was already in enough trouble. Instead, she shrank into her seat and folded her arms, awaiting her mother's wrath.

Paula sat with her head bowed, as if in prayer. 'Young lady, we'll say no more about this now, but when we get to your father in Chicago, we're going to have a serious discussion about the rules we have set down for you.'

Jazmin shook her head. 'Like they even matter anymore.'

'You say that to your father, Jazmin. Say that to him and we'll see if it matters anymore.'

Renata kicked her little legs and screamed even harder, causing O.B.'s ears to throb.

'Instead of sitting there sulking, why don't you see to the baby?' Paula said.

Jazmin huffed, unlocked her arms, and shoved a bottle half-full of juice into Renata's open mouth. The child immediately rejected it and continued to whine.

'Me and Bruno are gonna take a walk to get some air,' O.B. said.

'Oh no. You ain't goin' no place, Oswald,' Paula said.

'I'll be right outside, Mama.'

'Oh shit,' Bruno exclaimed from the back. 'The Colonel just farted.'

'Ewww.' Jazmin screwed up her face and covered her nose, ruining her good looks.

Sara just laughed and attacked her cheesy poofs.

It took a while for the dog's smell to hit the front of the car, but when it did, it hadn't lost any of its potency.

'*¡Guácala!*' Paula attempted to waft the meaty stench away. As soon as she began to wind down her window, the rest of the Gonzalez family did the same and they were no more protected than if they were standing in the road.

'That's it. I'm stepping out.' Bruno didn't wait for approval.

O.B. was halfway out before his mother realised. 'Stay close to the car, Oswald. Close enough to hear me calling you,' Paula said.

'That means we can go anywhere in the state,' Bruno whispered.

The first thing they did was to search between the piles of suitcases on the roof rack to find their skateboards and pull them down.

O.B. placed his boot on the tail of his board and examined the huge line of traffic that was snaking its way along Route 57, right up to the glistening cityscape of Chicago. 'Do you think he's still there?'

'Your Papa?' Bruno looked up at the lights. 'He wouldn't let you down. He's nothing like mine. He'll be there, cuz. You worry too much.'

'He didn't call us when the phones were still up.'

'Dude, do you have any idea how many people were using their cells when everything went to shit? The networks couldn't cope with it. They were flat-out crashing. At least that's what they said when the TVs were still up.'

'I guess so,' O.B. said.

The Gonzalez family weren't the only ones staying inside their vehicles, but many travellers had started to settle down for the long haul. Some stood outside chatting with other motorists. Some opened out the flatbeds in their trucks or placed down blankets in the back of their trailers. The lucky ones were the motorhome owners.

A pretty flash-looking one was sitting just behind the station wagon. It didn't seem like the kind O.B. had seen before – there was no overhang above its cabin; it looked more like a coach than an RV.

A guy was sitting on the hood of his car nearby, feeding peanuts to his kid and gazing up at the stars in the clear sky. The child couldn't have been any older than six. O.B. couldn't hear what his father was saying to him, but he could tell by his facial expressions that he was trying to be enthusiastic, attempting to turn the whole experience into an adventure. The boy continued to stare at the sky, but the man noticed O.B.'s eyes on him. For just a moment, his smile faded and a crushing weight of weariness pulled at his face, but once the child reached for another peanut, the man's smile returned and he managed to hold it together again.

O.B.'s focus was broken by a shout coming from about six cars further down the line. Everyone outside turned to see what the commotion was. The shout soon transformed into a wail of distress. It sounded like a woman, and she was calling out a name.

'Kevin! Kevin! Kevin!'

O.B. jumped onto his board and kicked towards the wailing. Paula waved from the window of the station wagon, too immobile and cramped up to do anything more. 'O.B., don't you leave my sight.'

'*Un memento, Mama*,' O.B. said, never looking back.

'Dude, let it be,' Bruno said.

O.B. skated right past him, going in the direction of the car. Bruno rolled his eyes and followed.

Once they got alongside the car, it was as O.B. feared. A black woman was cradling a young man in the back seat of the Ford Sedan. The door was open so the boy's skin could be kissed by the breeze that swept across the highway. His face was dripping with sweat and his skin was a shade of grey.

O.B. realised the teen must be really sick, but then he noticed that his eyes were open, and that they were dilated and unresponsive. He couldn't remember if he'd ever seen a dead body before. In a strange way, he thought the boy looked new, like he'd just received a fresh sheen of polish – a glow of deadness. His mouth moved slightly, opening a gap between his lips, as if he were somehow trying to force out a whisper from beyond the grave.

All the woman could think to do was stroke his hair and rock him like a baby. To her, he still was one.

Sitting behind them on the back seat, a girl not much older than the boy was gripping the woman around her waist and weeping into her shoulder.

'Dude, check it out,' Bruno whispered. He pointed to the teen's right arm, which was draped across his mother's lap.

O.B. saw it – the bandage wrapped around his forearm and the red stain that was growing beneath it.

'You know what that means. We have to get away from here.'

'So do they.' O.B. stepped off his board and approached the car.

'O.B., no.' Bruno thought about going with him, but the fear caused him to hang back.

O.B. knelt down by the open door, turning his eyes from the sight of the dead boy as a sign of respect. 'It seems hot in there,' he said softly. 'Why don't you bring him outside so he can get more of the breeze? I'll help you, if you like.'

The woman sucked in her tears and gazed up at him inquisitively. 'Yes. I think he would like that.' She ran the back of her hand over his brow as she spoke.

'OK then.' O.B. supported the boy's shoulders, careful not to handle him too roughly, and the woman shuffled from the back seat, holding onto her son's limp legs. Together they managed to lay him on the road, facing the stars. His mother stayed by his side, holding his hand. She began sobbing again.

Her daughter climbed out of the vehicle too, but remained on her feet. O.B. shared a look with her; one that told him she knew what would happen if they did not move away from her fallen brother. He hadn't thought far enough ahead. His only idea was to get the women to at least create some distance between them and the teen's corpse. Then he hoped that someone else would come to help. 'You look like you could do with some water and something to eat. Do you have any?' he asked.

'We have nothing,' the young girl said.

'We can help. My mama brought lots of stuff with us. Our car is just over there. Maybe you and your mom could come with us.'

The woman reacted to his suggestion by gripping her son's hand even tighter, throwing her other arm across his chest to shield him.

O.B. could see just how close her forearm was to his open mouth. 'Oh no, I didn't mean we should leave him alone. My cousin Bruno will take you over. I'll wait here and watch over him for you.'

The girl placed her hands on her mother's shoulders. 'Mom, we can trust him.'

'No,' the woman said. 'I'm not leaving him with you. You can go get it and bring it here if you want, but I'm not moving from his side.' She glanced around at the other motorists with suspicion, as if they were waiting to pounce and take away what was hers – the child that had gestated in her womb and grown into this young man, only to be burned out by an uncontrollable fever that had all but cooked his organs from the inside out.

'Come on, B. Leave it,' Bruno said, standing behind him and tugging at his arm.

'No.' O.B. tried to shrug him off.

'Forget it, you idiot. She's gone.'

O.B. stopped struggling to face his cousin. 'She's still here, Bruno. She's right here.'

'You know what I meant.' Bruno waved his hands in surrender. 'Whatever, man.'

They both flinched at the anguished scream of the young girl. The dead boy's hand flexed and closed its fingers around his mother's wrist. Something stirred within his grey eyes. Not life – a strange form of transient, necromantic existence that had become so common place in recent weeks. His open mouth widened further and forced out a gargled breath. He sat up abruptly, as if waking to an alarm clock, late for school. His head twisted mechanically in the direction of his mother, and in some obscure way, he seemed to recognise her.

'Kevin,' she sobbed. 'You came back for me.'

Of course, Kevin was no longer present – not in any real sense. What she was gazing upon with such heartbreaking maternal love was a human transformed. The creature lurched for her, gnashing its slathering jaws as it tried to take a bite out of her arm. The woman's daughter grabbed the creature's shirt and held it back just enough to keep its teeth from her flesh.

Against his cousin's protests, O.B. threw himself into the fray and started to prise the corpse's fingers from her wrist. They struggled. The tangle of bodies seesawed one way and then the other, but still the dead one wouldn't let go – its hunger was all-consuming. It turned back in anger and made a reach for its former sibling, who prevented him from feeding. The girl screamed and let go, falling hard on the asphalt.

The freed creature went back to its original prey, snapping its teeth in readiness. But before it could squeeze out a proper, gleeful groan, its face exploded, covering the distraught woman in blood, bone and sinew.

O.B. caught a grisly splash of gore across the neck of his shirt. Only then did he hear the shot. His ears ringing, he traced the sound back to a nearby Buick. The grey-haired man in the driver's seat was pointing the smoking Magnum right at them. O.B. got the impression he wanted to fire again, even though the creature had fallen still on the road. But the man withdrew his finger from the trigger and pulled his weapon inside his vehicle. He turned and stared through his windshield, as if he'd just witnessed someone else do it.

The woman fell onto her back, her son's brains sliding from her cheeks. For the first time since they had seen her, her weeping had ceased. She lay in silence, her eyes cold, her fists held up to her chin.

O.B. got to his feet. His instinct was to run as far away from the scene as possible, but then he saw how broken-hearted the teenage girl was. She called for her mother, already aware what had become of her. She was in hell, like they all were.

'B?' Bruno's voice had taken an ominous tone.

The moment O.B. turned, he saw it. The golden crown atop the Sears Tower flickered like a faltering heartbeat, then died. It initiated a chain reaction, and the window lights started to wink out on the building. The darkness spread to the street signs, lamps and houses until there was only shrouded outlines left of Chicago.

Only when it was as black as pitch did the groaning start. Most of the car engines on the highway had been switched off, so it was easy to hear, even in the distance. Soon, the other survivors noticed the sounds and stopped talking. It grew by the second, emanating from the depths of the forest. The trees began to sway and tremors could be felt right through the concrete road.

Bodies broke the treeline, flattening the undergrowth, each one more foul and gruesome than the next. Men, women and children inhabiting their new transitions. Their putrid flesh hung from their bones like an ill-fitting dress as they ploughed headlong towards the stationary traffic.

Everyone froze at first, marvelling at the sheer weight of numbers pouring from the woodlands. The people who regained their wits fast enough either fled in the opposite direction or desperately tried to gather their families before making their escape. For the scared and the selfish, a chance remained. The rest weren't so lucky. The forest edge was extremely close to the road. The dead were upon them before most had a chance to exit their vehicles.

O.B. ran back to the station wagon, his own weight slowing him down.

'Wait,' Bruno shouted.

O.B. managed to get close enough to see the car just as the dead swarmed it and the surrounding vehicles. The windows of the station wagon had been left open – all the invitation the creatures needed. They reached through and clambered inside the front and back. The screams of his family washed over him like a tide of sickness. He watched on, helpless, as splashes of blood coated the car's interior. The next thing he knew, Bruno had wrapped an arm across his chest to drag him away.

'We have to split, bro. We have to go now!'

The creatures descended upon the cars right next to them. The rotten net was closing in. O.B. turned his back on the station wagon, and the last thing he saw was The Colonel, trapped and still barking in the rear window.

His cousin guided him from there. He felt like he was having an out-of-body experience. Bodies ghosted by him. It was unclear whether they belonged to the living or the dead. The sound of screams was muffled. He glanced down to the black woman. She was still lying on the ground, her eyes fixed on the sky, her son's blood beginning to dry on her skin. Her daughter did her best to snap her out of it, but she was wasting her time.

O.B. could do nothing for them. Even as Bruno guided him to his board and ordered him to kick away, he was operating on autopilot. Just like the station wagon containing his family, the woman and her daughter fell into the swarm, where they were, devoured by twenty or so hungry mouths. The stumbling stampede dispersed across the highway like the blast from a fire bomb. The two boys weaved between the cars and fleeing survivors until they were clear of the horde. Even so, they kept on skating.

O.B.'s head cleared enough to hear one survivor call out as he watched the mass feeding frenzy unfold from a safe distance. 'It's over. It's all over.'

Chapter 2

By the time O.B. and Bruno came across the first road sign for Posen village, the dawn had already begun to break. The fact they had been able to use their boards most of the way had saved their feet, but they still needed to rest and find food and shelter.

Since they'd escaped the swarm, they had not set eyes on any of the dead and this served as a welcome relief. Thankfully, this didn't change as they strolled along Posen's main road. Concrete defence barriers were still in place, blocking off every route into the village by vehicle. Without soldiers to man them, they were easily negotiated.

O.B. placed his hand on an area of one of the barriers, scorched black by fire. Further down the road they came across the skeletal frame of a burnt-out truck. Bullet holes peppered the walls of the village bank on the corner. It appeared that the military had been forced to put up a fight before the evacuation, but it wasn't clear what they had been fighting against.

Bruno made a beeline for the car dealership across the street. Meticulously waxed cars were standing in front, and there were others in the showroom behind a broken pane of reinforced glass. He stared in envy at the gun-metal-grey Chevy Camaro at the centre of the display. 'That's my ride, right there.'

O.B. ignored him – too traumatised to take note of his cousin's trivial desires.

'We should boost this son-of-a-bitch,' Bruno said.

'Like you know how to boost a car.'

'Yeah. Well, we just need to find one with gas and the keys inside.'

'What we need is food and water and a safe place to sleep,' O.B. said.

Bruno admired the glimmering sports car for a moment longer. When he noticed his cousin was getting away from him, he shrugged and jumped on his board to catch up.

O.B. turned up his nose in disgust at the sight of the half-eaten corpse sitting upright against the wall of Davis Elementary School. It had been chewed down to its waist. At least thirty flies were picking through the open, decaying flesh. He averted his eyes before it made him sick.

Hundreds of white posters blew about in the cross-wind, rolling from curb to curb. One tumbled in O.B.'s direction and got snagged against his shoe. He crouched down and turned it the right way up. The picture featured a smiling child, messy hair and dimples in his cheeks. The text read 'MISSING PERSON: Simon Cunningham. 11 years old, white, slim build. Last seen on July 7 2016, wearing blue jeans and a green polo neck shirt. Has distinctive birth mark beneath left eye. If you have any information, please contact Posen Police Department on 0708-385-0277.'

O.B. couldn't take his eyes off the boy's photograph. How happy he seemed – how safe... loved.

'What are you lookin' at?' Bruno said as he walked over.

'It's a kid. He went missing around the time it all started. There's no one left to look for him now.'

Bruno smiled. 'I love you, cousin. You have a big heart. If it's any consolation, I'm gonna do my best to make sure it stays in your chest where it belongs. Now come, get up.' Bruno helped him to his feet and they wandered over to the steps of the elementary school.

The front doors were chained and bolted, but a window close by had already been smashed. 'Looks like this could have been locked up before the outbreak,' Bruno said. 'Schools store a lot of food for the students.'

'The freezers would have powered down weeks ago. It'll all be rancid now,' O.B. said.

'Not the canned stuff. We're bound to find something.' Bruno wasted no more time arguing. He knocked the remaining glass shards from the frame of the broken window with his elbow. 'What are you waiting for? You'll fit through here.' He climbed inside, leaving O.B. to stare at the opening.

'Just about,' O.B. said under his breath.

⁂

Although it was getting warmer outside, the gloomy halls of the school were deathly cold. Fortunately, there were no corpses of students or teachers rotting in the classrooms, but there were plenty of echoes of the vibrant hub that it used to be. School bags and children's jackets hung over the chairs, open books lay on desks, writing had been left on blackboards. It was clear that the evacuation of the school had taken place during class time.

Bruno nudged O.B. and pointed to the sign hanging from the ceiling in the corridor. It read 'Canteen'. 'There'll be a store room in there. No doubt,' Bruno said.

The grinding sound of their skateboard wheels reverberated around the empty, shadowed spaces until they reached the double doors of the canteen.

Bruno jumped down and kicked the tail of his board so he could catch it by its nose. 'Canned peaches, here we come.'

They had taken no more than two steps inside before the smell hit them. They knew what it was because they had smelled it on the highway on the previous night. All the tables and chairs from the room's centre had been removed, leaving just floor space. Lying there were at least a hundred body bags. Some of them were torn and looked as if they had been clawed open. The contents of the open bags were nothing more than greasy bones, with the odd piece of flesh clinging on. Pools of blood had collected and dried into the Linoleum. Some of it trailed in drag marks leading back to the stainless-steel serving counter and the kitchen behind it.

'We should leave,' O.B. whispered.

'Yeah, no shit,' Bruno said.

They heard a groan from behind the counter and three figures emerged, swaying, their arms limp and their teeth gnashing. One of them was missing an eye. Its cheek had also been shattered, creating a substantial dent in its face.

The boys jumped onto their boards and skated back the way they had come. O.B. wailed on the bar of the first fire exit, but it would not budge. 'It's locked.'

'Move. Let me try.' Bruno pushed him out of the way and swung on the bar, lifting his feet from the ground to get more leverage. 'Fuck!'

They continued on through the hall, but before they could reach the next exit, another group of corpses stumbled around the corner. The creatures were shoulder to shoulder, completely blocking the way and removing any ideas of somehow slipping by them.

'Up here.' Bruno turned towards the staircase and began leaping steps two at a time. O.B. took one last look at their creeping, decaying pursuers and followed.

By the time they reached the second floor, the dead were already clumsily climbing the stairs. O.B. leaned over the barrier and gazed down at them. One creature was pushing on ahead of the others, seemingly more nimble on its feet. The grey-haired corpse managed six steps before it lost its balance, veered left, and then toppled over the handrail.

O.B. turned around, and was startled by the look on his cousin's bloodless face.

'We're in deep shit, O.B..' Behind him, more of the dead were shuffling along the second-floor corridor. At first there had been none, and now they were everywhere. Bruno ran to the top of the stairs. 'We'll have to go back. Fight our way out.'

'Are you for real? There's too many. They'll eat us alive,' O.B. said.

They headed up the second flight of stairs to the third and final floor. No sooner had they reached the top than they were met by another dozen creatures stalking down the left-hand corridor. They reached out with emaciated arms into the empty space between them and their next potential meal.

'Now what?' Bruno said.

O.B. pointed to the other end of the corridor. 'Maybe there's a fire escape at the end.'

'And if there isn't?'

'Then we're screwed.' O.B. ran for it, his large belly bouncing from side-to-side as he went. He knew that if more wandered out of any of the doors ahead, of which there were many, it would be over. He figured he would keep running in the hope of knocking them down if any did come out. To his relief, he made it to the window in one piece, Bruno close behind. But when he tried to slide it open, it wouldn't budge.

'Come on, come on,' Bruno said.

'It must be jammed.'

His cousin stepped up to the frame and they both pulled at once. Even their combined strength didn't seem to have any impact. It felt like it was nailed shut. Just as they thought they would have to break the glass, there was a snapping of wood and a violent shift that caused them to stumble backwards.

Bruno shoved O.B. out onto the steel grating of the platform. As he climbed through the window himself, he glanced back at the gathering crowd of undead, who hadn't managed to get even halfway down the corridor.

Their shoes clanked down the first set of stairs, but O.B. stopped abruptly when he reached the next platform. 'They're gone.'

Bruno thought he meant the dead at first, but then realised he was looking over the edge. He dodged around his large frame and looked down at their new quandary. Something must have struck the fire escape. There had clearly been an explosion. Just like the barriers on the way in to Posen, the wall on the side of the school building was scorched. The last set of stairs had melted and contorted, and were impossible to use. Even for someone strong and athletic, the distance from the ground was too high to jump.

'There.' Bruno pointed just below the railing on the platform. The extra emergency ladder was still attached to the track, but because it was drawn in, it had been protected from the blast and remained intact.

O.B.'s head started to spin at the prospect of climbing over the railings and dangling his feet towards the first rung. 'I don't think I can make it.' Beads of sweat oozed from his face and neck. His hands felt like they'd been smeared in grease as he tried to get a firm grip on the rail.

'You have to make it. Now get over there,' Bruno said.

O.B. prayed for courage to suddenly take hold of him, but it never came.

'Buddy, either you climb over that rail, or so help me, I'm gonna push your fat ass over.'

O.B. turned to his cousin, hoping that he would lose his patience and do what he'd threatened. Just then, the glass of the window behind Bruno shattered, and before he could move clear, a wall of decaying hands reached through the empty frame and caught hold of him. His startled eyes fixed upon O.B. as he was dragged inside.

'O.B.!'

Bruno's tone was expectant as well as desperate, but his cousin had no idea how to react. Instead, he watched Bruno get pulled into the second floor corridor almost folded in two.

'Please. Help me. Please.' His screams coincided with the multiple sets of fingers punching holes into his skin, tearing at his flesh. 'Pleeeeeease. Pleeeeeease.'

O.B. coiled into the foetal position, pressing himself hard against the rail and crying helplessly. The last image of Bruno he saw as he disappeared into the belly of the ravenous horde would be forever burned into his memory. His shaved scalp was torn from the top of his forehead by a skeletal hand and peeled like an over-ripe fruit, exposing his skull beneath. Blood cascaded down his face like tears. His screams were soon drowned out by the chewing and tearing as the creatures feasted on everything he had. O.B. froze. His muscles locked in place. At that moment, the only thing he was able to do was to listen to his cousin being devoured.

'Hey, fat boy!' came a croaking voice from below. He looked down into the street and saw someone standing there with a shopping cart full to the brim. It was hard to tell, but he guessed it was a woman. Her limbs were painfully thin, her skin caked in dirt. A red beanie hat covered most of her greasy, matted hair. 'You gonna climb down that ladder, or do you wanna end up like your friend in there?'

He went cold and glanced back to the window. The dead were coming to the end of their meal, and they were just starting to build up an appetite.

'Look, either way suits me fine. There's enough of you to keep those sacks of shit busy for an hour. Means there's less of 'em around for me to avoid. Do what the hell you like.' The haggard woman began to push her cart away, and O.B. could feel his legs again.

He clambered over the rail and tentatively dangled one foot down to the ladder. As soon as he put his weight on it, the top section rattled along the track and stopped just above the ground. With every rung, he needed to stop climbing and take a breath, wrapping his arms around the frame, just in case he slipped.

By the time he got to the bottom, landing awkwardly in the street, the woman was already well on her way, checking for signs of danger as she went. 'Wait,' he shouted.

'Why don't you just ring the dinner bell, dickhead?' she whispered back.

'Where are you going?'

'Home,' she replied.

Chapter 3

O.B. followed his dirty new acquaintance right across to the other side of the village, but he still wasn't able to catch up with her. At a distance, he could appreciate just how malnourished she was. Her legs carrying her and her precious cart along were like two twigs. It would have been easy to mistake her for the other type of humanoid now sharing the planet with them. Despite that, O.B. was no match for her stamina and determination. Wherever 'home' was, it wasn't any of the scenic houses in Posen.

She led him to the outskirts and the one place left. The two-storey building looked high to him, one half fallen away in ruins. A broken sign lay face up on the derelict ground surrounding it. The lettering had faded, but he could still make out what it said: 'Gilded Paints'.

The woman battled to untangle the wheels of her cart from the rocks and waste that littered the ground. She managed to push through the furrowed terrain and was entering the broken shell of the factory just as O.B. finally caught up with her. The inside was much the same as the outside – nothing more than an industrial relic, with crumbling walls, dripping with moisture from the naturally cultivated rising damp. The whole place reeked of mould. O.B.'s skate shoes peeled away from the sticky substance coating the floor. He realised that his board was no longer tucked under his arm. He'd left it back on the platform of the fire escape.

The woman forced her shopping cart to the edge of a ramp that led down to the basement of the factory, and then turned to O.B. 'Don't be shy now. Help me with this shit.'

'Help you to do what?'

'To move it down below. Like I told you. This is home.'

He followed her down the ramp to a cast iron manhole cover surrounded by railings. The cover was flipped open and he could see a set of ladders descending into the darkness of the sewer system. 'Wait. You're going down there?'

'Don't get your panties in a twist. It's clear. Separated from the rest of the system by a locked gate. It stinks of shit, but what doesn't these days?' The woman reached into the cart and grabbed the two blankets from the top, pushing them into O.B.'s chest. 'Carry these.'

Now that he was able to get a good look at her, he saw that she was even more haggard than he'd realised. Her cheeks were sunken, her skin covered in red blotches and scabs. She noticed his stare and smiled. The cracks in her blistered lips separated like tiny mouths to reveal raw flesh in between. Her gums were enflamed and her teeth had succumbed to decay.

'Sucks, don't it?' the woman said. 'The only time in your life you might have had a chance with a pretty girl, and you get stuck with a dog like me.'

O.B. shook his head. 'No. Errm, I wasn't.'

'I ain't offended, kid. I haven't had a cock in me for about twenty years. Besides, you ain't exactly John Stamos yourself.' With that, she gathered up the canned meats and fruits from the bottom of her cart, dumped them into a plastic grocery bag, and began climbing into the sewer duct, leaving a stunned O.B. clutching the blankets she had thrust upon him. 'Well, don't just stand there. Your ass might just about fit through.'

Fearing he could not safely climb down using only one hand, O.B. decided to open out both blankets and tie them around his waist like a skirt. The pipe was even wetter and grimier than the factory. With each rung, the ladder got slimier. He felt drops of water fall onto his head and roll down the back of his neck. The drain below seemed to reach on forever. Occasionally, he lost sight of the woman in the shadows, and then she would reappear, contently splashing through the obnoxious sewer flow with her shopping bag as if she were returning home from a trip to the supermarket.

She set the bag down when she reached a fenced area. The small space was shielded from the damp and a mattress lay next to a freshly built campfire.

She sat down next the fire and grimaced, reaching down to scratch her thigh and pointing to the blankets around O.B.'s waist with her other hand. 'You can use them to sit on if you want.' She started to rummage around inside the bag, tossing cans of peaches and cured pork aside to get to the bottom. 'God knows why they locked up those freaks in the school. Maybe the townsfolk did it, or the soldiers before the evacuation. I got no idea. Either way, you and your buddy walked right into it.'

'He was my cousin.' O.B. sat down on the blankets and hung his head. Every muscle in his body ached.

'Gotcha!' The woman found what she had been looking for and held it up to her face. 'You don't know how long I've been searching for one of these. Some of the houses had electric ones that ain't worth shit now, but a lot of 'em didn't have any at all. I guess those idiots packed them before the soldiers shipped them off to the concentration camps. They probably thought it was gonna be like one big family holiday, huh?' She grinned at her own comment and her coveted prize – a plastic and metal can opener. She shuffled about and tilted her head like a curious dog, her attention drawn to the type emblazoned across the front of O.B.'s shirt. 'What in hell is The Vandals anyway?'

He kept his head in his hands, squashing the fat of his cheeks. 'A punk band.'

'That why you got all that shit in your hair?'

'Kinda.'

'My name's Darla – Darla Peatree. What do they call you?'

'O.B.'

Darla shifted her head again, every movement resembling a nervous twitch than a deliberate motion. 'You ain't telling me you were christened that? Must be short for somethin'.'

'Oswald Benedict.'

Darla gave a throaty cackle, so explosive that she almost fell backwards onto her mattress. 'What kind of faggotty name is Oswald Benedict? It sounds like a communist fucked a monk.' She continued to laugh until she was doubled over.

O.B. finally lifted his head – too weary to take issue with her derision. 'I was named after my grandfather.' He put his hands to his face again, this time so he could weep into them. He cried so hard that his whole body jiggled.

'Jesus. What's wrong with kids today? You should really learn to have thicker skin by now. I'm surprised someone with your ass wasn't bullied at school.'

'They used to call me beef trust. My skin's thick enough. They killed my entire fucking family. They climbed into the car and ate them alive. My mum, my little sisters. Renata was just a baby.'

Darla's expression soured. 'I suppose this is the part where you expect me to be the wise old shoulder to cry on. Well, save it. I had a mother who did a better job of nursing a bottle of vodka than me, and a daddy who liked to hold me a little too close, if you know what I mean. At least you had a family that loved you for as long as they did. Shit happens, kid.'

O.B. tempered his emotion and rose with a steely glare in his eyes. He headed back along the drain to the access pipe.

'Hey, where you goin'?'

'Away from you. I would have to be desperate to cry on your shoulder. You fucking stink.'

'At least stay the night. It's one extra day you'll be alive.'

O.B. kept on walking and Darla got to her feet and went after him. 'Look, here's the deal. I'm goin' back out there anyway. You help me do some more rootin' around and I'll shout you a decent meal. I guess you're always hungry, right?'

⊥

Back in the deserted streets of Posen, O.B. hung back, watching Darla scamper from house to house, collecting any extra food and odds and ends she could find. After a few minutes, he noticed another pile of missing posters for Simon Cunningham tumbling by on the breeze.

Over in the next street, a male police officer was lying face down in the road. Darla approached the corpse with interest, immediately stooping down to get underneath the body so she could lever it over onto its back.

As much as O.B. felt like walking away, his stomach was groaning and aching with hunger. Against his better judgement, he wandered over to where Darla was struggling to flip the body.

'Give me a hand with him, will ya?'

O.B. got to his knees and pushed the officer at his hip. Their combined strength did the trick. He then got up again and stepped back, alarmed by the bullet entry wound at the centre of the man's head.

Darla paid it no mind and proceeded to check his duty belt. His sidearm had already been taken; the magazine pouches were also empty, and his radio was gone. But to her delight, she did manage to retrieve a pair of handcuffs, pepper spray and an auto-folding knife from one of the back pockets of his pants. She searched his front pockets, but there was nothing of any use in them.

'What are you looking for exactly?' O.B. said.

'Whatever I can get,' she said.

He caught a glimpse of the wood finished handle of a Colt 38 poking from the back of her waist band. 'You already have a gun,' he said.

'Can't hurt to search for another one.'

'Do you have any ammunition for it?'

'Same amount I had when I found it.' Darla got up and wiped the sweat from her blotchy forehead. 'See, me and them got sorta an understanding. I don't get up in their business and they keep their noses outta mine, except when two idiots walk straight into 'em and get 'em all riled up.'

'Bruno wasn't an idiot. He only died because...' O.B. looked down at the specks of blood on the toes of his shoes.

'Don't beat yourself up about it, kid. Most people are still breathin' at someone else's expense. That's just the way things work now. Hell, that's pretty much the way it's always worked.' Darla dumped what she had salvaged into her grocery bag and moved on.

'So you lived on the streets before it happened?' O.B. said, following after her.

She sniggered. 'What's it look like? I hung around on the sidewalks of Chicago with the rest of the degenerates before this – goin' on twenty years. I look like I'm in my sixties, but I'm a lot younger.'

'How old are you?'

'None of your fuckin' business.'

'You were in Chicago?'

'Until those things started appearing. I was smart and got out early. The bums were the first to go. Exposed in the city at night, we started goin' missing one by one. The cops didn't give a shit. They never did. Then I found one of my buddies in an alleyway one mornin' – what was left of her anyways. Decided to move on before I ended up the same. I got as far as this place and then the main power grid went down and the army showed up. It's stayed pretty quiet so far. Just the way I like it.'

'My dad was in Chicago when it happened, but we lost contact with him. That's where I'm going – to try and find him.'

Darla sniggered again and gazed through the broken window of a convenience store. 'If your daddy stayed put, I wouldn't hold out much hope for him. If he had any sense, he would've made for the coast. That's what all the city folks were talking about doing before I left. Trying to get to the water and hire themselves a boat – steal one, if needs be. If your daddy's still alive, that's where he'll be.'

'Then I'll go to the coast,' O.B. said.

Darla blew through her teeth. 'Good luck with that.'

'Then come with me.'

'Why would I wanna do that?'

'To find somewhere better.'

'I've already found it. I have everything I need right here. Don't really fancy the idea of gettin' ate or shot up running a fool's errand for your sorry ass.'

'How long are you gonna last before there's nothing left to scavenge in this place?'

'Shhh.' Darla's ears pricked up. She held one of her scrawny hands to O.B.'s face and waited.

Sure enough, one of the dead stumbled around the corner, dragging its broken left leg behind it. The fractured bone created a bloodied bulge beneath its pants. It had yet to see them, and Darla intended to keep it that way. She shoved O.B. across the street in the direction of Posen's modest fire station. She kicked him once in his ass and then he entered through the open rolling doors of its entrance. They both crouched down and peered from behind the wall to watch the creature pass. As it was still in view, they were alerted to a new sound approaching from the road into the village. The grumbling tyre tracks of the heavy vehicle got louder, and soon they saw the robust shape of an armoured infantry carrier with five soldiers marching alongside it.

The men didn't seem to be concerned about the creature heading towards them. When it realised there was a chance of fresh meat nearby, it reached out its hands and started to growl softly, but the personnel carrier ran straight over it, mangling its brittle bones between its tracks, crushing it flat.

O.B. smiled and began to rise from their hiding place. Darla reacted swiftly, yanking him back into position. 'Don't you fuckin' dare,' she whispered.

'What do you mean? They'll take us in. Take us to one of the camps.'

'Make one peep, and I swear to God I'll put a bullet in you and leave you to bleed out.'

'What is wrong with you? They're obviously looking for survivors,' O.B. said.

'I don't deny that.'

'Then what the hell?'

'Just be patient, fat boy.'

Once the patrol reached the centre of town, the vehicle stopped. One of the soldiers got on the radio, but O.B. and Darla were too far away to hear what he was saying. Darla pulled O.B. behind the wall of the station as the patrolmen scanned in their direction. They seemed to be hanging around waiting for something – perhaps orders from their central control.

The soldiers suddenly raised their weapons in response to a noise coming from a house close by. A woman emerged from it, dirty and dishevelled, and holding a blanket around her neck. 'Oh, thank God,' she shouted. 'We thought no one would come for us.'

'Calm down, ma'am. You said we?' A soldier replied.

'Yes. My son. He's inside. He has a bad wound on his leg and he's lost a lot of blood. I don't know how much longer he would have lasted.' The woman's voice was strained, overcome by emotion and relief.

'We're not gonna get another chance to let them know we're here,' O.B. whispered.

'Just wait a minute,' Darla said.

'So there's just you and your son. You've not seen anyone else?' the soldier asked.

'No, we're the last.'

No sooner had the woman answered the soldier aimed his rifle at her head and opened fire. The single bullet cut into her skull and she collapsed into the blanket she had been holding.

O.B.'s instinct was to shout out, but Darla remedied that by cupping her hand over his mouth.

The soldier who had gunned her down signalled to two of his colleagues and waved them towards the house. They shuffled along the perimeter, covering each other as they went, and entered through the side door.

Thirty seconds later, Darla and O.B. heard two shots and saw the flashes behind one of the windows. When the men rushed back into the street, the radio operator got on his device again, and they soon began to leave Posen along the same road they had come in on.

'They executed them. Shot them down in cold blood,' O.B. said.

'You're catchin' on,' Darla said. 'You might just live a little longer after all.'

⚔

O.B. watched the flickering flames of the campfire and slurped back the last of the juice from the canned peaches he'd eaten. He lay on the double blanket and rested his head. It wasn't exactly comfortable; he could still feel the hard, cold concrete of the sewer floor, but he trusted Darla when she said that they were safe from the dead. He shut his eyes and tried desperately to block out the echo from the dripping pipes. In the darkness, he saw the clamouring hands tearing back the flesh of Bruno's scalp, and jets of blood splattering the interior windows of his mother's station wagon.

He sat up with a jolt and noticed that Darla's eyes were still open. 'Those pictures never disappear. You just start to remember 'em in less detail after a while,' she said softly. Even within the harsh croak of her voice, he sensed some semblance of empathy.

'I don't want to forget – ever,' he said.

'You might change your mind 'bout that.'

O.B. rolled over, pulling the edge of one of the blankets around his shoulder.

'I'll tag along with you – as far as the coast,' Darla said. 'If we're gonna stand any chance, we need to find a ride.'

'I can't drive.'

'Just as well I can then, idinit?'

'Thank you,' he said. The next time he closed his eyes, he was too exhausted to fight the images that flooded his brain, so he fell asleep to them instead.

Darla turned on her mattress and opened out the fabric drawstring pouch lying next to her – the kind a young girl would use to store her costume jewellery. She held the pouch upside down and three off-white rocks fell out of it. Darla pushed the rocks around on the mattress with the crusty end of her index finger. She leaned over them and breathed in, taking in their chemical odour through her nostrils.

EPISODE FOUR

Rich Man's Burden

Chapter 1

The controlled hiss of hydraulic brakes brought the truck to a stop. Salty and Raine peered through the mud-stained windshield at the car wreck blocking the road ahead. The car had slid horizontally across the road, preventing anything from getting past. There were dents and scratches across its bodywork, and both windows on the nearest side to them were shattered.

'This happened recently,' Raine said.

Salty concurred. He'd also noticed the plumes of steam rising from the hood that had been popped open by the impact. 'Whatever. Let's go move the goddamn thing.' He slipped the truck into park and jumped out onto the tarmac, hatchet in hand.

Raine sat staring at the wreck for a while longer, trying to see if there were any bodies inside it. When she felt Salty's eyes on her, she grabbed the assault rifle they'd obtained from the dying soldier and got out.

Salty walked around to the back of the truck and popped his head inside. The Grahams and the two young men waited in anticipation to find out why they'd stopped. 'Nothing to worry about, folks.' Salty made the remark with the nonchalance of a bus tour guide. 'Just a slight blockage in the road. We'll have it shifted and be rolling again in no time. Stay put.'

When he walked back to the front, Raine approached the wreck, inspecting the skid marks beneath her feet. 'Obviously spun out of control and hit the road barriers,' he said.

'Obviously.' Raine got closer, but she still couldn't see inside on account of the steam from the hood. Bending down, she squinted through the broken front window. Both seats were empty. A thick pool of blood had collected, and was mingling with the shattered cubes of glass at the footwell of the driver's seat. She shifted her attention to the back and heard a chewing sound over the hiss of the ruptured engine.

The driver's body had been dragged into the back seat. The flesh of his right shoulder and neck had been gnawed down to the bone and he was rocking slightly, as if he was still breathing. Before Raine could reach inside, the dead one that was feeding on the corpse sat up. A half-eaten piece of muscle hung from its rotting jaws.

The creature leapt forward and pushed one of its arms through the window, grasping the assault rifle. Raine refused to let go, struggling back and forth and trying to prise the weapon away from it. She tugged so hard that the creature slid out. As it did, the jagged shards of glass still lodged in the window track pierced the fragile skin of its stomach and sliced all the way down to its waist.

Raine fell with it, finally releasing the rifle so she could brace herself for the landing. The meat bag stood up, the weapon in its hands. It let out a slow groan of delight. Its serrated flesh flapped open, and its oedematous bowels and intestines slid past the lining of its stomach and splashed onto the asphalt. The stringy mess didn't steam. It was stone cold, but the stench that exuded from it was no less putrid for that.

She scrambled across the road with no regard for what might be behind her. The creature lifted its head to observe the haze from the sun. Then it fixed its eyes upon Raine. Before it managed to get more than a yard towards her, a hollow sound rang out as Salty buried his hatchet deep in its skull. Its eyes rolled back and it fell to its knees before tipping over completely onto its face.

Salty placed his foot on the small of its back in order to yank the hatchet free and plucked the assault rifle from beneath it.

As Raine dusted herself down, he was there to meet her. 'I don't pretend to know what all this silent brooding shit is. That's your business. But if you want to see your way past this, you better shape up, darlin'.' He forced the flat of the rifle against her chest and she snatched it away from him.

'Thanks for the concern,' she said, glaring.

'I don't want you gettin' the wrong idea. I don't give a donkey's dick what happens to you, but if you don't shake yourself out of this funk, when you're supposed to be backing me up, that's my ass.' Salty walked over to the car, reaching inside to release the brake. 'Maybe I should ask Mommy Graham to cover me next time.'

She didn't say another word. She just slung the rifle strap over her shoulder and helped him to push the bloodied wreck to the side of the road.

Vincent jumped from the truck and edged cautiously to the cabin, meeting Salty as he made his way back.

'What did I say, Vinnie?'

'I heard a struggle. It sounded serious,' Vincent said.

'Which is exactly why I told you to stay in the truck.'

'How much longer is it going to take? Emily's feeling a little sick with all the bumping around back there.'

'Jesus, has that kid got something wrong with her immune system or somethin'?'

Vincent rolled his eyes at Salty. 'I guess it's just the way she has been brought up. That's pretty much what you were thinking.'

Salty paused to smile, and before he could respond, Vincent continued. 'I know we aren't exactly adapting outside the confines of our comfortable lifestyle, but we're doing the best we can. We didn't have a choice when we were all thrown together.'

'No argument from me on all those counts. You don't need to do any of my thinking for me there, Vin. I may look stupid, but you'd be surprised.'

Unimpressed, Vincent was about to return to his family.

'Why don't you tell your wife you're gonna come sit up front with me? You can even bring the rugrat with you if you like. There's less bumping around in the cabin.'

'Why?'

"Cause Grace Jones in there is only fun to be around if you're in the mood for a staring competition. Besides, we're almost there.'

Chapter 2

Soon after Vincent went to sit up front with Emily on his lap, the vehicle left the main road and turned onto an unmarked stretch. Eventually, the road ended and they started bumping over the rocks and dirt of a beaten trail.

'Sorry about this, Emily,' Salty said.

'That's OK,' she said with a smile. Her father pressed her back against his chest to try to keep her still.

Any trace of suburbia was soon replaced by dense oaks, ashes and hickories, which engulfed the trail. The way ahead became narrow. The overhanging branches were almost touching the truck. Vincent half-expected to hear the sound of the side mirrors cracking as they were taken out by the long reach of the forest. The windows were rolled down, and the sweet scent of blossoming flowers and the calming fragrance of damp earth filled the cabin. Civilisation in general may have been dying and rotten, but this particular section of the natural world was still thriving.

Vincent glanced over to Raine, who was sitting right against the passenger door. She looked out to the forest and he could feel the distinct chill of her isolation. In contrast, their driver and guide looked almost smug behind the wheel, enjoying the intermittent rays of sun that kissed his face as they flashed through the tree cover.

'Isn't this more than a little risky? How do we turn around if we meet something coming the other way?' Vincent said.

'Don't sweat it, Graham. This won't last for much longer.' Salty was completely right. As they plunged even deeper into the woodland, the trail ended and the bumping stopped. They had hit a smooth piece of road again.

Vincent noticed its surface was almost white, free of any tyre tracks. The centre line had been marked with fresh paint. There was ample space on either side of them too – it was wide enough for two trucks.

'What is this?' Vincent said.

'It's the scenic route to our destination. My former employer had this road built from scratch. He regretted having to lay so much of it, but he needed the access to transport in what was needed.'

'Your employer?'

'Damon Warrington.' An even broader smile came over Salty's craggy face when he said the name.

'That sounds familiar.'

'It should. He was the previous owner of Uridium Technologies – a company that heavily invested in green energy and preservation about fifteen years ago. At 41, Damon decided to sell his business and retire. It fetched a little over 350 million dollars.'

'I know. I read about it,' Vincent said.

'Not too shabby for a retirement fund, eh?' Salty said.

Raine finally turned from the passenger window and spoke. 'Fat lot of good it will do him now.'

Salty shrugged, easing the wheel over as they approached the next gradual bend in the road. 'You'd be surprised.'

About a hundred yards ahead, a pair of antlers emerged from the trees. A buck stepped tentatively onto the asphalt and scanned in all directions, the surface of his tan brown fur glimmering silver in the sunlight.

'Daddy, look!' Emily shifted with excitement on Vincent's lap.

Salty eased down on the brake to give the animal some breathing room. The deer stood around four feet from his shoulders. He stared at the truck, twitching his ears in anticipation of danger. Once certain it was safe to cross, he placed all four hooves onto the hard surface. The doe and her two fawns came out of hiding and followed him.

The doe corralled the two leggy and vulnerable youngsters while the buck examined the way ahead. They only remained in view for a few seconds before disappearing into the treeline on the opposite side, but it was long enough for Vincent to appreciate their bond and the simplicity of their existence. It created a rare moment of stillness in his heart, making him wish that Kristin was sitting up front so she could experience it too.

Emily waved into the forest as the truck accelerated past the spot where the animals had made their exit. 'Stay safe,' she said.

'You ain't seen nothin' yet, darlin',' Salty said.

'OK, you have our attention,' Vincent said. 'What did Warrington build the road for? Where is it leading us?'

'As you can guess, Damon was more than a bit of a tree-hugger. He cared a lot more about conservation of the natural world than he did about money – dedicated his life to it. Success kind of fell into his lap on account of what he was good at, but conservation he had to work at. The main reason he retired was to buy up a nature preserve here in Ohio. Ever since then, it's been closed to the public, and he just kept expanding it until it was the largest in the country – private or otherwise. Has its own water system and off-grid power source – one even an apocalypse can't screw with.'

'How do you know all this?' Vincent said.

'Like I said, he was my employer. Even though it was privately owned, there were still lots of animals and land to attend to. He hired a full-time skeleton crew of staff to do just that.'

Raine, who had been listening with interest throughout his story, deepened her frown. 'What the hell did Warrington want with you?'

Salty chuckled. 'I know what you're thinkin'. You types take one look at me, the way I talk and dress, and you have me all figured out, right?'

'Surprise me,' she said.

'I know my white tails from my roe for one.'

'What?' Vincent said.

'I know deer. A friend of a friend got me the gig with Warrington two years back. He seemed to like my no-nonsense approach, and he was always good at figuring out if people really knew what they were talkin' about. He turned down plenty of folks with fancy qualifications. 'Cause he was self-taught, I guess. Probably the key to his success in the first place. He made me responsible for tracking the deer's movements within the preserve, controlling their numbers, catching them when they needed medical attention.'

'You were the park ranger?'

'You could call it that. Course, he had all kinds of brainiacs on the payroll – sub-contractors mostly: conservation scientists, wildlife biologists, botanists, landscape architects, organic farmers... But with any project like that, you always need someone on site willin' to get their hands dirty. Just so happens I was that guy. I would have come here right away, but the army didn't give me the choice.'

'How do you know someone else hasn't already claimed this place?' Raine said.

'For one, hardly anyone knows it exists. And for another, it's surrounded by a twelve-foot electric fence. There ain't much chance of the power being out.'

'So how do we get in?' Vincent said.

'Main gate has a combination key code. Just so happens I know it.'

Salty navigated the truck around the next bend that led to the final stretch of road before the gate. The steel surrounding the perimeter looked untouched, and they could see sections of cable from the electrified fence through the gaps in the trees.

The brakes hissed right on the doorstep of the preserve. Raine jumped out and immediately fixed her glare on the two security cameras perched on the top of the gate, moving back and forth on a motor.

'Like I said, power's still workin',' Salty swaggered to the back and slapped the flat of his hand on the truck's body to alert the others.

Adam got down and helped Kristin. Ethan exited the truck, rubbing the stiffness from the back of his neck.

Salty headed over to the chrome intercom panel and pushed the button to talk into it. 'It's Jake Masterson. Doctor Anders? Julia? Anyone else make it?' He waited for a response, but nothing came back through the speakers except for the whine of static. He stepped away from the panel and approached the keypad secured to the right side of the gate.

'Maybe Warrington changed the pass code,' Vincent said as he placed Emily on the ground and Kristin joined them.

Salty grabbed the bill of his cap and tilted it to get more air to his forehead. 'Before the shit-show, he travelled to the Antarctic with some of his buddies. They liked to climb in the cold for some goddamn reason.' He paused to think about what he'd said and smiled. 'Maybe it wasn't so crazy after all. Bet those son-of-a-bitches are safer than any of us. Anyway, he wanted me to come back here to do some more work after I'd visited my ex-wife.'

Everyone gathered in front of the truck and watched him place his hand on the keypad. Despite all his bravado about their potential sanctuary, he ran his fingers over the keys for a few seconds before he started to push them.

The escape and subsequent journey had taken a lot out of the group. They stood round-shouldered, staring dead ahead, like they were about to witness the opening of Pandora's box. Salty pressed down on the first key with his index finger. After hitting the sixth digit, he hesitated again, and then pushed two more. He drew his hand away from the panel, letting the others know the sequence had been completed.

He stared down at the red light, clenching his right hand into a fist. Just as he thought something was wrong, the red light winked out, replaced by a green one and a hollow buzz that rattled through the structure's metal. Almost silently, the door started to shift and open inwards.

Vincent felt Kristin's fingers interlocking with his. He met her smile and glanced down to their daughter, who was clutching her favourite stuffed bunny. In that moment, he felt like the luckiest man alive. That was a genuine possibility now.

Salty moved to the opening and turned to face the rest, wearing the goofiest grin you could wish to see. 'Ladies and Germs, welcome to Jurassic Park.'

The laughter that followed sounded more like a collective sigh of relief.

'OK, folks. If you'd like to resume your seats, I'll give you the guided tour of the facility.'

This time, they retired to the truck with their chests out and renewed energy.

⁂

'Woah.' Emily's eyes couldn't widen enough to take it all in. The preserve rolled out in front of them – acre after acre of lush green grass and plant-life. In the distance, they could see several towers, large bodies of water and modern buildings.

They passed various nature trails leading into the woodlands, and Salty hit the brakes on the truck again. To their right, huge rectangular panels tilted up to the sky, each one mounted on a tower. Everyone in the cabin shielded their eyes from the glare reflected from the panels.

'This right here is the heart that pumps the site with its blood,' Salty said. 'Our solar farm produces over one hundred megawatts of electricity. The grid runs right beneath us, powering everything from the water supply to energisers for the perimeter fence.'

Vincent gazed out of the window like an awestruck child. 'When you said you knew a place, you really knew a place,' he said.

'It just moved.' Emily pointed to one of the towers, looking at Salty to confirm she hadn't imagined it.

'That's right, kid. The towers are motorised, which allows the panels to track the sun so they have the highest output. Each one is made from cadmium telluride. Funny name, huh? It's a thin, state-of-the-art semi-conductor designed to absorb and convert sunlight.' Salty seemed pleased with himself, as if it was something he'd learned by heart and which he had been dying to repeat to someone. 'It delivers the smallest carbon footprint possible, the lowest amount of water usage and the shortest energy payback time. Unless these assholes find a way to block out the sun, we should do alright. Come on, let's get to the Management Centre and have a proper look-see at the rest of the facility.'

Salty stepped on the accelerator, and Vincent, Emily and Raine felt the glow of the redirected light on their skin for what they knew was the last time for a while.

The truck came to a halt again right on the doorstep of the hexagonal-shaped Management Centre. A four-pronged antenna rose up from its roof and artificial lights could be seen within.

Everyone got out. Adam immediately bent over, almost touching his knees with his head, stretching the back of his calves in the process. Emily rushed over to where he was standing and copied him, cheating by bending her knees and peering between her legs to smile back at Vincent, the ends of her pigtails trailing on the grass.

Vincent smiled at her and Kristin joined him. It was the first time they'd seen their daughter relaxed outside since the outbreak. The colour had returned to her bubblegum cheeks after the tooth abscess had made her so sick. Vincent turned to his wife and kissed her. 'Did you see the solar farm on the drive in?'

'I did,' she said.

'This place is astounding.'

Far to the south, Vincent spotted a huge section of dense forest situated inside the facility.

'Mommy, Daddy! Sailing ships!' Emily was standing on tiptoes to gawp at the lake about a quarter of a mile to the south. Sure enough, tied up at the jetty, a few rowing boats and two cutters were bobbing around in the water. 'Can we go see them please?' The young child clasped her hands together in expectation.

'Maybe later, sweetheart, but we have to make sure everywhere is safe first,' Kristin said.

'Awww.' Emily frowned and flung her hands apart.

'I know. Mommy's a spoil-sport,' Vincent said.

'You're so good at always coming out as the good guy,' Kristin said.

'That's 'cause I am.'

They continued to observe their daughter's excitement while Adam pointed out a flock of birds coming to rest on the lake's surface.

'OK, folks. Let's not get too distracted.' Salty started to back towards the Management Centre and waved everyone in his direction. 'You, where I can see you,' he said, gesturing to Ethan, who was lurking at the back of the group as usual.

The weary young man shook his head and approached. 'Can you see me well enough from here?'

Salty took another moment to examine his face. 'Yeah, that'll do.' His attention was drawn by Raine, as she walked past him purposefully, the soldier's rifle over her shoulder. She was heading away from the Management Centre in the direction of the aviary. 'Where in the hell do ya think you're goin'?'

'Don't know. What does it look like?' Raine snapped.

'First off, you ain't goin' anywhere until we have checked to see if the fences have been compromised.'

'Compromised. Big word for you.'

'Second, if you don't plan on usin' that, you may as well leave it with me.'

'Fine.' She took the rifle from her arm and tossed it to him.

He caught it, stepping back to absorb its weight. Raine remained outside and Salty led the rest of the group to the door of the Management Centre. He tried the handle; as he had expected, it was unlocked.

When the group moved inside, they were immediately struck by the cooling sensation of the air conditioning. Because they had either been out in the heat or cooped up in the truck, the cool air felt like a baptism. The building smelled of sanitised nothingness as they climbed down the set of stairs to the main room.

Salty held the assault rifle out in front of him and called, 'anyone home?'

The only response he received was his own smoky voice echoing back. All of the halogen strip lighting fitted around the circumference of the ceiling was fully operational. The banks of computer rigs still whirred beneath each desk, and the deer-head emblem of the Warrington Preserve was bouncing around the confines of each monitor like a stray bubble. Everything appeared to be primed for the beginning of a new day.

Salty ventured further into the building, passing the banks of desks, and the rest followed. He reached a large control panel. Above it, a wall of monitors displayed every camera feed on the entire site. There was a camera for each designated area and various numbered fence checkpoints on the perimeter. He handed the rifle to Vincent and sat down behind the controls.

The group crowded around the monitors and watched Salty scroll through each one: the solar farm, nature trails, both lakes, the aviary, power station, visitor centre, parking lot, Observation Towers 1 and 2, the bathroom block, clinic, picnic area, campsite, the lodge, and finally, the golf course and deer park.

Once he'd finished examining every site, he moved on to the perimeter fence cameras, taking control of the viewing arm so he could examine as much of the electrical boundary as he could.

He sat back in the swivel chair and adjusted his cap. 'Well, that's all 36 of em' along the fence, and I ain't spotted a single breach.'

'Or a single person,' Adam said.

'That's a good thing. Trust me. We don't need any complications. Although it would help to have a few qualified folks to manage the place.'

'So what's next?' Vincent said.

'From what the cameras say, it seems like good news, but there are plenty of blind spots – just so happens I know where they are. We'll need to split up if we're gonna cover all the ground before nightfall. I think y'all would sleep much better if you knew there were no surprises.'

'You've got that right,' Kristin said.

'Before we do, there's one last thing I wanna show you.' Salty jumped up from the chair and led them to the back of the building. It opened out into a viewing area complete with large chairs and artificial water fountains. Its centrepiece was a huge window that allowed them to look out onto the whole preserve.

They wandered right up to the glass – all except Ethan, who took the opportunity to drape himself over one of the cushioned lounge chairs.

'It goes on forever,' Kristin said.

'Close. You're lookin' at 820 acres of land. That's the sweet spot. Look it.' Salty pointed across the lake to the deer park. 'It has its own little ecosystem, full of wildlife. So long as we make sure the species remain sustainable, we should have all the food we could need for the rest of our lives,' he said. 'If things get hairy when we go out there, just wanted to let you know what we're fightin' for.'

Ethan raised his hand from the lounger. 'Erm, you can count me out of that. I'm vegan.'

'Like Doctor Spock?' Emily said.

The whole group burst into laughter. Her comment even raised a wry smile from Salty.

'Yes, Emily. Exactly like Doctor Spock.' Ethan's smile soon faded when he saw that Vincent was glaring at him. He leaned back in his chair and looked at the ceiling.

'Anyways, we do this right, we got it made.' Salty looked Ethan's way. 'As for you, there's plenty of mushrooms growing all over.'

'Great. Mushrooms are my Kryptonite.'

'Well, I guess you're shit out of luck.' The wiry-looking man stood proud, surveying the preserve like he'd built the place with his bare hands. 'Let's get some air, people. I don't know 'bout you, but I ain't much for breathin' this reconditioned crap.' He went back into the main room and searched the storage locker against the left wall, taking three walkie-talkies from their charging bays and carrying them out to the front entrance.

As soon as they emerged, Raine looked to them for confirmation.

'Looks good, but the cameras can't see everything,' Salty said.

Raine nodded and started to head towards the aviary again.

'Hey, wait a sec,' Kristin called after her.

'I'll check the north fence,' she said without looking back.

Kristin gestured to Salty to say something, but he just shrugged. 'Seeing as she's got the north side, I'll take the east. Mrs. Graham, will you oblige me?'

'Sure,' she said.

Vincent glanced down to her leg, noting the fact she still wasn't able to put her full weight on it. 'Your ankle?'

'It's easing now, really.' She pushed the Beretta into his hand. 'It'll be fine. I'll be fine.'

He accepted the gun and smiled. 'OK, but what about Emily? I don't like the idea of her running around this place until we know for sure it's safe.'

'I get that, Vin. Doesn't change the fact I need you out there – if we're gonna get this done before we lose the light,' Salty said.

Vincent stood and pondered what to do. 'Adam.'

'Yes sir?' The young man approached him with his usual wide-eyed exuberance.

'Will you stay here and keep an eye on Emily until we get back?'

'Of course, Mr. Graham. Whatever I can do to help.'

'Thank you.' Vincent smiled. 'That OK with you, pumpkin?'

'Sure, Daddy.' Emily ran up to Adam and playfully punched his thigh. 'I won't be too much trouble.'

'Be nice to Adam. Me and your mom will be back before you know it.'

Salty grabbed Vincent by the wrist and pulled him to one side, keeping one eye on Ethan. He was currently strolling around the walls of the Management Centre with his hands in his pockets.

'Looks like you're stuck with the day walker. Check out the east.'

'No problem,' Vincent said.

'Hey.' Salty forced him closer, narrowing his eyes. 'Bein' vegan don't make him a saint. Don't drop your guard for one second,' he whispered.

'I won't.' Vincent brandished the parting gift from his wife.

'You know how to use that?'

'I think so.'

'Let's hope you have the guts to pull the trigger when the time comes. That little girl needs her daddy.'

'Let me worry about that,' Vincent said.

'Fine. Let's get goin'. We've wasted too much time already,' Salty said, handing him one of the walkies he'd found. 'Long as you stay clear of the trees, you should spot one of those things comin' from a mile away. If you do, make sure you use the walkies. I set them all to the same channel.'

Vincent and Kristin kissed Emily and joined their partners to head off on their search.

Chapter 3

Raine waited until she was adjacent to the twenty-metre-high observation tower before gazing up at it. The tall wooden structure creaked gently in the wind, its shadow shielding her from the sun. She thought she noticed it swaying. Not possible, of course. A trick of the light. Or maybe it was due to lack of food and sleep.

Away from the glare, she could spot the radio antenna and TV transmitter mounted on the insulators on the roof. The door at the foot of the tower stood ajar, revealing the first few steps of the spiral staircase.

She took a peek into the stairwell. It was empty – no dead, no blood. She counted all fifty three steps, pushed open the hatch at the top, and climbed into the observation room.

The place looked lived in. There were candy bar wrappers on the desk. A baseball jacket with an Ohio State Buckeyes patch lay over the back of a lazy chair. The cold coffee and milk in the mug had separated and the coffee had turned to an indiscernible sludge. On the other side of the room, a table housed a TV set and a longwave radio unit.

Raine lifted herself up and walked over to the table, sliding her finger through the layer of dust that had settled on the TV screen. She ran her hand across the transmitter and then switched it on. She turned the dial, searching through all the channels, looking for anything other than the crackle and hiss of static. As she'd suspected, there was nothing but dead air. She cut the power and wandered over to the desk, smirking at the monthly video game magazine lying open there. After rifling through a few of its pages, she closed the magazine to look at its cover.

An object had been hidden beneath the publication, and it caused her to raise her eyebrows when she finally saw it. A set of high-powered binoculars – something she could use. She picked them up by their strap and hung them around her neck.

The pinch from the cramp in her calf muscles and the bottoms of her feet made her wince. The distressed leather of the lazy chair seemed inviting all of a sudden. Raine sat on it and rested her boots on the edge of the desk.

As she was about to sit back and relax, a strong musty smell hit her nostrils and she straightened up again. The unpleasant odour was coming from the drawer below her left arm. She gave it a tug, but it didn't want to budge. A second, sharper encouragement caused the jam to clear and the drawer to slide open. The source of the smell soon became obvious. What used to be a cream cheese bagel was sitting on top of a greasy napkin; it was so infested with mould, the fuzz on its surface resembled a miniature of the preserve's forest. A bunch of keys and a Rubik's Cube sat next to it. Raine put the keys in her pocket and pondered over the multi-coloured puzzle, rotating it through her fingers. She tossed it in the air and caught it; a smile of reminiscence broke across her face – she remembered... She gripped the cube tighter to prevent the memory from fading, but no matter how hard she squeezed, it continued to decompose.

Frustrated, she got to her feet and ventured out onto the perforated steel of the observation deck. The tower certainly served its purpose; she had a panoramic view of the entire facility. Even after Salty's boasting, it was hard to appreciate just how large the place was until it was laid out in front of her: acres of lush green grass and forest, punctuated by eco-friendly structures and bodies of water. She could see all the way to the tops of the surrounding fences.

The weight around her neck reminded her of the binoculars. She lifted them and scanned for the whereabouts of her companions. First she looked east, towards the parking lot and a rather futuristic, dome-shaped building, but try as she might, she couldn't pinpoint anyone.

She gave up and turned her attention north, spying the second observation tower on the edge of the deer park, and the walls of the facility's power station.

Finally, she spotted signs of life. Adam was next to the Management Centre, carrying Emily on his shoulders. She was using him as her own observation tower, stretching out one of her dainty arms to point out a shifting flock of birds heading towards the lake.

Further away to the northwest, Raine found Vincent and Ethan walking together. They were just about to pass the glowing panels of the solar farm on their way to the woodland on the other side.

She scanned west to the main gate where they'd entered from, and then behind her to the fence. She locked on to a figure moving through the trees beyond the confines of their potential safe haven. She could tell by the shrivelled skin and its repetitive motions that it was one of the dead. It constantly plodded towards the electrified cables, only to be knocked back again – its movement was relentless and without thought. It was impossible to say when this back-and-forth had begun, but it would never stop – at least not until its flesh and muscle had fallen away and its bones had crumbled.

Something about that idea made Raine's blood boil, so intensely that she knew she wouldn't be able to rest knowing it was there. She lowered the binoculars and frowned in the direction of the fence.

Chapter 4

Beyond the glare of the mounted solar panels, Vincent licked his dry lips as he trudged towards the nature trails. Ethan had been lagging behind since they started the search. Although Vincent was just as suspicious of the group's most peculiar member, he was pretty sure his distance wasn't intentional. The more time he had to observe him, his movements, the shape of his body beneath his loose fitting hoodie, the more apparent it became Ethan was struggling to keep up. From his face, he seemed no older than 25, but his physical condition suggested a man twice that age. Vincent didn't peg him for a hellraiser. Drugs, he thought. Probably drugs.

He dropped his backpack on the ground and knelt to reach inside it. He felt something cold on the back of his hand. He saw it was a grey shirt, damp with sweat. He recognised it as the top Adam wore to jog around the refugee camp. He rested his arm against his knee and sighed.

'What is it?' Ethan asked.

'It's nothing really. I must have picked up Adam's pack instead of mine.' He delved through the pack again, eventually placing his hand on what he was looking for. 'It's OK though; Adam has water in here too. Would you like so—'

Vincent turned, holding the bottle, and to his surprise, he saw Ethan almost on top of him. He took a step back as they made eye contact, and Vincent thought he saw Ethan withdraw his outstretched hand back to his waist.

The young man straightened his stance. The shadows cast by his hood blackened and elongated the dark patches under his eyes. He seemed ill at ease, like a guilty child. 'No thank you, Vincent,' he said. He paused for a moment, and then walked on towards the trails.

Still on his knees, Vincent watched him, waiting to see if he glanced back. He ran his fingers over the ridged front of the walkie clipped to his belt and onto the handle of the Beretta tucked in his pants.

Chapter 5

Adam watched Emily swinging her left leg to kick the surface of the grass, almost losing her balance as she followed through. She pushed her tongue against the inside of her cheek, creating a bulge.

'How's your gum feelin'?'

Emily shrugged. 'OK. Sore, I guess.'

'Just keep gargling that salt water. It'll stop it from getting infected again.'

'Urgh.' Emily pulled her face. 'Maybe the abscess is better.'

'You don't mean that.'

She focussed on the ground. Taking a short run up, she flipped onto her hands and arched her body over to land back on her feet. She finished the move by pushing out her chest, adopting the stance of a gymnast at the end of a routine and looking thoroughly pleased with herself.

'That was impressive,' Adam said.

'I know. I wasn't too good at it when I was at school, but I had plenty of time to practice at the camp.' She soon lost interest in cartwheeling and returned to kicking the grass. 'What should we do now?'

Adam gazed over to the open door of the Management Centre. 'I think your dad packed those playing cards before we left. Your mom left her bag inside, so if they're there, we could play Go Fish.'

'Boring. I want to do something out here,' Emily said.

'Just think of all the exploring we will be able to do when the others have made it safe.'

'Are there lots of animals around here?'

'For sure. There's deer, foxes, coons, woodchucks, squirrels, mice, and a whole lot more, I reckon.'

The talk of animals excited her. Adam could see the warmth pipe into her face. She paused for thought, curling her lip.

'We could go to the lake and play cards down by the boats.'

Adam's pale blue eyes flickered. 'Erm, I don't think that's such a good idea, Emily.'

'Salty said as long as we stay clear of the trees, we will be able to see the monsters coming from a mile away.'

'Yeah, but your dad said we were to stay put.'

'He also told you to keep an eye on me.'

'Yeah?'

'Well, how can you keep an eye on me if you're here and I'm way over at the lake?'

'Emily?' Adam raised his eyebrows.

She smirked, a glint of mischief in her eyes, and then took off across the grass, giggling with every gleeful step.

Adam was shocked at how much distance her little legs had already covered in just a few seconds. 'Emily, wait!' He had no choice but to chase after her.

Chapter 6

The steel frame of the aviary arched against the landscape. It was hands down the biggest bird house Kristin had ever seen. From where they were, she could hear the gentle buzz of insects darting around the botanical gardens. But there were no birds – not a single chirp or wing flap.

As they got closer, they understood why. Both doors to the structure had been left wide open.

'Someone had the sense to let them out before they abandoned ship. That tells us somethin',' Salty said.

'Tells us what?' Kristin asked, still gazing into the dome.

'Someone was here during the outbreak. They knew no one was ever coming back.'

'I remember how it felt back then. Even when whole cities were being locked down and martial law had been instigated, I still believed the authorities would stop us from going under. How stupid was that?'

'Pretty stupid, but I guess if you've had a private school education and work in a well-paid job so you can live in a fancy home, provide for your kids and pay medical bills, makes it hard to realise by just how thin a thread everything is hanging.'

Kristin turned from the aviary and regarded Salty's tattered clothes and weather-worn complexion. 'What about you? You worked here; Warrington obviously trusted you. He didn't sound like a guy who would short-change his employees.'

'It was a good gig; I'll give it that – probably the best I've had, but it wasn't always that way. Not nearly.' He hawked up some phlegm and spat it onto the grass nearby.

'Come on,' he said, flicking his head to the east. 'Time's a wastin'.'

They followed the main road until they came to the visitor centre – the largest building on the site. Panels of concrete and glass had been assembled to form an almost perfect cross.

'Even though he closed it to the public, he left everything in there just the way it was.' Salty smiled. 'Except for one thing. He had a fancy cocktail bar installed. He might have had a stick up his ass about purifying the planet, but he had a weakness for liquor.'

'You admired him,' Kristin said.

'Can't say as I agreed with everything he stood for, especially not his politics, but he was a man who knew what he wanted outta life. There wasn't too many of them around. Even less now,' Salty said.

'We going to take a look?' Kristin said.

'Nah, we'll check it out later. There's somewhere else we need to go first.'

'Where's that?'

'It's right up ahead.'

Behind the visitor centre there was a circular building with a glass roof. Salty quickened his pace when he saw it and Kristin strode alongside him. The doors were unlocked and they wandered into the reception area. Kristin noticed the public information posters about deer physiology and diet. She realised they were standing in what used to be the preserve's animal clinic.

Salty behaved like he knew the place well, slipping behind the counter and entering the door to the rest of the building. An intense smell caused him to recoil and cover his mouth with the cuff of his plaid jacket.

'Christ! What is that?' Kristin moved to his side, pinching the end of her nose.

'You're doing it wrong. Breathe through your nose. Close your mouth. Trust me, it's better.'

'Sounds more like you want me to shut up.'

'That's just an added bonus.' Salty pushed on through the corridor to another door on the left. He gave it a kick to reveal the animal holding area. There were eight cages, four stacked upon four. Six were empty, but the other two contained rotten carcasses. Salty approached the first one and peered inside. It was obvious from its pointed, but now rather shrivelled tail and the streamlined shape of its skeletal body that it was the remains of a fox.

'How terrible,' Kristin said. 'They would have starved to death in there.'

'Nah, they didn't suffer. Take a look.'

She edged closer to the bars. 'What am I supposed to be looking at?'

'See how clean the insides of the cage are? No way they wouldn't be scratched up if this critter was still alive.' Salty stood straight, confidently waving his hand. 'These guys were euthanised. They were probably too sick to be released like the others, so it was the kindest thing.' He coughed a little and moved into the next room. This one had a sign on the door that said 'Supply Room'.

He flipped the switch on the wall and the blue neon bulb flickered for the first few seconds. He tapped the glass of each cabinet standing along the back wall. Kristin noticed his lips moving as he muttered something under his breath. At the end of the row, he knelt down next to a set of metal drawers and pulled out the one at the bottom. He lifted a black case from it, flipped the latches, and opened it up.

'We've been rolling together for a couple of days now, but just one glance at y'all and I knew I was gonna be doin' all the huntin' once we got here. I thought this might be more to your likin'.' Salty held up the largest object in the padded case and showed it to Kristin.

The scoped rifle's slender stock and barrel looked almost futuristic to her.

'We can use it for tagging, and for killing for food – all silently so we don't attract unwanted attention at the fences every time we bag a deer.'

Kristin stared uneasily at the weapon.

'Don't worry. You'll just have to knock em' out. I'll do the dirty work,' Salty said. 'We got more than a year's worth of sedatives. By then, I reckon we might be pretty handy with a bow.' He placed the rifle carefully back in its case and smiled.

Kristin hadn't seen him this relaxed since their intense first encounter. The calmness seemed to take the edge off his sharp, angular features.

He took a step back to admire the cabinets full of barbiturates, antibiotics, and anti-venoms. 'I thought for sure one of them would ransack this place.'

'Perhaps they did plan on coming back,' Kristin said.

'Maybe... it's ours now though.'

⚔

Kristin was more than thankful to be outside again and to have the smell of dead animals blown away by the clean air of their natural surroundings, but the sickly odour seemed to cling to her clothes. She bent over and tried to spit the taste of it out of her mouth. When she lifted her head, Salty was already well on his way towards the second lake of the facility, ignoring the picturesque log cabin to the north. She examined his destination and realised what had caused him to make haste.

One of the sailboats had broken free of its mooring and floated clear of the jetty. It was now grounded on the bank of the lake – one side held firm by the wet dirt and the boat bobbing on the water's edge. Its sails were up too and the wind caught them sporadically, threatening to drag the vessel onto dry land.

Kristin did her best to jog over to catch him up, but her injured ankle remained weak, forcing her to move with more of a limp.

Salty reached the boat and looked inside, then immediately took a step back, placing his hands on his bony hips and staring up at the pale blue sky. He walked over to Kristin before she could get to the bank, holding up his hands.

'What is it?' she said.

'You don't wanna see it.'

She pushed passed him and put one foot on the deck. A body lay sprawled over the cockpit, half-covered by the main sail. Flies were swirling around the bloodied corpse. Judging by the tone and tightness of its grey skin, it hadn't been dead long. She could tell by the polo shirt and shorts that it was the body of a male, but his sex certainly could not have been identified from his face. His features and brain matter were scattered across the deck like macabre jigsaw puzzle pieces. A pistol rested in the grip of the man's right hand. Kristin covered her mouth, fearing she might throw up. At least they were out in the open; it would be easier to escape the smell than it would have been the animal clinic.

'Did you know him?'

'Yeah,' Salty said with a sense of resignation. He climbed into the boat and stood over the body, first checking the pockets of his shorts, then starting to prise his rigid fingers from the gun handle. 'His name was Stephen Schneider. A herpetologist – studied reptiles and such.' He retrieved the pistol from his former colleague and opened the chamber to check if it was worth the trouble. Five bullets remained. 'Makes sense he'd take himself out on the water. We should go. We'll come back and bury him once we've checked the fences.'

Salty turned his back on the suicide and jumped off the deck onto land, expecting Kristin to follow. Kristin lingered, staring at what was left of the scientist, his hopes and dreams spilled over the cured wooden panels. As she was about to leave, she spied something poking from the clenched fist of his left hand. She stooped and carefully pinched the end of it between her finger and thumb so she could pull it free. It was a note, no bigger than a match book.

'Come on, Mrs. Graham,' Salty urged from the bank.

'One second.' She unfolded the lined piece of note paper and read the eight words scribbled across the middle. 'I'm sorry. I could not endure without you'.

Chapter 7

Vincent froze when he heard the rustling sound, and reached for the gun tucked in his pants. A shape skipped through the leaves and fallen branch wood just ahead of him. Something small – no bigger than a woodchuck. He relaxed his stance and took a breath.

Behind him, Ethan bent over on his haunches, struggling to breathe. Sweat glistened on his face as the sun peeked through the trees. 'You alright?'

Ethan smiled. 'Exercise was never really my thing.'

Vincent noticed how pale he looked. He couldn't resist the temptation of asking the question, hoping that, in his desperation, the young man would just come clean that he needed a fix of some sort. 'Is... is there anything you need?'

Ethan paused to consider Vincent's awkward delivery and nodded, indicating he'd expected Vincent to imply something of that nature. 'No, Vincent. Nothing rest won't cure.'

'We'll rest for a while then.' Vincent removed his pack and threw it down, then sat himself against the nearest red maple trunk.

Ethan was only too happy to hit the dirt directly opposite. He adopted his usual position, drawing his knees up to his chest so he could lock his arms around them and then rest his head on top.

Vincent leaned back and closed his eyes for a moment. Suddenly, his ears were filled by the background noise of the occasional screeching bird and little snaps and shuffles within the undergrowth. Once Ethan had started to calm down and had wiped the sweat from his forehead with the sleeve of his hoodie, Vincent felt obliged to break the silence between them.

'So, how did you find yourself here in the States?'

'I guess you could say it was a work commitment.'

It then became clear to Vincent that he seemed to carefully consider every response whenever he was asked about his personal life. He'd been doing it ever since they'd encountered him, in fact. 'What kind of work did you do?'

Ethan looked directly at him and smiled again. 'She envies you, y'know.'

'What?'

'Your wife – the way you are with Emily.'

'You seem to take a lot of interest in us.'

'It's prudent to know who you're dealing with,' Ethan said.

'I agree.'

Ethan relaxed his shoulders and sighed. 'What I said to your daughter before...'

'It doesn't matter. We cleared that up, didn't we?' Vincent said.

'I was only trying to help her. She's going to have to grow up faster than you'd like, the way things are.'

'And that's for me to handle,' Vincent said.

'Of course. Who am I kidding? I wouldn't know the first thing about bringing up a child. I couldn't even take care of myself before this. Hence why I'm still trying to catch my breath.'

'Didn't you have family? A girlfriend?'

'I was estranged from my parents. I hadn't spoken to them for about three years. I tried to call them when things got bad, but so many people were doing the same thing. It jammed the whole network. As for girlfriends, I've never had the pleasure.'

'Never?' Vincent felt guilty that he'd imagined some junkie hanging on to Ethan's every word – a girl who used to be pretty before the drugs had washed her out.

'Not really. A few pretend ones, but they weren't interested in me.'

'After your money, huh?'

'Yeah... something like that.' Ethan's eyes rolled back, as if he was drowsy. He ran his hands through his hair and licked the dry surface of his lips.

'Take some water,' Vincent said.

'I'm fine.'

Vincent stretched to kick the backpack towards him. 'Quit playing the martyr and drink.'

Ethan disentangled his limbs and grabbed the pack. He dragged it over and reached inside to locate the bottle. As quickly as he'd started, he stopped rummaging and stared up at Vincent, his expression grim.

'You find it?'

He didn't answer. Instead, Ethan threw himself to the ground. His body rigid, he shook wildly like he was in the middle of some sort of seizure.

'Ethan?' Vincent crawled to where he writhed about. The young man was unresponsive. His eyes were open, but vacant. He was unaware of Vincent leaning over him, trying to snap him out of it. 'Ethan? What can I do?' He thought about shaking him, then suddenly remembered that you are supposed to leave the sufferer of a fit to just go through it.

His body began to shake even more violently. His mouth opened and he let out a groan, as if he was in pain. Vincent saw something clenched in his right hand. It appeared to be a piece of fabric of some kind. Ethan held it so tightly that he couldn't be sure what it was.

There were no signs of the affliction abating. If anything, it was getting worse. Vincent fumbled around on his belt for the walkie. He would call Salty. Since he seemed so well-equipped for dealing with everything else, perhaps he'd received first aid training as well. Before he got chance to hit the talk button, Ethan stopped shaking and he became completely still, eyes open.

Vincent leaned over him again, placing his cheek close to his mouth. He couldn't feel any breath against his skin and he knew time was too short for his new redneck friend to help him out with this one. He would have to attempt CPR and hope for the best.

As he placed his hands on Ethan's chest, he took a sharp breath in and jolted upright. Vincent jumped in fright, but Ethan held on to him, grabbing the front of his shirt like his life depended on it. The look in his eyes suggested he'd emerged from the darkest nightmare imaginable.

'Jesus, you scared me. You were out for a moment. You were—'

'We have to find her,' Ethan whispered. 'We have to find Emily.'

Chapter 8

Adam picked the last of the mushrooms in the patch and placed it into the cradle he'd made with the bottom half of his sweatshirt. He glanced over at Emily, who was about to pick a large one from the bank of the lake side.

'Not that one!' he said, shuffling towards her, careful not to spill the mushrooms he'd collected. He moved his hand underneath the cap of the fungus in question and peeled it back, running his fingers through its ribbed gills. 'See how white they are?'

'Yes,' Emily said.

'That tells us this one is probably poisonous.'

Emily pressed her finger against its spongy surface. 'It would give me a belly ache if I ate it?'

'Yep. Maybe worse than that. Some of them can make folks really sick.'

'Gosh. You know an awful lot about mushrooms.'

Adam laughed. 'Not so much. Just the basics. My dad taught me. We don't want you getting sick, not after your abscess.'

'No. That was horrible, and I still have to take these tablets. They taste nasty.'

'Usually, the nastier they taste, the better they are for you,' Adam said.

'That's what my dad says.'

'We were awful worried about you. I was awful worried about you.'

'Really?'

'Of course. Y'know, that day in the medical tent, that wasn't the first time I saw you. The first time, you were with your mom. She was collecting you up from the school-house. I remember the wind had picked up that day, and I was standing pretty close. So close, I even caught the scent of the shampoo on your hair. It smelled of fresh apples.' Adam closed his eyes to savour the memory. When he opened them, Emily noticed they looked different. There was something else behind them. A type of hunger that she didn't understand, but one that instinctively raised the fear within her.

'I know your dad probably tells you this all the time, but you're a very beautiful girl, Emily.'

'Erm, I am?'

'The fact you don't realise how much, is what makes you beautiful.' He reached out with the back of his hand and brushed his fingers over the trembling skin of her knees. 'Your skin is so soft.' His words began to trail off into more of a whisper. He touched her leg again – this time closing his fingers around the puppy fat of her calf.

Emily tried to pull away, but Adam's grip tightened. 'I think I'd like to go back and wait for my mom and dad now.'

'But you said you wanted to come to the lake with me. You said it like you meant it. I knew you were flirting – you've been doing it ever since we got out of the camp.'

'I don't know what you mean, Adam. I want to go back.' She again attempted to free her leg, but the fit young man was far stronger than her. 'I thought you were my friend.'

'I am your friend. I could be so much more if you'd let me.'

'Please, I don't understand.'

'Then let me help you.' Adam released her and reached up to her face. 'Look around you. This place we've found is paradise, and we can keep the monsters out so they can never hurt us again. This could be the start of something special for you and me. I know I might seem old to you, but I'm not all that old. I still remember when I was in third grade. It wasn't so long ago.' He smiled, tracing his fingers along her neck.

Emily dug her chin into her chest bone. She didn't like the tingling sensation created by his touch. It made her body hurt.

'What's ten years, Emily? What's ten years? I bet that's about the same gap between your mom and dad.'

'My mom and dad are grown-ups.'

Adam shook his head. 'Don't you see? None of that matters anymore. We don't have to do what we're told. There's no one around to make us. We're free, Emily.' He touched her leg again, sliding his hand up to her inner thigh.

'No!' Her statement was as firm as it was loud. She wedged the flat of her foot into his chest and scrambled backwards over the bank of grass and dirt.

Adam raised his hands and bowed. 'OK, OK. I'm sorry. I was moving way too fast. I understand how this can be scary and overwhelming at first.'

'I want to go back to wait for the others,' she said.

'Sure. Whatever you want, but you gotta promise me you won't say anything about this to your parents. It's complicated stuff. They wouldn't see things the way we do.'

'I don't know what you're talking about.'

'Of course you do. You're just confused.'

'No, I'm not. I thought you were being nice to me because you were my friend, but now I don't think you are. I think you tricked me and you touched me in places you shouldn't. That's why you don't want me to tell 'cause you know you'll get into trouble.'

Every one of her words seemed to stick into him like the point of a knife. His smile evaporated and tears welled in his eyes.

'I don't want to be your friend anymore, Adam.' As Emily turned to stand up, he pounced on her, grabbing her wrists and pushing her into the ground. She began to scream, thrashing her head back and forth because it was the only part of her body she could move.

He sat on her legs and squeezed down hard on her wrists, cutting off most of the blood supply to her hands. 'Please be quiet,' he said.

'Let me go!'

'I can't let you up until you promise not to tell.'

'I promise. I promise,' Emily wept.

'Why don't I believe you?'

She saw it again. Only for a brief moment, but she recognised it as the hunger – the darkness behind his eyes. Another shadow loomed overhead, rising up behind Adam. The haggard waif descended, its sunken eyes fixed on him. It latched onto the boy's back and opened its receding jaws, biting deep into the side of his neck. The bite severed his jugular and the flesh tore away like rice paper. Adam tried to scream, but blood instantly filled his throat and all he could do was gargle and choke on it. The red torrent poured out of the wound and onto Emily. She screamed and received a mouthful of blood in return.

The creature took a second bite from the same place, snapping a tendon and removing another chunk of flesh. Adam was still able to somehow hold himself up, and his blood soaked the little girl underneath him. It completely coated her neck and face, drowning her hair, turning it jet-black. She felt pressure at the tops of her arms. Something else had hold of her. It pulled her out from beneath the carnage and she found her voice once more.

Her screams were short-lived. The embrace that enveloped her was warm and the body possessed a familiar smell. She gazed up into the distraught eyes of her father.

'Emily?' Hardly able to recognise her through the gore, Vincent desperately tried to wipe it away from her face.

The creature realised it had company and picked itself up, leaving Adam to bleed out as he gargled his last. It headed towards Vincent and Emily on the ground. It stretched out its arms and moaned, slobbering from its latest feed.

Ethan ghosted beyond his fellow survivors, wielding a twisted branch at his side. He swung it awkwardly when he reached the creature, but managed to connect with its loose jaw. Its body made a half-turn on impact and fell down. Before it had a chance to rise again, Ethan brought down the branch into its face, vertically, like a spear. He repeated the violent thrust four times, until its fragile skull caved in and its brain matter bubbled to the surface.

Still panting from their sprint to the lake, he fell over and crawled to the backpack Vincent had been carrying. He reached inside to retrieve the piece of fabric he'd been holding in his grasp during the seizure.

Vincent looked up from his daughter and realised what the fabric was. A pair of children's pink underwear with a cartoon bear patch sewn on the front.

In the midst of frenzy, Ethan began to burrow into the loose earth with his fingertips.

'Where did he get those?' Vincent said. 'Did he—'

'No, he stole them from a clothes' line back at the camp.' Once the hole was deep enough, he threw the underwear into it and covered it over.

Vincent brushed Emily's brown hair away from her face. She shivered, eyes fixed on her father. 'It's OK, sweetheart. You're safe now. Everything's gonna be fine.'

She didn't respond to him. Although she was staring straight at him, her eyes seemed as dead as the thing that Ethan had put down. 'I'm so sorry. Daddy should never have left you.' He leaned over and kissed her forehead.

Ethan turned to face them, rubbing his hands together to get rid of the dirt. 'I hate to be the bearer of more bad news, but judging by the clothes that thing's wearing, it wasn't an employee. Which means either it somehow got in here before it turned, or there really is a breach in the fence.'

'Then we need to find out where it came from, right now,' Vincent said.

Ethan got to his feet and gazed at the rotten body. A portion of flesh had been opened up on its flank. The cut seemed crude, like it had gotten snagged on something sharp. He looked beyond it in the direction they had come from, and noticed some of its entrails on the ground and a few splashes of red staining the grass. 'It came from the woods, not far from where we were before.' He turned back to Vincent. 'Is she OK to come with us?'

'I'll carry her, but we can't just leave him like that. He'll become even more dangerous if we do.'

Ethan was trying to avoid facing the obvious, but he knew Vincent was right; they couldn't leave him like that.

Adam was lying face-down in a pool of his own blood. He'd already stopped breathing and his left hand twitched involuntarily.

Emily remained unresponsive, and Vincent clung to her like he never wanted to let her go again.

'I'll do it,' Ethan said, rolling his eyes at the thought.

'Are you sure?'

'You are otherwise indisposed right now, and I don't see that redneck running to our rescue this time.' He took a deep breath and blew it out quickly as he tried to psych himself up. He went to the bank of the lake and picked up a stone, about the size of a football. He could scarcely lift it higher than his hips, it was so heavy. He carried it over to Adam's body, standing close enough for the growing pool of blood to lap at the toes of his shoes.

On the first attempt, he dropped the stone from waist-height. It struck the back of Adam's head, leaving a dent in his skull. Dismayed, Ethan locked eyes with Vincent, but all he could do was press Emily's face even closer to his chest.

Ethan rolled the stone and picked it up again. This time, he used all of his strength to bring it level with his chin, then threw it onto his target. The cracking sounds confirmed the job was done, that it had torn through the flesh and bone. Adam's head opened up like a freshly beaten piñata.

He reeled away from it and fell on all fours, throwing up what little he had in his stomach. He tried to heave again, but nothing came up.

'Come on, sweetie. We gotta go. It's OK; Daddy's got you.' Vincent struggled to his feet, lifting his prostrate daughter with him. He walked over to where Ethan had fallen. 'Are you OK?'

'Do I look OK?' Ethan replied.

'Of course not, but we have to hurry.'

Ethan nodded and took one last look at the sticky patch of bile he'd left in the grass. They tried to run to the nature trails, but their fatigue and Emily's dead weight conspired to hold them back.

Ethan collapsed against a tree, wheezing from the exertion. Vincent couldn't feel his arms anymore. Emily hadn't moved or spoken a word since they'd found her. Adam's blood had dried in crusty patches around her hairline like a crimson halo.

Vincent pressed the back of his hand against her forehead and drew away, shocked at how cold she felt. 'We need to get her to Salty.'

'We have to go on, Vincent. We're almost there,' Ethan said.

'You go. I have to do what's best for her.'

'What's best for her is finding that breach so we can plug it. She's just in shock. She's...' Ethan noticed that Vincent had been distracted by something. 'What is it?'

'Can you smell that?'

Ethan did his best to take in a deep breath through his nose. 'It smells like ash.'

They ploughed on into the woods to the outskirts at the northwest corner of the facility. They saw the singed grass first, then the toppled tree burnt black by fire. It had smashed into the wire cables on one section, cutting some down and weighing down the rest until they almost touched the ground. Over by the nearest energiser pylon, a charred mess of bodies had been welded onto the surface of the metal.

'Jesus. What happened here?' Ethan asked, open-mouthed.

'I think I can guess.' Vincent surveyed the scene. 'A bunch of the dead pushed themselves up against that part of the fence. It must have shorted out and caused a fire that caught hold of the tree, bringing it down onto the fence and taking out the conductors.'

'At least we know how it got in,' Ethan said.

'Here.' Vincent pushed his hip out towards him. 'Grab the radio and let the others know.'

Ethan unclipped it from his belt and flipped the switch on the side. 'Salty, are you there?'

After a brief hiss, a voice came back. *'What are you doin' on this channel? Where's Vincent?'* The grizzled tones were unmistakeable.

'Never mind about that. We need to talk. Something's happened.'

'I asked you a question, Twilight. Where's Graham?'

Ethan shook his head and waved the walkie back at Vincent. 'Arsehole only wants to talk to you. Do you want me to take Emily?'

Vincent didn't answer. He was frozen just like his daughter, eyes fixed over Ethan's shoulder. Before Ethan could ask him what was wrong, he heard the snap of branch wood behind him and got the distinct sense of being watched. He turned sharply, expecting to see one or more corpses stumbling to get to them. Instead, he saw two men who looked very much alive. The one on the left was smiling. He was black, short of stature and bald. The other guy was at least two hundred pounds and was sweating like a dog. He was not helped at all in dealing with the afternoon heat by his long, slicked-back hair and biker beard. They were both dressed head to toe in combat gear, strapped with bandoliers. The short guy had a six-shot revolver and the fat one was cradling a shotgun just beneath his bulging gut, and had a large black hold-all on his back.

The short guy's grin widened, a twinkle reflecting from his gold front tooth. 'Well, shit. Ain't this somethin'?' he said.

Episode Five

Kill Switch

Chapter 1

Vincent's eyes darted between the two men. Even though they had only just reached the facility themselves, these men still felt like intruders. He waited for them to raise their weapons. He thought about reaching into his pants for the Beretta, but due to Emily's current state of paralysis, there would be no way of getting to it in time.

Ethan had nothing to aid them in their defence either. All he could do was stay on his toes, ready to run.

'Woah there,' the short man said, raising his hands and dangling his pistol from one finger by its trigger guard. 'We don't mean you no harm. We're just lookin' for a place to lay our hats is all. It's pretty funky out there.'

'Where did you come from?' Vincent said.

'We got in through there.' The short man pointed to the gaping wound in the fence. 'But Kansas originally. The name's Fukes, and this right here is my good friend Harley.'

Harley raised one finger from his right hand, then placed it back onto his shotgun. It was impossible to tell if he was smiling under his dense beard, but his eyes suggested not.

'Aww, don't mind him. He ain't as mean as he looks,' Fukes said. He turned to the damaged fence, observing the mass of broken cables and charred bodies with his hands on his hips. 'You really should do somethin' 'bout that. It's handy for us it was here though. We buzzed the main gate for a long time and nobody came.' Fukes faced them again, gazing at each of them in turn. He gave off an air of confidence that was both disarming and dangerous in equal measure.

His inquisitive stare came to rest on Emily, still frozen in time.

'She yours?'

'My daughter,' Vincent said.

'She hurt?' Fukes leaned forward to wave his hand in front of her face.

'She was attacked.'

The stranger immediately withdrew. Behind him, Harley adopted a tighter grip on his weapon. 'She bit?' Fukes asked.

'No. She's in shock. I need to get her back to the others.'

'Yeah. I heard your friend talkin' on the radio. How many of you folks are there?'

Before Vincent could answer, Ethan butted in. 'Two: the guy on the radio and Vincent's wife.'

'Ain't you the lucky one?' Harley said, staring at Vincent, his jaw wagging violently as he chewed on some bubblegum.

Fukes had zeroed in on Ethan after he spoke. 'You a Brit, kid?'

'Unfortunately, yes.'

'Ain't no shame in dat. Worked with a British guy once. Good guy – trustworthy. Those kind are hard to come by.'

Vincent checked Emily's temperature again. Her skin felt like ice. He took one panicked look at the two intruders and whispered 'I have to get her back' to Ethan.

'Sure,' Ethan said. 'Can you wait here while we go get our friends?' he said to Fukes.

Fukes huffed. 'I'd sure be grateful if we didn't have to wait right next to this hole. You never know what might come strollin' by.'

Regardless of how suspicious he was of the men, Vincent wasn't prepared to wait any longer. He took off, back through the woods towards the centre of the complex, cradling the back of Emily's head so as to not damage her neck.

He left Ethan standing alone. Both sets of steely eyes were now upon him, asking him to make a decision. 'OK, follow me,' he said. He broke into a jog to try and catch up to Vincent, and the men followed close behind.

Once they'd emerged from the treeline, Vincent had blazed out in front, walking at a pace that only Fukes was sufficiently in shape to match. However, he purposely hung back with Harley, who was struggling to carry his own weight and the heavy black hold-all over his shoulders.

Ethan glanced back and saw the top of the large bag bobbing around behind his head. Harley's face was drenched with sweat, his skin bloodshot. Ethan was still holding the walkie in his clammy grip. He flipped it so it faced the right way and held it up to his ear. But before he could press the talk button, he heard footsteps pounding up beside him.

'Hey,' Fukes said, flashing his gold tooth. 'I was thinking you don't look like nature-preserve types. How you get inside?'

'The other man we're with, Jake. He used to work here.'

'Lucky for him, so lucky for you, huh? This is certainly a sweet place to be right now – no doubt.' Fukes pirouetted so he could get a panoramic view of the lake, the deer park, the solar farm, and everything else beyond. 'Plenty of food, a place to grow crops, shelter, technology and those high fences. Hey, maybe later when you've found your buddies, me and Harley could give you a hand pluggin' that leak.'

'Yeah,' Ethan said. He reached up to massage the back of his own neck and swallowed hard. 'That would be helpful.'

'Hey, you don't look too fresh there, hoss.'

Fukes was right. Ethan had broken into a cold sweat and his skin had turned a queasy shade of grey.

'It's OK. I'm just...' Everything was closing in on him. The whole preserve seemed like it had been reduced to the size of a basketball court. He felt sick to his stomach and his mouth was bone-dry. He closed his eyes and blocked out Fukes's voice for a moment, taking deep breaths through his nose and out through his mouth. When he opened his eyes again, the walls of his world began to retreat and the wave of nausea passed.

'You still with us?' Fukes said.

'When Vincent's daughter was attacked, one of our own was killed.'

Fukes nodded. 'And you had to make sure he wasn't comin' back again, right? Never gets easy, but it does get easier.'

Ethan had regained his wits enough to focus on Fukes, and was staring at him long and hard. 'I'll have to take your word for that one.'

'Whatever, man. Just tryin' to help.' Fukes slowed down, dropping back to rejoin his counterpart so they could engage in a whispered conversation. He couldn't hear what they were talking about, but Fukes glanced up and smiled at him.

He lifted the radio to his ear and pressed 'talk'. 'Salty, come in.' Nothing but static. 'For God's sake, come in, you moron. I haven't done away with Graham. He's fine, but we have a problem.' Ethan was so frustrated with the lack of response he entertained the idea of bouncing the walkie off a nearby rock.

Shortly after, the waves of nausea washed over him and his surroundings began to shrink. He closed his eyes and heard the distinct crack made by Adam's skull again. Then he saw the blood – so much blood.

Much of the journey back was a blur for him, although he did recognise the severe orange hue burning from the edges of the solar towers. His vision sharpened when they got close to the Management Centre. He scanned for signs of the others, but it seemed deserted, door ajar like Adam and Emily had left it.

Vincent staggered on ahead and went inside. He ran down the steps in search of his own backpack and found it on the floor near the banks of computers. He took out a cotton blanket from it and knelt down, laying it across his lap. He wrapped Emily in it, pulling it tight around her up to her neck. Her eyes were still fixed, and a blank, expressionless face stared back at him. A wax sculpture of his daughter. 'Emily, please don't do this,' he whispered. They were just words, but in the cool air of the facility, her eyes flickered and she inhaled her first deep breath since he'd found her.

Ethan used the handrail to help himself down the steps and to prevent himself from keeling over. 'Still nothing?' he said.

'She moved her eyes. Where the hell are Kristin and Jake?' Vincent said.

'I tried them again. Nothing.' Ethan winced as he got the flash again. He couldn't get Adam's shattered skull out of his head. To make matters worse, just then, their two unwelcome guests entered the building.

Fukes reached the edge of the stairs and surveyed the operational technology below – the flickering lights and monitors. 'This is some Star Trek shit, right here!'

'Bet you can get porn on those things.' Harley's fat face was greasy with sweat. He flinched as Fukes jabbed his toe into one of his shins and glared at him.

Fukes left his counterpart to stew on his chastisement and moved down to where Vincent held his daughter in desperation. He rubbed his chin, tilting his head to one side as if he were a doctor assessing a new patient.

'I seen someone act like this before. When I was a kid, there was this boy, Charlie, who lived in my neighbourhood. He was one of those quiet ones – timid as a mouse. Always clinging to his momma. The other kids would always make fun of him. Anyway, he had this little white rabbit – y'know, one of those freaky albinos with pink eyes. I think his momma got it for him 'cause he didn't have any friends. He used to spend all of his time with it.'

As anxious as he was about the men, Ethan couldn't stay on his feet any longer. He slid to the floor, his back up against the side of the digital map table.

Harley plodded down the steps, relieving himself of the hold-all immediately after getting to the bottom. It landed on the floor with a weighty thud.

'He used to take it to the local park and let it run around, but he'd always corral it, talk to it, that sort of thing.'

Harley sniggered, much to Fukes's displeasure. The rotund man shrugged. 'I still wanna hear about the bunny,' he said.

Fukes continued. 'One time, me and my buddies were playin' in the park near to Charlie and his rabbit. An older boy from the neighbourhood showed up with his dog off its leash. Y'know where this is goin', right? This dog was a mean ol' bastard – had been in lots of fights, had a gnarly flap of skin where one of its eyes used to be.

'Poor Charlie couldn't do shit about it. The rabbit was so tame. It didn't even try to run away. He watched the dog tear it to pieces. By the time it was over, it was just skin and bone. Charlie didn't say much of anythin' after that. He just lay in bed like a vegetable. "Catatonic shock", they called it. His mom moved him away a couple of months later, so he could be closer to the hospital. Never did find out what happened to him. Course, I'm not sayin' that's what is happening to your girl.'

'It's not,' Vincent said. 'She'll be fine.'

'Hey, man, it's just a story,' Fukes replied.

'Ethan, the bag, please.' Vincent reached for the backpack and Ethan roused himself enough to toss it over to him. He took the bottle of water from it, pouring some of its contents over his fingers and then transferring them to Emily's lips. The moisture made contact with their dry surface, then rolled to the corners of her mouth and down her cheeks. 'Try the radio again.'

Before Ethan could act on his request, Emily blinked twice, let out a long breath, and focussed on her father's face. 'Hey, baby,' he said smiling.

Her weak voice hissed through her barely moving lips. 'The monsters.'

'It's OK now – the monsters are all gone. Daddy found you. I'm so sorry I left you alone. I won't ever do that again. I promise.'

Emily's eyelids soon grew heavy. She tried to open them again, but the same thing happened. 'I'm really tired.'

'Then go to sleep.' Vincent caressed the loose strands of hair hanging over her forehead and wiped the tears from her eyes.

'There you go,' Fukes said as he crouched next to them. 'Like I said, it was just a story.'

He cranked his neck to relieve some stiffness. Vincent noticed that on the side of his neck he had a tattoo of a large snake, coiled around a medieval dagger.

'So I guess we wait for your friends to get here, then see to your daughter and we can have a chat about me and Harley stayin' for a while. What you think?'

Vincent coughed to clear the tightness from his throat before responding 'we can discuss that, but the guy who got us here's not likely to be keen on the idea.'

'He in charge?'

'No one's in charge. He just helped us find a safe place.'

'Well, if he led you here and kept you safe, I'd say he's in charge, even if it ain't official an' all that. Don't worry, Vincent. We'll have a nice civil conversation with your man. I'm sure he'll come around to our way of thinkin'.' Fukes paused and looked around at the walls of the Management Centre. 'This is a big ol' place. Plenty of room for everyone. If we stayed over at the other side of the facility, we'd hardly ever see each other.'

Vincent cast a nervous glance at Ethan, but the young man seemed to be suffering, holding his head in his hands. 'I can't speak for Jake; we've only known him for a few days.'

'What about you, Vincent? What did you do before all this?' Fukes said.

'Me? I... I wrote fiction.'

'Really? Anything I'd know?'

'No. I'd just sold my first novel.'

'So how did you get by?'

'My wife was a human rights lawyer in the city. I stayed home and looked after my daughter.'

Fukes rested back on his heels, giving Vincent's words careful consideration. 'A house husband, huh?'

Harley, who still stood over Ethan, sneered at Vincent, curling his lip in disgust.

'I gotta say, Vin, you're a bigger man than me. I couldn't have it that way round. Not at all,' Fukes said. 'Kind of knocks nature's balance off-kilter in my eyes.'

Vincent caught sight of the black hold-all Harley had thrown down. 'I enjoy being a father. It's something I'm good at.'

Fukes nodded and stroked his chin. 'I can definitely see that. Shame about your book though. I haven't found anythin' decent to read for months. What was it about?'

'It was a romance,' Vincent said.

Harley could not help but release a deep, grimy snigger.

'"Course it was.' Fukes smiled.

'Fukes likes the dirty ones,' Harley said.

Fukes smiled faded. 'Harls, why don't you make yourself useful and go see if Jake and Vin's wife are on their way.' He spoke calmly, but Vincent could tell there was anger simmering behind it.

Harley looked despondently to Ethan sitting on the floor.

'He's fine,' Fukes said.

'Yeah, sure.' Harley lifted the shotgun to rest it on his shoulder and climbed the stairs to the door.

'We don't want your people bein' all spooked when they get back and see us in here. They may think we're up to no good. Folks were too hasty even before the dead started comin' back. Does this Jake fella have a firearm?'

'A pretty big one.' Ethan suddenly piped up, seemingly back with them again. 'Not that I know anything about guns.'

'Ethan, ain't it?'

Ethan nodded.

'Now, you're a real interesting guy.' Fukes stood up and walked over to him.

Ethan saw that, hanging from his belt, he had a walkie-talkie of his own – a little older and more beaten-up than theirs. 'You'd be surprised how many times I've heard that.'

'I don't think I would,' Fukes said.

Vincent couldn't take his eyes off the hold-all. The silver pull of its zipper sat at the end closest to him, but it was just out of reach. He slowly shifted Emily's head from his lap and onto the floor without waking her.

'See, the problem with interesting guys is they overthink things,' Fukes continued. 'They let shit go round and round in their heads till it eats them up. I can see you're still findin' it tough – maybe because of what you had to do when your friend got himself bit.'

Vincent leaned towards the bag, keeping one eye on Fukes, and with the other, making sure he didn't accidently bump Emily. As he stretched his fingertips out, a few centimetres from the pull, the sole of his shoe created the tiniest squeak on the floor's polished surface. Vincent heard it, but Fukes didn't. His back remained turned. Vincent gained enough leverage to place his hand on the hold-all's black canvas.

Vincent's face went numb with the sound of the slide and snap of the loaded shotgun above his head. 'No one told you you could touch that, asshole.'

This got Fukes's attention. He saw Harley aiming the shotgun at the top of the stairs and lowered his hands towards him. 'Woah, woah, woah – let's calm the fuck down. There's no need to be popping off shots at each other.' He wagged his finger back at Ethan, and the broadest smile broke over his face. 'Y'know, as soon as we first saw you two, we knew you weren't the kind of folks who'd go pulling guns at the first sniff of an outsider. You're reasonable people, after all. Get Vincent's shooter, Harley.' Fukes looked at Vincent. 'Give Harley your weapon, buddy.'

Vincent reached down carefully and slid the Beretta from the top of his pants and handed it, handle-first, to Harley. The hulking man struggled to bend enough to take it from him, sticking the end of his tongue out as he fumbled.

'I knew you'd be curious about the bag. It's hard to miss. Don't worry, we'll get to that. First things first.' Fukes drew his own gun and shoved it in Ethan's face. 'I want you to try and get your mate on that radio again. That's what you Brits say, right? "Mate"? Tell him to meet you here.'

'Should I mention you?'

'Erm, I don't know, Ethan. Should you mention us?'

'Probably not?'

'See? Interestin' people are usually smart too.' He thumbed back the hammer on his six-shooter. 'Call him.'

Ethan lifted the radio to his mouth. 'Salty, come in.'

To his surprise, Salty's voice came back immediately. *'Where's Graham?'* He was breathing fast.

'He's fine. Where the hell did you go? I've been trying to get hold of you.'

'Yeah. We ran into a couple of former employees up at the lodge. They were former in every sense. Tell Graham his wife's OK.'

Fukes glanced at Vincent and Emily. 'Looks like your lucky day,' he said.

'We've been having some troubles of our own,' Ethan said.

'What kind of troubles?'

'We found a breach in the fence near the nature trail.' Ethan considered mentioning that they had been attacked and lost Adam, but he held his tongue, keenly aware of the gun barrel aimed right at him.

'*We're on our way,*' Salty said.

'We're back at the Management Centre.'

'*Why aren't you dealing with the breach?*'

Ethan paused to take a breath and Fukes raised his eyebrows, covering the trigger. 'I'll fill you in when you get here.'

'*You better,*' Salty said.

'Over and out.' Ethan dropped the radio to his lap and Fukes uncocked his weapon.

'You're a good man, Ethan. We'll get this all cleared up in a minute,' Fukes said. 'In fact, you're pretty congenial yourself there, Vincent. Makes me wonder how you two boys and the kid managed to last so long out in the open. There's your wife – obviously wearing your balls as a necklace, but I still don't see her as the survival type. That leaves us with the good ol' boy. I guess he did a bang-up job of protecting you.'

'We were part of a camp, southwest of here,' Vincent said.

'Military?'

'Yes, but it's gone now. The soldiers cleared out of there.'

'So they just bailed on the civilians?'

'Not exactly,' Vincent said. He looked away to check if Emily was still asleep.

Fukes pondered his cryptic reply and soon worked out what it meant. 'Wait, what? They cut loose, but didn't wanna leave any potential gut-bags behind?'

'They called it mercy.'

'Y'know, that's smart. I mean, that's what I would've done.'

'Damn straight,' Harley added.

'You see, house husband, there's never been anythin' but two types of people in this world – thinkers and doers. Me and my associates, we're doers. If we see somethin' we want, we don't just think about it. We reach out and take it. In polite society, men like us were seen as outcasts, because we didn't do it with fancy suits and a fuckin' business degree. But now, in this jungle, we're goin' right back to the old rules.' Fukes shrugged at him. 'We fit into this terrain better than you and Rainboy over there. As for your daughter – I hate to be the one breakin' it to ya, but she's just an accident waitin' to happen.'

'Don't talk about my daughter,' Vincent said.

Fukes shook his head knowingly and smiled. 'There's nothing like fatherhood to get the blood pumpin'.'

'You talk about being smart,' Ethan said. 'Why lug a useless bag of money around with you in a world like this?'

'Woah there, I was just jokin' with the Rainboy thing,' Fukes said.

'Lucky guess,' Ethan said.

'"Cause it's our haul. We spilled blood for it,' Fukes said.

'Some innocent teller?'

'No, my fuckin' brother, you piece a' shit.' Harley spat the words across the room at Ethan, raising his shotgun once again.

'Five of us hit an armoured cash transport just outside of Lawrence, Kansas. And we pulled it off – almost,' Fukes said. 'Came away with just over a million, but we didn't get away clean. Will took a bullet to his chest.'

Vincent saw Harley curl his lip and grunt. He kept his grief at bay with anger. Vincent could only imagine what he must have done with the security guard who fired the shot.

'We barely made it out, but Will didn't last long. By the time we got to Missouri, he'd already passed.'

The hollow clanging echoed through the Management Centre as Harley booted his foot against the stair rail.

Vincent noticed Emily's eyes flicker immediately after the sound. Then they closed again.

'An old school buddy of mine had a farm out in the prairie region. He was one of those full-scale preppers. Not the butt of everyone's jokes no more. Law of averages: bark at the moon long enough, one day you're gonna be right. Anyways, Spittoon hooked us up. Helped us bury Will. He had one of those futuristic bunkers out back. Forty feet down, air filtration unit, its own power source, all the fuckin' canned food you could eat. We stayed down in that hole for two whole months, waitin' for the heat on the robbery to cool off. Then one day, Spittoon doesn't show up to check on us. We waited for another week before we went above ground. And we found it like this. Like I said, we're just lookin' for a place to stay, just like everyone else that's still breathin'.'

'You and your friends?' Ethan said.

'That's right. We split the money when we split up to scout for supplies.' Fukes smiled, flashing his single gold tooth as he stared down at Vincent. 'What you reckon, house husband? Think we can all get along after our little misunderstanding?'

'I can't see that working out well, no. When Jake and my wife get back, we should all just take a breath, and then our group will be on its way. We'll take some food and clothing and be gone before nightfall,' Vincent said.

Fukes nodded, covering his top lip with his bottom. 'I don't know, Vincent. Let's just have ourselves a chat and see what happens.'

Harley, alerted by something, jogged to the door, his stride awkward. 'They're comin',' he said, peering outside.

Fukes pointed to Ethan on the floor. 'Stay put,' he said, then looked at Vincent. 'A lot depends on you now. Could decide which way this thing goes.' Fukes went to the top of the steps and waved Harley back. They dragged Vincent and Emily under the stairwell with them and waited.

As the footsteps and muffled voices drew closer, Fukes trained his gun on Vincent and Harley pointed his shotgun at Ethan, in case he got any ideas about signalling to the others before they had got down the stairs.

'You in here, Graham?' Salty wandered in first holding his hatchet, fresh blood dripping from its blade, the assault rifle slung over his shoulder.

'Vincent?' Kristin shouted. Vincent was desperate to call out to her, but Fukes's eyes instructed him to reconsider.

When Salty reached the top of the steps, he saw Ethan slumped on the floor. 'What in the hell are you doin?'

Ethan opened his mouth to speak and then closed it again.

Salty ran down to him, and both intruders emerged from the stairwell to flank him.

As soon as Salty heard the click from the hammer of Fukes's pistol, he froze.

Harley flicked the shotgun barrel to his left to direct Kristin down the steps.

'Lose the chopper, green bean,' Fukes said.

Salty let go of the hatchet and it clanged against the hard floor.

'The rifle next. Nice and easy now.'

He twisted his slim frame to slide the strap from his shoulder, but as soon as it was free, he swung it back, striking Fukes's wrist with the rifle butt. As he was about to plant his fist on Fukes's chin, Harley stepped across and leathered him on the side of his head with the heavy end of his shotgun. Salty fell face-first, going limp before he hit the ground and dropping the assault rifle.

The weapon slid over to where Ethan was sitting. He shuffled towards it, but Fukes had already recovered and placed his boot on it. 'Don't let your asshole friend's stupidity catch on. Spraying bullets around just ain't you.'

Kristin noticed Vincent and her sleeping daughter under the stairwell. She tried to go to them, only to feel one of Harley's strong arms across her chest. He positioned himself behind her, his hot breath on her neck as he took a powerful whiff of her hair.

'Jackpot,' he said, sniggering.

Kristin's eyes fixed on her family.

Vincent stood and squared up to the hairy biker. 'Get your hands off of her.'

'Let's stay cool,' Fukes said. 'Vincent, I don't know whether you've noticed, bud, but you ain't really in a position to be callin' anything right now. So just sit back down and see to your girl. That's what you're good at, right?' Out of the corner of his eye, Fukes caught sight of Ethan crawling towards Salty. 'Where're you goin'?'

'Checking if he's still breathing.' Ethan reached the body on the ground and placed his hand between Salty's bony shoulder blades.

'He'll wake up with a shitty head is all. He should've done as he was told, and that's what y'all gotta do: sit tight and wait for our associates to get here.

No one else has to get hurt.' Fukes relaxed his stance. His pistol hung loose in his grip. He swaggered further into the Management Centre, his attention caught by the glow from the security monitors beyond the banks of computers. He wandered over to them and examined each monitor in turn. 'Y'know, you owe Yosemite Sam even more than you realise for leading you to this place. In fact, I'm gonna thank the motherfucker as soon as he wakes up.' He hit the console of one of the monitors and cycled through the locations of the facility. The golf course, the scenic lodge, the east lake, the parking lot and the observation tower to the north.

Ethan watched from afar, expecting Fukes to freeze on one camera and lean in so he could get a better image of Raine making her way towards them. Instead, Fukes lost interest in the security feeds and walked back. 'If we do cosy up together, I think we'll take whatever's on this side of the park. That way we can keep an eye on you from here. Whaddaya say, house husband?' Fukes then broke into song. 'Ebony and ivory, live together in perfect harmony.' It made him laugh so much that he couldn't sing anymore.

'I hear it's gonna get real cold this winter,' Harley whispered in Kristin's ear. He pushed his body tighter against her. She tried to wriggle away, but his grasp was too powerful. She could feel his pelvis grinding against her backside. Fortunately, his gut was so large he could barely get his groin to make contact.

Vincent watched on, simmering with rage. It was taking everything he had just to stay on the ground. Such was his torment, he unknowingly squeezed on Emily a little too hard and she opened her eyes.

'Mommy?' she said, as she focussed on Kristin and the dirty bearded man who was holding her from behind.

'It's OK, baby. Mom's just fine. You stay put.' Kristin fought back the tears so Emily wouldn't see her crying.

Harley pressed his tongue against the back of her neck and she cried out in shock. Any assurance that Emily had felt disappeared and she started to hyperventilate. 'Mommy?'

'For God's sake. Aren't you going to stop him?' Vincent growled, directing his anguish towards Fukes.

Fukes rolled his eyes and approached Kristin, moving his gaze over the curves of her body. He then looked at Harley, nodding his head towards the door. 'You wanna take this outside? No need for the kid to see.'

'No!' Vincent sat Emily on the floor and started to get up again. He'd only got to his knees before Fukes turned his gun on him.

'I know what you're thinkin', Vin: you wanna kill me, right?'

'Yes,' Vincent said, clenching his jaw tight.

'Truth is I don't take any pleasure from it. I just know what makes people tick. That's why they follow me. And what makes Harley tick is ass. As long as he gets some, he continues to cover mine. It's how my world keeps turnin'. So you'll just have to suck it up.'

Vincent's whole body shook. He was so overcome with emotion he couldn't force another word out.

Fukes smiled. 'It's one of those things where you gotta swallow your pride and get over it. It's gonna get a lot worse when our buddies arrive. You see, they both like ass too.'

Vincent had forgotten about his daughter in that moment. He stared down the barrel, ready to meet what came from it when he tried to rush their captors. He happened to glance at Kristin. Through her tears, he saw a calmness in her eyes. She lifted her hands above her waist and opened them, telling him to hold back, and somehow, he found the strength to do so.

Ethan watched it unfold. He also thought about making a run for them, but Harley had the drop on him. 'You're fucking psychopaths!' he muttered.

'Little melodramatic, don't ya think?' Fukes said. 'Last time I checked, mental health was determined by a shrink. Don't see many around these days.'

'Let's go.' Harley shoved Kristin towards the steps.

'Mommy will be back soon,' Kristin said. She mouthed the words, 'I love you' to Vincent.

Vincent bowed his head, defeated. He put his arms around his daughter again and covered her face.

'Nothin's really changed in this world. You still gotta compromise. Some folks have to compromise more than others,' Fukes said.

Outside, Harley dragged Kristin around to the side of the building by her arm and threw her against the wall. He licked his lips and moved his hand down to his inner thigh, damp with sweat. He rested his shotgun on the ground and stepped up to her. Pushing her hard to the wall, he began massaging her shoulders with his thumbs, leering over her cleavage.

Kristin raised her chin in defiance, never averting her gaze from his. 'Just get on with it, and keep your filthy hands off my daughter.'

'She's safe. I don't do kids, lady.'

'You think that redeems you somehow?'

'Yeah, it does. Little girls are innocent, but big girls always know their shit.' He pushed one of his large thighs between her legs, forcing them open. She did her best to resist, but her shoes slid on the concrete base surrounding the Management Centre. 'Bitches who've been married as long as you have, they get their second wind.' He reached up and undid the top three buttons of her shirt to reveal the trim of her black bra. 'They experiment to keep their relationship fresh. Keep their husband satisfied. Now you're gonna show me the things you showed him.'

Harley used his other hand to unbutton the flies of his jeans while he ran his fingers down her neck and over her breasts. 'I'll decide whether you've shown me enough, but don't worry, I won't make you go all out. I want you to save some surprises for the other times. We're gonna have a whole lot of time. Now take off that bra and show me them titties.' He took one step away from her so he could get a better view.

Kristin almost gasped when she saw Raine looming up behind him. Somehow, she'd managed to get a few feet away before she'd even noticed. Raine's expression was ice-cold. She didn't acknowledge Kristin; her focus was on the back of the intruder's head.

Kristin knew she still had a captive audience. Harley was already sliding a clumsy hand down the front of his pants. She took control and unbuttoned the rest of her shirt, opening it to show the flat of her tummy.

'Oh yeah,' Harley purred. 'You work out, don't you? You business types always look after your bodies. It's how you get ahead. Sucking that cock all the way to the top. I can't promise mine will smell as sweet as theirs, but it'll definitely make an impression.'

Kristin slid one finger under the left strap of her bra and unhooked it from her shoulder. Harley's greasy face gurned with approval. 'That's it. Just go with it. It'll be a lot less painful.'

Raine's shadow was now covering him, and her fists were clenched.

'I can't promise that,' Kristin said.

Harley frowned. 'Huh?'

Right before Raine pounced, Kristin looked into her eyes – the deadness she saw there scared her. She locked her right arm around Harley's neck. Her tight, sculpted muscles popped and her bicep pressed into his throat. The big man tried to call out, but could only choke. She pulled upwards with all of her strength, pushing down on his shoulder with her free hand. Harley flailed hopelessly, forced onto tiptoes. He groaned and grabbed at Raine's arm, but there was no leverage for him to exploit.

Raine gritted her teeth and twisted. The snap that came after was clean and final. As soon as his body went limp, the weight became too much for her and she dropped him. He landed awkwardly, one of his legs bent underneath him, the fractured vertebrae pushing out the skin on the side of his neck.

⁂

'Fukes, stop this. You can stop this,' Ethan said. 'If you're really considering letting us live here, how do you think it's going to work if you let this happen?'

'Save it, Ethan,' Vincent said. He glared at an empty section of floor, still comforting his traumatised daughter.

'Vin gets it: there's got to be some give and take,' Fukes said. 'Later on, we're gonna help you fix that fence. One of our buddies used to work in construction. We'll have it up in no time and keep these bastards out of our patch. There's enough food and power to go round.'

'That sounds just like Disney World. We're all going to be so happy together,' Ethan said.

Fukes bent over to get closer to him. 'I might make you my errand boy. You can shine my fuckin' boots every time you open that smart ass-mouth.'

Ethan raised his eyebrows and sighed. 'I've never seen a pair of jackboots on a black guy before, but I guess there's a first time for everything.'

Fukes put his foot into Ethan's chest and forced him flat on his back. 'I can't see how this arrangement will ever get boring.' After he spoke, Fukes heard the light patter of feet on the platform. He looked up to see that Raine had already launched herself from the stairs. He raised his gun to get off a shot, only to be kneed in the chest and knocked to the ground. They both scrambled to get up and started grappling with Fukes's six-shooter.

Raine caught hold of his wrist, trying to force the gun away from her. As its barrel moved towards the area where Vincent and Emily were sitting, Vincent turned his back on the struggle to cover his daughter. The gun went off and the bullet struck him.

Raine regained her balance and thrust her knee into Fukes's stomach. Winded, he dropped his weapon, then countered her blow with a right hook. She took it full on the chin and stumbled into the digital map table. Before she could recover, he was onto her, his hands closing around her throat. Now face to face, they glared into each other's eyes. Fukes grimaced, flashing his gold tooth, as the pressure to her neck began to close her airways.

Kristin made her way down the steps, still shaken by Harley's assault, wielding his shotgun. But however much she tried, she couldn't get a clean shot at Fukes without running a serious risk of hitting Raine in the process.

Contorting herself, Raine managed to break his hold, twisting his arms at the elbows until they locked. The next thing he felt was Raine's forehead connecting with his nose. The cartilage crunched on impact and they released each other. Incensed by the sting and sudden rush of blood from his nostrils, he kicked out and Raine walked into it. The toe of his boot thudded into her crotch. The vibration it sent through her pelvic bone turned her stomach and she doubled over.

Fukes was now standing over her, raising his fist. Kristin screamed. She ran at him, holding the shotgun over her head, her open shirt flapping at her sides. He welcomed her charge with a slap to the face that sent her skidding to the floor.

Raine recovered and threw herself into the fight again, wrestling face-to-face with Fukes. He got underneath her and hoisted her onto his shoulder. He carried her around the table and tossed her, screaming, into the banks of computer desks. Her elbow shattered a monitor screen, before she rolled off one of the desks and smashed down on a computer rig.

Struggling to breathe through his broken nose, Fukes turned to search for his gun. Ethan jumped on his back, straddling his waist and clinging to him like a limpet. Fukes twirled round several times in an attempt to free himself, but Ethan sank his teeth into the man's ear. Fukes cried out when he felt the bite cut into his connective tissue. He bent on one knee to shift his weight and Ethan toppled over his back, landing at his feet.

Fukes reached up to the bloody, chewed-up mess at the side of his head, feeling the uneven ridge where the top of his pinna used to be. His face tightened with rage and he stamped down on Ethan.

Ethan did his best to protect his head as the blows kept coming. One stamp connected with his ribs, knocking the wind out of him. Just as he realised he no longer had the strength to protect himself, Fukes stopped.

Ethan peered through his fingers and saw Raine had returned. She was holding a broken shard from the casing of a computer rig. She'd already shoved the jagged piece of carbon into Fukes's neck, puncturing his larynx. He clawed at the offending object, but didn't have the energy to remove it. Panic welled in his eyes, and his breaths turned to desperate gargles. Raine had twisted it deep, and as she yanked it from the wound she'd created, a jet of blood sprayed her face and chest.

Still gargling, Fukes dropped to his knees. Ethan scrambled backwards before the criminal could fall face down on top of him.

In the wake of so much violence, the Management Centre was suddenly plunged into silence – the only noise was the gentle hum of the computer servers.

Kristin shook herself from her daze and raced over to her family. Vincent gingerly turned his body so he was no longer shielding Emily. He winced as he tried to move his arm, and Kristin saw the bloodied hole in his shirt. 'God, you've been shot.'

'I think I'm OK,' he said.

'Mommy.' Emily crawled over her father and put her arms around Kristin.

'It's OK, baby. Daddy's fine; we're all fine.' She pushed her fingers through the hole in Vincent's shirt and tore the material open. She was relieved to see that there was both an entry and an exit wound. The bullet had missed the bone and passed straight through the muscle. They both looked up when they heard the broken shard fall from Raine's hand and hit the floor.

She walked towards them, stopping short of Salty's unconscious body. She was panting like a wounded animal; she was drenched in sweat and blood, her body at breaking point.

Ethan, Vincent, Kristin and Emily all stared at her in awe and in fear, unable to process the burst of brutality they had been caught up in and how they had somehow all survived it. Raine was keenly aware that their eyes were on her, and responded by glaring back at them.

Their stare-off was interrupted by the stuttered hiss of a radio transmission.

Ethan checked his walkie, but it wasn't coming from there. Bruised and stiff from his beating, he crawled over to Fukes' fresh corpse and lifted his jacket. Fukes' walkie was still clipped to his pants. The hiss from its speaker was soon replaced by a human voice.

'Hey, Fukes. Come in, you asshole. We're on our way.'

Episode Six

The Breach

Chapter 1

The voice crackled through the speaker of the walkie again. *'Just makin' a stop first. We've found a nice haul nearby. Be a couple of hours.'*

The group listened intently, delaying their next breath.

'You fucks better roll out the red carpet, cause we've hit pay dirt.' There was a pause, and the voice returned. *'Hey, you found any pussy in there? Deer or coyote 'll do. I ain't proud right now. Haha.'*

The two women shared a look, Raine's eyes wandering down to Kristin's open shirt and the pink skin of her midriff.

The radio clipped to Fukes' body fell silent. Raine recommenced her panting and bent over to pick up the assault rifle. The others were still mesmerised by the beast she'd unleashed from within. 'The showers?' she said.

'Head east. The bathroom block is between the visitor centre and parking lot,' Kristin said as she applied pressure to the wound on Vincent's arm.

Raine pointed down to her feet, where Salty was lying motionless. 'Somebody better see to him.' She then stormed out, leaving the rest of them to deal with the aftermath of their violent struggle.

'Come on, baby. Get up.' Kristin put her arms around Vincent's waist and helped him to his feet.

He grimaced, trying to keep his arm still.

She guided his hand to the bullet hole and pressed against it. 'Keep pressure on it.'

Clinging to her father's shirttails, Emily followed them to the nearest chair. She hugged him as soon as he sat down.

Kristin went to work, tearing the sleeve off her own shirt to fashion it into a tourniquet. Ethan gazed at the dead body and the blood pooling in front of him. He felt something rolling around in his mouth – a bitter-tasting gristle. He realised what it was and spat it out immediately. He wiped a hand across his mouth and noticed Kristin struggling to tend to her husband.

'Can I do anything to help?' he asked.

'I think I saw a first-aid kit fixed to the wall back there,' she replied.

Ethan stepped over Fukes, careful not to touch him, and headed further into the building.

Kristin pulled the torn piece of fabric tight above Vincent's wound. He gritted his teeth and sucked in. Her open shirt caught his attention, and so did the bruise forming around her left eye where Fukes had struck her.

'Are you OK?' he asked. He reached up to her cheek.

'Fine. There was nothing you could have done but what you did,' she said.

Emily forced her way in between them and buried her face into Vincent's lap, smearing the dried blood still in her hairline onto his jeans.

'She was attacked. She became non-responsive for a while due to the shock. We need to keep a close eye on her,' he said.

Kristin frowned at the knowledge of her daughter's experience. Then she paused for thought, looking around at the centre's open-plan layout. 'Where's Adam?'

Vincent felt Emily's arms tighten around him at the mention of the boy's name. 'He had to... go,' he said.

Before she could respond, Ethan got back, holding a plastic first-aid box. He passed it to Kristin, who opened it up and picked out saline solution, antiseptic, sterile gauze pads, and bandages. She also removed a small glass container full of an off-white liquid and handed it to Ethan.

'It's ammonia – for him.' She looked over to where Salty lay.

'Right.' Ethan took the bottle and moved to the man's side.

Kristin soaked some cotton wool in saline so she could start to clean the entry and exit wounds.

'As soon as this is dressed and Jake's back on his feet, we should grab what we can and get out of here.'

'I'm not so sure that's a good idea,' Vincent said, straining to speak through his discomfort.

'What?'

'Things are bad, but do you really think it will be any better out there?'

Kristin's eyes widened in disbelief. 'Vincent, you were just shot. I presume Adam's dead, and Emily could have been too.'

'I know. I was there.'

'So why are we even discussing this?'

'OK, say we go. Say we just pack up and leave before those other men get here. Where do we go? Do you know of a place? If you do, please tell me and I'll be right behind you.'

She shook her head. 'This is insane.'

'Twenty minutes ago our daughter was catatonic. Look at us – we're in no shape to go anywhere right now.'

'So what do you suggest we do? Do you think we can stand another fight like that one?'

'They won't be able to get past the main gate unless we open it for them, but Ethan and I found a hole on the west side of the fence. We have to see to that right away.'

Ethan flipped Salty onto his back. It didn't seem as though the fall had caused him any serious facial injuries. When he waved the smelling salts under Salty's nose, his nostrils twitched and he began to stir. His eyes opened and focussed on the ceiling, and he immediately sat up with a jolt, then relaxed a little when he saw Ethan leaning over him. To his right, he noticed Fukes, lying in his own blood.

'What happened?'

'Miller. Miller happened,' Ethan said.

'Miller?' Salty groaned.

'Yeah. She... she changed.'

Salty reached up to feel the sore bump on his head. 'Any ideas who they were?'

'Bad news. They got in through that hole I told you about.'

'There really was a breach?'

'An electrical fire must have brought a tree down on the cables. It's a mess.'

'Yeah. That falls into the "no shit" category.' Salty groaned again, putting his head in his hands.

'It's not over yet,' Ethan said. 'They have some friends. We just heard them over the radio.'

'They know about this place too?'

'They must have communicated with their friends when they discovered it.'

Salty didn't need to hear any more. He started to get up. 'We have to get set – put a gun on the gate.'

Ethan placed his hand on his chest and eased him to the ground again. Under normal circumstances, he wouldn't have stood a chance of overpowering Salty, but he was more than a little woozy.

'Outta my way, Twilight.'

'You were just out cold. How far do you think you'll get before you keel over? You need to stay put until you've recovered.'

'Ha. And have you running the show?'

'No, thank God. Vincent and Kristin are here, and Miller's about somewhere, I guess. We lost Adam though. He was killed by one of the dead. Must have gotten in through the breach.' The memory of what Ethan had been forced to do to stop the young man from coming back was still fresh.

Salty turned slowly to see the Graham family huddled together, and Kristin dressing her husband's wound. 'You get bit?'

'Shot,' Vincent replied. 'A lot happened while you were out.'

'Evidently. Where did Miller go?'

'To get cleaned up,' Kristin said.

'Shame about the boy. I liked him,' Salty said.

Ethan and Vincent thought about speaking up, but they both remained silent.

'If no one has any objections, I say we dress these wounds and get over to the visitor centre,' Kristin said. 'Jake and Emily can get some proper rest there and I'm sure we'd all feel a lot safer being closer to the parking lot.'

'Who's going to watch out for those assholes?' Salty said.

'On the radio they said they were a couple of hours away. We should post someone here to watch the monitors.'

'I'll come back once I've helped you get over there,' Ethan said.

After Kristin had secured the bandage around Vincent's arm, she saw to Salty's head injury, wrapping it with a dressing. She and Ethan helped the wounded men into the truck and told Emily to sit up front with them as they drove east to the much larger visitor centre facility.

▲

The automated doors slid open and the five survivors staggered through in a huddle, bloodied and bruised, into the foyer. The floors were polished and a large welcome sign hanging from the ceiling greeted them.

To the left stood a C-shaped reception desk, a sizeable photographic image of a woodland stag mounted on the wall behind it. On the opposite side was a souvenir kiosk that had carousel stands full of hard-back books on wildlife and conservation, motif pens, small-scale models of the animals that existed in the preserve, T-shirts, caps, and twelve-inch prints taken at various periods of its history.

Vincent noticed that the till register had been removed and wondered why any part of the kiosk was still remaining. 'I thought you said Farrington closed this place to the public?'

'He left everythin' pretty much as it was. He used to invite his family and some kids from the charity he was patron for,' Salty said.

A little further ahead they came to a movie theatre, where once a film on the preserve's history and development was screened. It now lay idle.

Emily was drawn to the flashing digital panels from a section called the Discovery Station. She let go of her father's leg and plodded over to it. The panels had been placed low to the ground, so you didn't need to be tall to use them. Each one contained interactive information about a particular animal or type of vegetation, which you were able to toggle through using two push-buttons.

There were also three microscopes fixed to separate desks, but she could only reach high enough to touch their bases.

'What is it, honey?' Vincent had noticed that she'd strayed and was now standing next to her again. 'Woah, how cool is this? You could learn a whole lot looking through those. You could be the next park ranger in no time.'

Emily didn't smile. Much to his dismay, she just gave him a brief look and then turned back to the panels.

Ethan approached one of the microscopes and peered through its lens. Beneath the slide was the delicate structure of an insect wing. The patterns created by the fusion and cross-connection of veins were both beautiful and oddly reassuring to him. It represented a snap-shot of the finer details of life, or at least the remnants of it.

'Can I see it?'

The sound of Emily's weak voice caused him to remove his eye from the viewer. He glanced to Vincent for approval and the child's father nodded.

'OK, take a look.' He grabbed her around her waist and lifted her up to it. 'See it?'

'Yeah. It looks complicated,' Emily said.

'That's the way it supposed to look,' Ethan said.

They made it to the lounge area and collapsed into the leather sofas there. In the right corner, next to the staircase leading to the second floor, was a sophisticated-looking cocktail bar surrounded by mirrors and decorated with stainless steel and soft-wood furnishings.

Kristin set down the first-aid kit and the medical case they had found in the military truck. She began to examine the centre-piece of the lounge: a tubular glass tank that reached all the way up to the next floor, its interior lit with blue neon, which illuminated the coral and seaweed inside. Bubbles rose to its surface.

'Farrington had all the fish removed 'cause he was against them being confined. He just kept the feature 'cause he liked it.' Salty eased back on the sofa to rest his bandaged head.

'I can see why he would want to spend most of his time in here,' Vincent said.

Kristin ran her fingers down the glass of the aquarium. 'And where is he now – this Farrington guy? Anyone know?' She turned to face them. 'I can see how taken you are with this place, but do I have to be the one to state the obvious?'

'Kris.'

'No, Vincent. We almost paid for having something that others want, and it's not over yet.'

'This time we'll be ready for em',' Salty said.

'Even if we are ready, there'll be more. Do you really think a handful of us can defend something this size indefinitely?'

'You wanna go back out there? Into that shit?' Salty said.

'As much as I don't want to burst the bubble of our industrious leader, I'm inclined to agree with Kristin on this one,' Ethan said. 'I have a bad feeling about this place.'

'No one asked you for your fuckin' opinion,' Salty said.

'You said a bad word.' Emily pointed an accusing finger at him.

'It's OK, sweetie. We're just talking.' Vincent stroked her hair and laid her back down on the sofa. 'Close your eyes for a little while. I'm still here.'

'Instead of arguing about this, we should be fixing that gaping wound in the fence,' Vincent said.

'How big's this hole? Will the truck block it off?' Salty said.

'Sure. It'll be big enough, but how do we get it past the trees?' Vincent asked.

'The perimeter around the facility is about twenty feet wide. All someone needs to do is come at it from the north side of the gate.'

'I'll go,' Kristin said.

'No you won't.' Vincent tried to get up, but she pushed him down again.

'You've lost too much blood already, and you need to rest. Besides, I'd feel better if you were with Emily right now,' she said.

'What about you, Twilight? Can you drive a stick or does your skill-set begin and end with gettin' the heebie-jeebies?' Salty said.

'I'm not so good at driving stick. I'm used to automatics,' Ethan said.

Salty croaked out a laugh, but soon wished he hadn't as his head throbbed under the strain. 'Jesus H. Christ.'

'It's fine. Ethan fought for us back there. He took a beating for it too. He should go back over to the Management Centre so he can watch the gates. I can handle myself behind the wheel. My dad was a long-haul driver. I grew up in them,' Kristin said.

Vincent stood and returned the Beretta to her. 'Keep following the west fence into the nature trails and you'll see it.'

Ethan handed her his radio. 'You better take this too. I won't be far away if you get into trouble. I can keep an eye out for you on the monitors.'

'You're not going to get into trouble, are you?' Vincent reached for her hips, barely making contact with the tips of his fingers.

'I'll be inside the cab and I have this.' She brandished the gun. 'See you soon. See you soon, Emily.'

'Bye, Mommy,' Emily said, her eyes half-closed.

Kristin made her way towards the entrance. Her ankle had loosened and her limp was hardly noticeable.

'I better go too. I'll grab one of the spare radios when I get there. Keep you posted,' Ethan said.

Before he could leave, Vincent called him back. 'Listen, I'm still trying to get my head around what happened out there, but what you did for my daughter, and what you had to do with Adam, I—'

'I did the world a favour, as far as Adam's concerned – even a world as fucked up as this doesn't deserve someone like him.'

'Nevertheless, I saw that kid – how he was. And I saw you. What I'm trying to say is I was wrong.'

Ethan frowned and his eyes glazed over. 'You were wrong about him, but you were right to be afraid of me.'

Vincent didn't respond. He had no clue what the young man meant by it. Instead, he watched him trudge across the polished floor with his hood up and his hands in his pockets.

Chapter 2

Kristin froze in the dirt on her way to the truck. She saw a lone figure approaching from the southeast, next to the clinic. The person was striding in her direction with some purpose. She wanted to believe it was Raine coming from the shower blocks, but it couldn't be: this person's hair had been shaved right down to the scalp.

The sky was turning a sickly colour as the day ebbed away, so it took her a few minutes before she could distinguish their facial features. Her cold flush subsided when she realised it was Raine after all, but she still couldn't explain her appearance. Her lack of hair made her seem harsher – more unforgiving. Raine held the assault rifle tight to her shoulder, her body rigid.

'What's with the hair cut?'

'Seemed appropriate,' Raine said.

'What you did in there—'

'What?' Raine squared up to her as she got close, inches from her face, cutting into her with her stone-cold stare. 'You gonna tell me you understand what that was?'

Kristin had to break eye contact, and she certainly didn't have an answer to her question.

'Nah, didn't think so.' Raine continued.

'Raine, those men are coming. We have to—'

'You don't have to worry about them anymore,' Raine said. She walked beyond the visitor centre and up towards the south fence.

Kristin couldn't afford to go after her. She climbed into the truck, cranked the stiff gears, and manoeuvred it in the direction of the main gate. She found that she was a little rusty with her driving, but she'd handled bigger rigs than this in the past. She thought about the times she'd sat up front with her father on his shorter trips. How she used to stick her head out of the open window on the highway to feel the wind blow through her hair. She tried to imagine how those familiar stretches of road would look now: silent, desolate – dead.

Chapter 3

Salty grunted in his sleep and rolled onto his side, pushing his face into the sofa's leather. He'd fought against his tiredness, but the blow to his head had weakened him and his body needed to recover.

Now the talking had stopped, the first floor of the visitor centre began to feel eerie to Vincent. The only sound he could hear besides an occasional moan from Salty was the gentle bubble from the empty aquarium. He knelt by the sofa next to Emily, propping his injured arm against one of the cushions.

His little girl lay with her eyes wide and alert, staring at the interwoven pattern of vines on the ceiling tiles. Vincent noticed her hair had started to become lank and greasy. Her bubblegum cheeks didn't seem quite so full anymore either. A few flakes of dried blood still clung to the edge of her forehead. He didn't want to brush them away, as it would draw attention to them and her ordeal. 'Could you at least try to close your eyes for me?' he whispered.

Her stare remained fixed on the ceiling. 'Every time I do, I see things. Things I don't want to.'

Vincent lowered his head, holding back a scream of frustration. 'I know. It's just that, sometimes, people see things and they can't ever make them go away. Usually, it's only a few unlucky ones that go through that, but things have changed. Now it happens to all of us.'

'What do those people do about it? If they can't ever make the pictures go away?'

'They learn to live with them somehow. It's hard, but they find a way.'

'Because it's better than not being around anymore?'

'Yes, sweetie. That's exactly right.'

Emily swallowed hard and finally looked at him. 'I think I'll do the same.'

Vincent shook as he fought back the tears and tried to get his words out without falling apart in front of her. 'You want to be around at least as long as your daddy.'

'Nah, that's too old.'

'Oh really?'

'Yeah.' Emily let out the tiniest giggle. Then a smile lifted her cheeks. It was a moment he wanted to capture and seal in a bottle because he dared not dream of it happening again. The smile was interrupted by a long yawn that elongated her face and caused her nostrils to flare.

'Come on now. Scooch down.' Vincent eased her along the sofa cushions so her head was flat against them, covering her with the blanket he'd taken from the Management Centre.

'Will I dream?' she asked.

'You might, but I'll be right here waiting for you when you wake up.'

Her eyes finally closed and Vincent felt safe to wipe the moisture from his cheeks.

Chapter 4

Kristin rammed the truck into reverse and rolled back level with the west fence. She could see the main gate and the access road on the other side, curving right into the forest. It was empty, for now. Her gun and radio lay on the passenger seat of the cabin, just within reach. She shifted into first and drove on into the gap between the fence and the trees surrounding the nature trails.

Through the spaces of the electrified cables, the stumbling dead were already beginning to swarm towards the facility. Their mannerisms – their flailing limbs and twitching heads seemed aimless, but their collective movement certainly wasn't. They had all found their way to the same place, as if summoned by something silent and unknown. It was then that Kristin recalled what Sergeant Banks had told them the night they escaped from the FEMA camp. He said that the herds the soldiers had been tracking migrated to the nearest coastline.

The charred debris and the twisted metal up ahead indicated she was close to the breach. She changed up again and eased the accelerator. Not only had the dead found their way through the forest, they were converging on the hole. Before she could reach it, one of the fragmented herd crossed the perimeter and stepped onto the scorched ground. At first, the creature had its back to the truck, but it turned in stages to reveal the melted features of a woman. Most of her hair had fallen out, leaving surface fuzz over her wrinkled scalp, like the skin of a giant insect. Her slack-jawed expression caused her to drool through her fractured rows of teeth.

Kristin noticed that her right eyeball was missing from its weeping socket, and there was a red strip of material hanging beneath her armpit. As she faced the cabin, Kristin feathered the brake. A dirty, shrivelled mess sat inside the carrier fixed to the woman's chest. Its small, diseased-ridden legs started to kick out and it turned its head towards the oncoming vehicle. The child could not have been any more than a few months old when it died. A sizeable section of its cheek was missing, and the flesh around the wound was stretched crudely. It wasn't difficult for Kristin to piece together what must have happened.

She reacted by moving the truck closer to the fence. Even though she quickly straightened up, the side mirror caught against one of the cables and was promptly taken out and bounced under the rear wheels. She abandoned the brake and accelerated again, pushing hard down.

The truck was just about to hit her, and the mother looked like she was almost cradling her baby. Then she reached out into the glare of the headlights and roared. Her body hit the cabin's windshield like a sack of bones in loose skin, leaving a circular patch of spoiled blood on the glass. What was left of the body got chewed up as the truck ran over it.

Kristin felt a violent jolt as the front fender crashed into the jagged shards of metal sprouting from the damaged fence. Her seat belt snapped her back and prevented her from hitting her head on the dash. The vehicle juddered and stopped, Kristin's foot forcing down the brake. Steam hissed out from the hood and in through the crack of the driver's side window. She shook herself and leaned forward to check out the damage. Not only was the front of the truck impaled on one of the fence supports, she'd also overshot the breach, leaving a part of it clear.

The dead were attracted by the noise and made their way towards it, more purposefully than before. At least twenty of them reached up to the cabin, groaning. Kristin snatched at the stick to slip it into neutral. She turned the key in the ignition, and it spluttered into life on the first attempt. When she tried to shift into reverse, the stick wouldn't budge.

The first creature to get to the passenger window tapped against the glass with the stump of its right arm. The flesh had been shredded up to half-way down its radius and ulna bones.

She grabbed the stick with both hands and leaned back to yank it into gear. The grinding sound filled the cabin again, and the stick remained fixed. Multiple hands slapped against the right side of the vehicle as the dead clamoured to get inside, leaving smears of blood and grease on its body.

Kristin glanced at the gun and radio before she gave the stick one last tug. With another jarring, mechanical snort, it moved back and lodged into the reverse slot. She eased on the gas, and the truck began to pull away from the damage, minus some of its front-end, which was still impaled on the jagged metal. Spinning the wheel, she drove into the perimeter, sandwiching the animated corpses between the fence support and the truck. As one of the skulls shattered, it fractured the passenger window.

She managed to back up far enough to fully block the hole before the leaking engine gave out and it grumbled to a halt. She could still hear the hands slapping the exterior on the opposite side. Taking a moment to breathe, she pushed the sweaty strands of hair from her face, snatched up the Beretta and walkie, and jumped out of the cabin.

Chapter 5

Ethan turned his nose up at the fat fugitive slumped against the side of the Management Centre. Harley's body had already begun to stink. His head was twisted and his vertebrae protruded from his neck.

He reluctantly sifted through Harley's pockets, coming away with six shotgun shells and a half-eaten packet of watermelon bubblegum. He put his finds into his own pockets and faced the dimming sky. Dusk had well and truly fallen. The light filtered through the clouds as a peculiar shade of blue grey, tainting the grass and the tops of the trees.

The temperature had also dropped a few degrees. When he ventured inside the building, the large open spaces were cooler than outside. Blood marked the spot where Salty had been knocked down. Chairs had been overturned and one computer rig was in pieces. Each of these signs reminded him of their violent encounter – and nothing more than Fukes's body. The pool of blood had already started to congeal around him.

Ethan stepped over his legs, making a concerted effort not to look at him. He made for the security monitors and took a seat in front of them. He took a deep breath and tried to rub the tiredness from his eyes, remembering he had not eaten all day. Sitting in a room with a fresh corpse was not at all in his comfort zone, but he did not fancy the idea of dragging it outside either.

He ignored the smell and the grumbles in his stomach to focus on the security feeds, switching from one camera to the next on 60 second rotations. He noticed one screen had switched to footage of the main gate and rolled his chair closer. The road leading in was clear, and the shadows were so thick that the trunks of the trees in the surrounding forest seemed to blend into one mass.

Another camera, positioned on the west side of the preserve, displayed the image of the military truck wedged awkwardly in the breach.

The next monitor showed Kristin on her way back, looking dishevelled but still in one piece. The solar panels no longer retained their glow without any sun to power them.

He caught a glimpse of the interior of the visitor centre just before the feed changed, and then placed his head on the desk, tapping his fingers until it cycled back around again. In the lounge, Salty lay with his arms over his face, so it was difficult to be sure whether he was asleep. Vincent was kneeling by the sofa next to Emily, his head on the cushion next to her stomach. He almost felt jealous of them, even if they were sleeping with one eye open.

The crackle of the radio behind him sent a cold jolt through his gut. *'Hey, Fukes, Harley. This isn't fuckin' funny anymore. Over.'* This time, the gruff voice on the other end sounded agitated. *'Come on, sound off. We ain't heard shit from you in three hours.'*

Ethan did not move from his seat. He just stared at the radio, which was still attached to Fukes's belt.

'OK, you better have run into trouble. We're packing up and comin' straight over there.'

There were no more transmissions after that.

Ethan rose from the desk and walked over to the body. As he bent down to reach for the walkie, he thought about what he could say in response. He wanted to confidently announce to them there was a small army behind the fences, and they had stripped their colleagues of their weapons and sent them on their way.

He plucked the device from Fukes and tucked it into his own jeans, making sure it was the opposite side of the walkie from the facility.

Chapter 6

Vincent lifted his head from the sofa, the front of his hair sticking up after his brief nap. He couldn't understand what had woken him so abruptly, but then he heard the hollow clunk of boot-heels on the hard floor of the foyer.

Kristin looked like she'd been through the wringer. Her clothes were damp with sweat and her limp had returned. He rushed over to her, searching her body for cuts and scratches, and cupping her face in his hands.

'Jesus. Are you OK?' He picked away some of the strands of her hair so he could properly see her face.

'The hole is covered, if that's what you mean. I hope those vehicles in the parking lot will start because the truck won't get us another mile. How's Emily?' She tried to peer over the back of the sofa to get a glimpse of their daughter.

'Better. She's sleeping.'

Kristin went to her. The little girl had fallen asleep with her mouth open. Being under the blanket had caused her cheeks to flush. She felt compelled to lean over and kiss her forehead, but she didn't want to disturb her rest. She remembered watching her sleep as a baby, how peaceful she had always looked. This serene image of Emily was suddenly supplanted by the memory of the decomposing mother she'd encountered at the breach and the half-eaten child she had been carrying. She shut her eyes and turned away, trying to erase it. When she opened them, Salty was stirring on the sofa opposite. He pushed himself into a sitting position, holding his head, as if he feared it would fall off if he didn't.

'Shit. What happened?' he groaned.

'It's done. How are you feeling?' she said.

'Like I got the mother of all shine hangovers. I'll live.' The wiry man snorted and reached for his cap, perching it on top of his head, above his bandage.

'Have you heard from Ethan yet?' Kristin said.

'Not yet,' Vincent replied.

She walked to the aquarium where they had left their bags and unzipped one of them. Taking out a bottle of water that only had warm dregs at the bottom, she chugged it back, then discarded it on the floor.

'Slow down,' Vincent said. 'Take a seat.'

Kristin shook her head. 'I'm going to search for food. Where is it kept?'

'There's a restaurant upstairs. The kitchen is always pretty well-stocked. There's some canned and frozen food too,' Salty said.

'Even better.' Kristin proceeded to empty out the contents of each bag. A power ball that Emily had packed fell out and bounced over to Vincent.

'Kristin?' he said.

'We take as much as we can carry. Leave some space for medical supplies from the clinic.'

'What are you talking about?'

'I know what's up her ass,' Salty said. 'Thought we understood that the answer was no the first time you asked.' He scowled, looking like he was determined to get up, even if he had to fall back down again.

'All we established was that I'm the only one who can see this place for what it is.' Before she could go anywhere, Vincent caught hold of her.

'Kris, wait. Even if we can get one of those cars to start, where are we gonna go in the middle of the night?'

'The coast. It's virtually a straight shot to Jersey from here.'

'You hankerin' for a swim, Mrs. Graham?' Salty said.

'Travelling through those other cities? We'd never make it on the highway,' Vincent said.

'Then we'll go around them.'

'Ma'am, I think maybe you've been out in the sun too long today,' Salty said.

'Jake, please.' Vincent held his hand up to warn him off.

Kristin ignored them both and continued to gather up the now-empty bags.

'Y'know, I was dumb enough to think I'd gotten through to you. Now it's clear you're outta your goddamn mind,' Salty said.

'It was your call to lead us here and I'm grateful – I really am, but you don't get to decide whether my family stays. We'll speak to Raine and Ethan – see what they want to do.'

Salty rubbed his sore head, suggesting the current conversation was only making it worse. 'Fair enough, but I get to decide what you take from this place. The vehicles and medical supplies stay where they are.'

Kristin threw the bags down in disgust and strode to the sofa, where he sat down. 'There are four cars on that lot, and you've got more than enough meds, you son of a bitch.'

This time, Salty found the strength to stand. 'Mind yourself, Mrs. Graham. Court's in recess right now.'

As Vincent moved to get in between them, the fizz of static came through his radio – Kristin's too. *'Erm... you there, guys?'* Ethan said. *'We've got company.'*

Satisfied that Salty and his wife had put their personal feud on hold, Vincent snatched the radio from his waistband and answered 'we read you, Ethan. We'll be right there.'

Salty grabbed the shotgun they had taken from Harley. He then handed Vincent Fukes's six-shot pistol. 'You better wake the rugrat.'

Chapter 7

The gentle hum of the light around the facility started to rise as their photocells activated in response to the descending dark. Ethan was occupied with one particular monitor inside the Management Centre. He'd altered the settings so it continued to show the feed from the main gate. The lights there had not fully charged yet, and the two men outside with their Hummer kept momentarily disappearing in the pockets of shadow under the trees.

They had pulled up right next to the car Fukes and Harley arrived in. Both men were prowling from one side of the gate to the other, peering through the fence and occasionally punching numbers into the control panel.

Ethan was unaware that he was biting his own fingernails as he watched every move and gesture they made.

'*Helloooooo?*' Again the voice crackled through the radio that he'd placed on the desk next to him. Ethan saw one of the men had raised his walkie to his mouth. '*Look, this ain't fuckin' funny, man. You gonna let us in or not?*'

The door to the Management Centre slid open and Ethan spun on his chair to see the rest of the group enter – all except Raine.

Emily walked unaided, but still clung to her father's arm.

'Where's Miller?' Ethan said.

'We don't know,' Kristin said. 'I saw her just before I took the truck to the fence and she wasn't in a good place.'

'Screw her. We've got more pressing shit to worry about,' Salty said. 'What are they doin'?' He made it to the monitors first, leaning in next to Ethan.

'They're just standing at the gate. They've tried to communicate a couple of times.'

'Have you spoken to them?' Vincent said.

Ethan shook his head.

Before Vincent could sit down at the desk, the radio hissed again. *'Hey, we ain't dumb enough to think someone ain't listening. We know our friends are in there.'*

Salty looked back at Kristin, who was now comforting Emily. 'You sure you plugged that leak?'

'There's no way they can get through. There are too many of those creatures gathered around it anyway,' she said.

Salty searched the other monitors for confirmation that the breach had been blocked, and he found it. There were at least thirty of the dead, either trying to clamber up the side of the truck or trapped between it and the fence.

'We just want our friends back. You let us in and there ain't no need for this to escalate.'

Vincent grabbed the radio from the desk and answered. 'My name's Vincent Graham.'

'What are you doin'?' Salty said.

Vincent ignored him and continued. 'We were brought here by an employee of the facility. What do you want?'

'Just to work this out,' the man said. *'We'd feel a little better about things if you told us why you got our buddy's radio.'*

Vincent paused for thought before he went back. 'It's complicated.'

'It always is. Now, I know you ain't about to spin some bullshit. So where Fukes and Harley at?'

Vincent turned and saw Fukes's corpse, lying exactly where he'd bled out. 'They're here – with us.'

'OK, so put 'em on.'

'That's not going to be possible.'

'Why's that?'

'They held us at gun point. They were going to rape my wife. We had to stop them.'

This time, the pause came from the other end of the transmission. *'So by "stopped", you mean killed them, right?'*

'We were only defending ourselves. They attacked us.'

'*Well then, Vincent Graham. You tell your wife from me, it ain't over for her yet. When I get in there, I'm gonna fuck her in the ass while you watch. Then I'm gonna gut her like a fish. Then I'm gonna—*'

Salty snatched the walkie from Vincent and screamed into it. 'Set one foot past that fence, we'll turn you as stone-cold as your friends. You hear me? This is ours. It's ours!'

Vincent reached over him to try and take the radio back. They both rolled around on the desk, tugging at the device. Their momentum took them into the wall, and the radio smashed against it. Its case shattered and its electronic guts spilled out onto the floor.

Salty wriggled out of Vincent's grip and pushed him away. 'Get the hell off me,' he spat.

Everyone looked at the contents of the broken device in stunned silence.

'That went rather well, I thought,' Ethan said.

Salty didn't take his eyes off Vincent. 'You lay on hands again, Graham, you're gonna be pickin' your teeth off the floor.'

Kristin put herself in front of Salty. 'This chest-beating isn't helping. What are we going to do?'

'You said it yourself. Those things are startin' to gather on the west fence. It won't be long before they make their way over to the gate. They can't stay there forever, so we just wait 'em out.' Salty's shoulders rounded and he backed away from the group, taking up the shotgun again.

Emily sat on the chair, quietly munching on a cereal bar Vincent had discovered earlier at the visitor centre. She chewed it right down to the edge of the wrapper, then decided to push more of the bar from inside of it.

The night was completely upon them now. The mounted lamps around the facility projected all manner of menacing shapes onto the floors and walls. Many of the structures suddenly became giant beasts, stalking the grounds of the preserve. In every dark corner they had a glimpse of something rotten, ready to stumble out into the light.

Kristen and Salty sat close to the monitors. Salty spent the time unloading and reloading the shells in the shotgun so he could count them.

Vincent noticed the two men outside were moving further along the fence, presumably looking for a way in. It made him feel grimy, but he prayed that they would encounter the dead gathered near the truck and end the anxiety his group were feeling. Sadly, the men became aware of the creatures before they reached them and kept their distance.

'Will they get in, Daddy?' Emily whispered, her mouth still full of toasted oats and nuts.

'I don't think so. Everywhere's locked up pretty tight.'

She discarded her wrapper on the desk and turned to catch a glimpse of Fukes's face down on the ground. Kristin had covered him with a blanket, but it wasn't quite big enough to mask the circle of dried blood around him.

Vincent realised this and twisted her chair back towards the screens. 'Try and pretend he's not there, sweetie. We're going to move him soon. I promise.'

'What are they doing now?' Emily pointed to the monitor that was broadcasting the images from the main gate.

Vincent leaned in and squinted to see them through the shadows. Both of them were crouching close to the base of the fence, just twenty yards or so from the gate. They appeared to be fixing something to one of the supports where the energiser was housed. One of them got up and tracked back to the Hummer. When he emerged from the back, he was carrying a large metal spool of wire.

'Is anyone else seeing this?'

As soon as they heard Vincent's comment, Kristin, Salty and Ethan gathered around the screen and watched the men make their preparations.

'Jesus H. Roosevelt Christ! They're armin' explosives,' Salty said.

'What?' Vincent almost pressed his nose against the screen to get a better look.

'That's C4. When it blows, it's gonna make that breach we had look like a pin-prick.' Salty lifted the shotgun and pumped the fore-end. 'You two up for this?' he said, looking at the Grahams. 'You wanna leave – I get it. But you need to fight before you can do that now. Not for this place – for yourselves and your daughter.'

Vincent and Kristin stood and pulled out their weapons.

'What about you, Twilight? Are you gonna contribute?'

Ethan reached into his pocket and handed Salty the five shotgun shells he'd retrieved from Harley's body.

'I guess that'll have to do,' Salty said.

'Ethan, will you stay here with Emily?' Vincent said.

'No, Daddy.' Emily jumped down from her seat and threw her arms around her father, but was barely able to reach up to his waist. 'Please don't go. You promised.'

'Sweetheart, it's OK. Your mom and I won't be far away, but you can't go outside with us. It's dark and the bad men are out there.'

'But what if they come here?' she said.

Vincent pushed her to arm's length and held her chin up so she was forced to look in his eyes. 'Emily, listen to me. They won't get past us. I won't let anything hurt you. OK?'

Although she tried her best to be brave, she couldn't stop the tears rolling down her cheeks.

Vincent took her hand and placed it into Ethan's. 'If they do get through, take her somewhere and hide,' he whispered.

'Sure. That's something I'm good at,' Ethan said.

'They're moving the vehicles,' Kristin said.

Sure enough, one man backed up the Hummer so it was well clear of the fence, then returned for the second car, while his counterpart rolled out the spool of wire.

They watched it all unfold on the monitors, helpless to do anything about it. When they saw both men retreat to the road, they knew what was coming next.

'What are they doing now?' Emily said.

'Cover your ears,' Vincent said.

The sound of the explosion roared across the grounds of the facility and into the building. It appeared as an intense white flash on the monitor, and then the screens flickered, as did the lights and every other piece of electrical equipment.

'Bastards,' Salty groaned. 'Bastards!' He ran for the door. Vincent and Kristin followed, trying to stop him from doing anything impulsive.

Emily tried to go too, but Ethan held her back. 'Let go of me,' she said struggling.

'We have to stay here.'

'I don't want to.'

'I'll be honest with you, Emily. I'm a crap babysitter. Just the thought of being responsible for a child terrifies me, but the monsters are out there, and I don't want them to get you.'

Now that he'd mentioned the monsters, Emily stopped trying to squirm out of his grasp and went to sit back in her chair.

Once Ethan was satisfied she wouldn't run, he turned his attention back to the security feeds. The section of fence that had borne the brunt of the explosion was nothing more than a mangled collection of smouldering metal. The Hummer burst in through the opening, knocking aside the debris in its way.

⊥

Outside, Salty raced towards the fire, still unsteady on his feet from the concussion. The Grahams tried to keep up, shouting after him. The Hummer seemed to spot them and changed its direction accordingly.

Vincent lunged and almost grabbed the back of Salty's shirt, but instead stumbled and fell into the grass.

'You stupid sons of bitches ruined everything!' Salty stood his ground, panting after each word as he lifted the shotgun and took aim at the oncoming vehicle. 'This was ours. Ours.' The first blast of the weapon missed its target. It was too far away, but that didn't stop Salty firing three more rounds.

The Hummer responded by increasing its speed, heading straight for him, lining him up in the beam of its headlights.

Before he could get off another shot, the pop, pop, pop of rapid fire rang out from somewhere above them. Kristin was helping her husband back to his feet and they both hit the deck. The shots were precise – there was not a single stray bullet. They peppered the windshield of the Hummer, turning it white with fractured veins of shattered glass. Full of holes, the vehicle veered away from Salty, over the road, slamming into a nearby tree at high speed. The front end crumpled like a toy, but the sturdy trunk didn't even shudder on impact.

Bemused and out of breath, Salty lowered the shotgun, first looking at the steaming wreck, and then up to the observation tower. He caught a brief glimpse of someone moving around on the top platform before they were shrouded by darkness. Exhausted, he dropped to his knees, the fresh, gaping wound in the fence never far from his mind.

Vincent and Kristin crept towards the ruined Hummer, aiming their pistols at it. Vincent hung back when they got close, but his wife didn't stop.

'Kris, wait,' he said.

'Wait for what? We have to know. Just cover me.'

Vincent gripped the gun tighter to steady his hand and Kristin crouched low as she approached the driver's door. She yanked its handle twice before it opened. The fumes from the engine filled the Hummer's interior, clouding the two bodies slumped over the bloodied dashboard. Each splinter of glass that covered the backs of the two men was stained red like macabre confetti. Their torn fabric of their clothes showed signs of exit. The driver had been struck by one shot, which had blown out the back of his head and splattered the roof with his brain matter.

Kristin recoiled, almost vomiting as she stumbled back to her husband.

'Are they?'

'Yeah. They are,' she said.

The soft squeaking sound of rubber soles on moist grass came from behind them, waking Salty from his haze of self-pity. Raine walked towards them from the observation tower where she'd got the drop on the second wave of intruders. She was striding with purpose again, her assault rifle still hot from its short but violent burst. She never once glanced at the Hummer. Even when her face caught the light, not a flicker of emotion could be found there.

'We get what we need, check those vehicles for gas, and leave tonight,' she said. Her tone suggested this wasn't being offered up for discussion.

Before anyone could respond, the lights powered down around the whole facility and everything went black.

'What's happening?' Ethan called from the entrance to the Management Centre. He had Emily with him, and he was protecting her with Salty's hatchet.

'Stay where you are,' Raine replied.

Another flicker and the exterior lamps dotted over the preserve found their glow again.

'The back-up generator just kicked in,' Salty said. 'But it can only provide power for the basics – everything else is on lockdown.'

'Was it the explosion?' Vincent said.

'Must have caused a surge. I think I can fix it, but I'll need tools and I'll need to find my way around the power station,' Salty said.

'No one's fixing anything. We're leaving, now,' Raine said. She continued her purposeful journey past the Management Centre.

Ethan finally allowed Emily to slip his grasp so she could run into the waiting arms of her father.

'I know you didn't want this, Jake, but I don't see what choice we have now,' Kristin said.

Salty got up off his knees and smiled sarcastically. 'Don't worry, Mrs. Graham. You got your wish. We're headin' back out into the big bad world. I personally can't wait to navigate that forest in the middle of the night, not knowin' if we're driving headlong into a herd or another group of murderous sons-of-bitches. But I guess we should look on the bright side. It'll be so dark out there we won't be able to see each other die.'

Salty carried on ahead alone and the Grahams shuffled back into a protective huddle, Emily at the centre.

'Don't go without me.' Ethan turned back for the door.

'Where are you going?' Vincent said.

'There are a few flashlights inside. I'll just be able to find them in the dark.'

When they reached the visitor centre, Raine had already forced open the automated doors, now inactive due to the loss of power. She was upstairs rifling through the food in the storeroom of the restaurant's kitchen. 'Someone go out to the lot and check those vehicles,' she said.

'I'll go,' Vincent said. 'Where are the keys?'

'Here.' Raine fumbled around in the darkness and slid the bunch of keys she'd found in the observation tower across the floor to him. 'They're labelled.'

Vincent guided Emily to Kristin. 'I won't be long. Stay here with your mom.'

'Be careful,' Kristin said, putting her arm around her daughter.

'I will,' Vincent said. 'Just be ready when I get back.'

Ethan came up behind Salty and held out one of the flashlights he'd found. Salty shoved his arm away. 'What the hell would I want with that, Twilight?'

'To see where you're going?'

'I see exactly where we're goin'.'

'You two, get over here and start making yourselves useful,' Raine said.

Chapter 8

The man in the passenger seat of the Hummer woke to the smell of blood; he could taste it in his mouth. He lifted his head from the dash and sat back. The cubes of shattered glass jingled as they fell from him and into the footwell.

He felt the blood from his wounds sticking his clothes to his skin. There was no pain at first – not until he tried to move, at least. When he found the strength to twist his neck, he saw what was left of his associate. He'd taken enough bullets to kill five men. Tugging on the door handle and leaning forward, he managed to tumble from the wreck onto the soft ground. It was only as he stood and straightened himself that the pain set in, causing him to curl into a ball again. He'd taken one shot to the centre of his left shoulder; another had ricocheted through the hood of the vehicle and entered the top of his thigh. However, the real wound, the one that convinced him he was not long for this world, was the hit to his gut.

His injuries made it excruciating to move, and he could see from the deep red trail collecting in the wet grass that he was bleeding out fast.

He turned to the east, towards the glow of the torch beam bouncing around near the entrance to the visitor centre. He wasn't confident of making it over there before he got too weak, and he had no idea whether his gun had fallen on the ground somewhere in the dark or if he'd left it inside the Hummer. He shuffled around gingerly and looked west towards the hole they had blown in the electric fence. Even through the oil and gore, an unmistakable smile of satisfaction could be seen on his face. Suddenly, he found the will to walk a little further.

Chapter 9

Raine collected two packs full of canned food and passed one to Kristin. She then grabbed another one containing frozen meat and handed it to Salty. 'Are there any ammunition supplies on the facility?' she said.

'There's nothing in here except for tranquilisers. Farrington loved security, but he was no fan of firearms.'

'Shit.' Raine took up one more bag for herself and left the storeroom.

'We're gonna need a lot more than a few pop-guns to find our way on the road,' Salty said.

'Yeah, I get it – you think we should stay. But you'll just have to suck it up,' Raine said.

Salty got out of her way so she could start down the stairs. 'What made your balls just drop, Miller? Could have done with your help long before now.'

Raine stopped and half-turned. 'There's an explanation, but it's not something I feel like sharing with you.'

At that moment, Vincent returned, pushing the entrance doors shut behind him. Kristin ran to the middle of the staircase to meet him, hand in hand with Emily. 'How were they?'

'The pickup has three-quarters of a tank left. Sedan has about half, if that. I couldn't even get the Ford to start.'

'It'll have to do. Let's go,' Raine said.

The whole group headed for the door, following Raine's lead.

'What about the medical supplies?' Kristin said.

'There's no time,' Raine replied. She stopped in her tracks, skidding on the polished floor and causing everyone else to pile into the back of her.

The wounded man appeared at the entrance and fell against the glass, smearing his blood over it.

Raine dropped the bags of food and flipped the assault rifle by its shoulder strap and took aim.

'No, Miller.' Ethan grabbed the weapon by its hand guard and forced her to point it away from the door. 'Just wait a second.'

She had no clue why he wanted her to, but she knew by now to trust him when he gave a warning. The dying intruder smiled as more blood poured from the bullet holes in his body. He extended his middle finger to flick them the bird. Then, out of the darkness behind him, they began to appear: the rotten deceased, putrid and chattering, coming to the end of their hunt. More and more of them surrounded the entrance to the visitor centre, all hungry for this slab of meat who had offered himself as bait. His final 'Fuck you' to his killers. As soon as they got within reaching distance, they were on him, tearing and biting at his already dripping body. The man's satisfaction was quickly replaced by terror. The blood from the gunshots was nothing compared to this massacre of the flesh. His eyes popped, his intestines spilled; the only thing that made him recognisable as what he used to be were his screams. He was literally turned inside-out by the gaggle of hands, and pieces of him were passed around to fill as many mouths as possible.

Vincent and Kristin were so transfixed by the horror, they didn't think to shield Emily from it. She saw it all, every last gruesome drop of dismemberment.

'Good God.' Ethan turned away and retched. 'Miller, the door,' he croaked.

Raine reached out to Vincent. 'The keys.'

Salty snatched them from his hand. He found the correct one as he made his way to the entrance, jamming it into the lock and twisting it. He backed up to the rest of the group and watched the multitude of hands claw at the panes of glass. Their groans sounded like a celebration – celebrating the pleasure of their latest feed and the promise of more to come.

The dead knew they were in there. All they had to do was to break through the thin barrier that separated them. More and more heard the call and joined the feeding frenzy. The glass started to buckle under their collective force.

EPISODE SEVEN

Bugs in a Jar

Chapter 1

The tortured faces peered into the visitor centre, withered flesh peeling away when it was pulled from the glass. The front entrance was smeared with the insides of the man who had led the herd there.

Raine grimaced at the deathly figures awaiting them outside, picked up her bags, and marched in the opposite direction. 'Take it there's a back door to this place?'

'Course. Fire exit,' Salty said.

The group followed her through the lounge to the exit under the staircase. Raine yanked the push-bar and flung the door open. The fenced-off parking lot was less than fifty feet away. As she stepped onto the concrete, she heard noises coming from the left of her – something was dragging on the ground. Popping her head around the open door, she saw twenty or more creatures shuffling from the side of the building, and then just as many coming from the other direction.

They spotted her, reaching out with their skeletal fingers and groaning in collective acknowledgement. The dead shifted their tired bones to quicken their pace. Raine stepped back and shoved the others inside. 'Go, go.' She slammed the fire door shut just as the creatures reached it. 'Shit!'

'What now?' Ethan said.

'I shut it,' Vincent said. 'After I checked the cars, I shut the gate. They can't get into the lot.'

'Great, but how do we get to it?' Ethan said.

Raine took some deep breaths, gently tapping the back of her head against the door. Without a word, she marched into the lounge again to face the hungry dead pounding on the glass at the front of the building. She crouched behind one of the sofas, urging everyone else to do the same. 'Best to stay out of sight. We don't wanna rile them up any more than we have to.'

'That glass is reinforced, but if they keep piling pressure on it, it's gonna break sooner or later,' Salty said.

'So it's not safe here. Is there any way onto the roof?' Ethan said.

'There's a skylight. We go up there and there's no coming back,' Salty said.

'Will you two just shut up and let me think for a minute?' Raine snapped. She gazed over to the bar, and then into the foyer. Seemingly unperturbed by their enemy, she moved from her hiding place, walked to the foot of the staircase and pointed to the polished floor. 'Here.'

'Here what?' Salty said.

'We'll fortify this area. When they come through the entrance, we can fight our way out.'

'Excuse me?' Vincent said. 'I don't know whether you've noticed, but we're not soldiers. We have a little girl, for Christ's sake.'

'And I'm giving her a shot. You wanna take your family and make a run for it out back, be my guest.'

Her words struck a chord; he pulled Emily close to him.

'We don't have much ammunition,' Salty said. 'Few rounds each for the handguns, a couple of mags for your rifle, maybe twelve shells for this, if we're lucky.' He held out the shotgun.

'We have a cocktail bar full of alcohol,' Raine said, raising her eyebrows.

'I don't fancy being inside this place with fire dancing around,' Salty said.

'If we're not out of here pretty fast, we won't be leaving anyway.'

Ethan ran his shaking hands through his hair and locked eyes with Raine. 'So how do we do this?'

'We grab whatever we can find to put obstacles between them and us so we can slow them up.'

'OK. Like she says, we don't have much choice.' Kristin got up and stood next to Raine. 'Let's get to work.'

The three men looked at one another, realising that regardless of whether or not they liked Raine's plan, it was the best and only option they had.

'Ethan, with me,' Raine said. 'Come help me search for things we can use for our special cocktails.'

He did as she asked without any questions and followed her up to the second floor.

Meanwhile, Salty, Kristin and Vincent were forced to work mainly in the dark, using their flashlights by cupping their hands over the beams to lessen the glare. The only other source of light came from the emergency lamp just outside the front entrance. First, they moved the furniture from the lounge area, all save the sofa Emily was sitting on, and turned each piece upside down, positioning it in a staggered formation around the foyer. Next they took down the interactive panels in the Discovery Station and broke them up, propping them horizontally to act as reflective screens.

The rest of the materials were pillaged from the souvenir kiosk. The metal-framed carousels and wooden shelves were emptied of their merchandise and added to the makeshift barricade. As Raine had instructed, they left a small alcove clear near the foot of the staircase where the group could operate from.

Tired and sweaty, the three of them stood back to admire their peculiar assault course. It looked like something children would construct for a game – if any children could have had the will and physical strength to make it happen. But this was no game. They only needed to gaze beyond the barricades to the mountain of rotten bodies pressed against the glass to be reminded of that. A few of the dead had wandered off, but the rest were still clamouring to gain entry, excited by the increased activity inside.

⚔

Raine dropped the box of cotton napkins she'd found in the upstairs restaurant onto the bar next to Ethan. He looked inside it, noticing the two containers of rubbing alcohol.

'It's a shame we don't have enough of this to use for the whole thing, but under current circumstances, we're just gonna have to use it to douse the wicks. It will make them more effective as fuses.'

'OK,' Ethan said, not sounding entirely focused on what she was saying.

'When it comes to the heart of the thing, we'll have to make do with plain old liquor.' Raine took a bottle of gin from one of the mirrored shelves and set it on the bar. 'Look for the bottles with the highest alcohol content. Gin, rum, whisky, vodka – it doesn't matter which.' She grabbed one of the napkins from the box and tore it down the middle, wrapping it around the neck of the gin bottle. 'Tie it off like this – just until you're ready to light them. When you are, open out the wick, soak it in the rubbing alcohol, and push it inside the bottle. Got it?'

'Errm, yeah. I've got it.' Ethan collected some vodka from one of the shelves and started to wind the other half of the torn napkin around it. 'Don't take this the wrong way, Miller, but you scare the shit out of me.'

'Keep going until you run out of spirits,' Raine replied.

'That's it. That's everything,' Kristin said as she joined them at the bar. 'We could check the second floor if you don't think it's enough.'

Raine surveyed the barricades in the foyer again. 'It's enough for what we need. Aside from the catering carts, there's nothing worth using up there.'

'Right then.'

'Good.' Raine turned away from her to face the shelves of liquor.

'We're not the enemy, y'know,' Kristin said.

Raine nodded. 'It's not you.'

'Then what?'

'You just focus on the demons out there; let me worry about mine.'

Kristin managed a half-smile. 'However much you try and pretend you're alone, you can't ignore the fact that you aren't.' She walked away, leaving Raine to her thoughts.

'I made another one!' Ethan beamed with satisfaction at his freshly made Molotov cocktail.

'That's good,' Raine said. 'Let's start on the rest.'

When they'd finished each bottle, they lined them all up on the edge of the bar and joined the others.

⚔

Raine sat on the fifth step of the staircase, so she took an overview of the foyer and the bizarre-looking obstacle course they had created, each piece of upended furniture and bookshelf staggered around their little shoehorn.

The creatures were still present in force at the entrance. No matter how much their minds had dulled since their demise and reanimation, they were smart enough to remember why they pounded against the glass. Raine had been listening to their desperate moans in the background for such a long time it had got easier to block it out. Not completely, but just enough to make it bearable. She gazed down to their station – all of their bags were now stored at the foot of the stairs.

Kristin rested with her back against a chair that had been turned upside down. She held the Beretta in her lap and stared at its steel surface. Ethan used the bar to prop himself up, sipping from a square tumbler with a measure of gin in it. Vincent knelt by the one sofa which they had left as it was and faced the empty aquarium. He gently stroked her hair, whispering in her ear. The girl turned over. She blinked, her mouth a tight line, then she shut her eyes again as hard as she could. However effectively Raine had managed to block out the night calls of the dead, it was obvious that Emily had not been as fortunate. Salty wasn't in sight so Raine twisted awkwardly to peer through the gaps between the steps. He lingered at the back of the first floor, his ear pressed to the door of the fire exit.

She almost wanted the glass to break now if it had to. The longer they waited like this, the more strung out everyone would be when they finally had to fight. She imagined herself walking to the front entrance and smashing the butt of her rifle into one of the panes to help them along.

Salty's footsteps echoed beneath her as he made his way into the lounge. She could tell by the look on his face that the back exit was still occupied by hungry mouths. When he noticed Ethan drinking at the bar, he joined him.

'Got any more of that?' he said.

Ethan smiled and reached for another glass. 'I saved one bottle. We ran out of wicks anyway.' He poured a generous double helping of gin into the glass and slid it over to Salty.

The wiry man gratefully took a gulp of the rich liquor. He reached into his pocket and produced a Zippo lighter from it. 'Here,' he said. 'It's more reliable for the fuses than that plastic one-dollar piece of shit you got.'

As he held it out, Ethan noticed the starred 'X' of the Confederate flag embossed on its face. 'A light and no smokes? That's why you've been such a pain in the ass.'

'Nah, I've never been one for the old cancer sticks – more of a cigar man. Belonged to my ex-wife.'

'Oh.' Ethan's smile faded and he sensed the pain behind Salty's craggy expression.

Salty broke eye contact with him and looked into the foyer instead. 'How's that ankle doin', Mrs. Graham?' he said.

'Better, I guess. The pain comes and goes,' Kristin said.

Salty glanced over to Vincent and Emily on the sofa. He scratched his head through his bandage, careful not to press too hard into the bruise. 'Can't really blame the kid for being wired. I think your husband's fightin' a losin' battle there.'

'He'll get her off,' Kristin said. 'When Emily was four years old, she suffered from night terrors. She'd wake in the middle of the night soaked through with sweat and she'd wander around afterwards, talking gibberish until we managed to convince her that she wasn't in the dream anymore.

'Sometimes, she'd scream the house down. It made her scared to fall asleep, anxious in the daytime, unable to concentrate or eat properly. We didn't know what to do with her.

'Of course, we tried everything. Drugs, child psychotherapy. None of it was particularly effective. As soon as she'd come to the end of a course of treatment, the terrors would start up again a week or so later.

'Vince always read to her at bedtime – fairytales mostly. In her nightmares she was terrorised by an evil witch. She'd stalk her – steal her away in an old sack over and over. She remembered every detail. Vince decided to incorporate the witch into a story of his own. He wrote the general outline and memorised it, building the tale each time he told it to her. He told her how the witch was ultimately defeated by the love the girl in the story had for her family.

'After a few weeks of telling that story, the nightmares seemed to lose their grip on her. The bags disappeared from under her eyes, she asked for the night-light to be switched off. A different little girl altogether. So don't worry – he'll get her to sleep.'

'It sure sounds like your husband could tell a good one, ma'am. I wish I could have read his novels,' Salty said.

'Yeah. Me too,' Kristin replied.

'It might not be a bad idea for us too,' Raine said. She'd been listening from her vantage point on the stairs the whole time. 'To get some sleep, I mean. We'll get enough warning if those doors give way. I'll take first watch. You guys do what you can. Five minutes is better than nothing.'

Vincent crept around the foot of the staircase, taking a quick look back at the sofa where Emily lay. 'She's finally down,' he whispered.

Kristin smiled and glanced over to Salty at the bar.

'Hey, Vincent, fancy telling me a bedtime story?' Ethan said.

'I think you should tell us one,' Raine said, directing her attention to Ethan. 'We'd all like to know a little more about you.'

All of a sudden, Ethan didn't look so relaxed. He stopped leaning on the bar and straightened up. 'Oh, my day-to-day was pretty dull, but I guess telling you about it would have the desired effect of putting everyone to sleep.'

'Not your day-to-day. Why don't you tell us how it is you knew about what Spears was planning with the supplies back at the camp?' Raine said.

'Yes, I'd like to know that too.' Vincent added his voice to the question, but he really wanted to know how he'd discovered that his daughter was in the care of a would-be child molester.

Ethan looked at their expectant faces. He shrugged and knocked back the last of his gin. 'I suppose in light of current events, it won't hurt to have you see me as an even bigger freak than you do already... I'm what some might call psychometric.'

'What the Sam Hill is that?' Salty said.

'I can obtain information, either in a vision or sensation, by touching an object.'

'Wait. You're trying to tell us that you can see the future by touching shit?' Raine said with a smirk.

'I never claimed to have precognition. I can only see or feel things that have already happened, but sometimes, from that, I can figure out what's going to happen next.'

'And how long have you been able to do this?' Vincent said.

'Since I can remember.'

Salty's eyes widened as the penny finally dropped in his mind. 'Shit, kid. I knew I recognised you from some place. You're that TV guy, aren't you?'

'I've been on TV, yes. A lot more than I ever wanted to be.'

'Yeah. He helped the police crack big cases. That's why he was in the States when it happened, right? I saw him on The Queen Latifah Show.'

'You watched Queen Latifah?' Raine said.

'Yeah, so what?' Salty said. 'This is the guy who solved the Kenny Thompson case.'

'The missing boy? I remember it,' Vincent said.

'Not so missing anymore. The story broke just before God called happy hour. Kenny Thompson went missing from his family home one afternoon. Chicago P.D. had been lookin' for him for over two weeks and found diddly-squat, not one trace of the poor little bastard. Then this guy shows up.' Salty nodded towards Ethan.

Ethan avoided their stares and poured himself an even bigger measure of gin.

'Go easy on that,' Raine said.

'It's my last one. I promise,' Ethan replied.

'Now that you mention it, I did read something about them getting help from a psychic in the paper. That was you?' Vincent said.

'It was him alright,' Salty said. 'He'd come recommended. Made a name for himself as a consultant for the police in Great Britain.'

'I didn't really help all that much. I just pointed them in the right direction,' Ethan said.

'My ass,' Salty said, giving him a sideways glance. 'Detectives gave him Kenny's jacket, the one he supposedly was wearin' before he got snatched, but he got nothin' from it. Then they ask him to visit the Thompsons' home, see if he can pick up any impressions there. And he does – from Mr. Thompson.

'Within a couple of days, he'd led them to a lock-up, where they found the Thompson's car that they claimed had been stolen by their kid's abductor. They found traces of Kenny's blood and a couple of strands of his father's hair in the trunk.

'After they dropped that revelation on their prime suspects, Mrs. Thompson broke. Turns out, daddy liked to drink, and when he did he'd get a little handy with his fists.'

Ethan took another large gulp of gin.

'The evening before they'd reported the abduction, Thompson came home shit-faced from a bar. Him and his wife had a fight and he was layin' into her. Kenny got outta bed and decided to get in his father's way. He caught a blow and hit his head on the dresser. Rather than go to the cops, that son of a bitch made her promise to keep it a secret, to help him dump the body in Lake Michigan, and stick to his bullshit about it having been a kiddie-snatcher. They tried their luck, but they didn't bank on The Sixth Sense here. Yes sir, y'all lookin' at a bona fide celebrity.'

'Quite a story,' Raine said.

Salty shook his head, bewildered that she didn't seem impressed. 'It ain't no story. This guy's the real deal.'

'He's your great white hope now? You've been spending most of your time telling us how useless he is.'

'Boy's obviously a fairy. No offence,' Salty said.

'Oh, none taken. Not an observation I'd disagree with,' Ethan said.

'But he's got somethin' we can use to our advantage.'

'I never pegged you as someone who believed in all that supernatural crap,' Raine said.

Salty chuckled. 'We live in a world where a virus brings folks back from the dead, and you think ESP still sounds kooky?'

'Whatever it is you do, I don't care. It's the only reason my daughter is sleeping soundly on that couch,' Vincent said.

'I'll second that,' Kristin said.

'Let's face it, none of us would be here if it wasn't for him,' Vincent said.

Ethan shrugged and finished what was left at the bottom of his glass. 'It's also the reason I'm spending the apocalypse with you fine folks. I was in my hotel room ordering room service, ready to fly back to the UK the next morning, when they evacuated us from the city and brought me to Indiana and that awful camp.'

'Do you know what happens next?' Vincent said.

'I told you. I can't see the future. I can only say that I have faith in Miller.' Ethan raised his glass and a wry smile to the woman on the staircase.

'Just focus on those bottles lined up over there and leave that one alone,' Raine said.

'Ah, let the kid drink. It'll make him less of a pussy when they come pourin' in here,' Salty said, taking a sip from his own glass.

'Ten minutes of being a fairly decent human being and now, within the blink of an eye, back to an asshole,' Ethan said, mildly amused by his drinking partner.

'Hey,' Raine said, raising her voice a little and looking at Salty. 'You got your head on for this? I'm gonna need you on point.'

Salty met her stare. 'One thing you can always count on with me, I won't hesitate. If things go south, then I know what to do too.' He turned back to Ethan, a mischievous glint in his eye. 'Want me to do you first, Twilight?'

Ethan's grin broadened. It completely changed the way he looked. To the others, it was like another person had suddenly replaced the young man they'd been travelling with. He was inebriated for sure, but still had his faculties about him. 'You see, we hear so many horror stories about rednecks back in England – fucking their siblings, cutting hitchhikers up into little pieces – but this one has a genuine heart of gold.'

Vincent laughed until his legs gave way. He slid down next to Kristin and put his arm around her. She welcomed the contact, leaning forward to rest her head against his shoulder.

'You on the next watch?' she said.

'In an hour – if the glass holds out that long,' he said.

The warmth from his body made it harder for her to stay awake. On the cusp of sleep, her voice thinned out as she spoke. 'Don't forget to let the dog out before you lock up.'

'Yeah... sure.'

Chapter 2

Emily heard the gentle bubble from the aquarium before she opened her eyes. She felt something cold around the edges of her face. She sat up on the sofa and realised her hair was damp. Her clothes were too – they were soaked through with sweat.

Her bunny rabbit toy lay on its side across her lap, its tattered left ear sticking up toward her. Its ear was in such bad shape because their dog, Tugger, used to chew on it when she wasn't looking – only the left one though. Her dad told her he was a Rhodesian ridgeback. No matter how many times he said it, she could never pronounce the breed correctly, but she didn't really care – Tugger was Tugger.

She tried to conjure his face from memory – his black jowls and his wet, twitchy nose, but she couldn't. The image just would not materialise in the darkness. Frustrated, she hopped down from the sofa and scampered out of the lounge.

Raine lay against the rail on the stairs, her eyes closed. Salty and Ethan were lying on the bar, also asleep. Emily stood on tip toes to get a better view of the two rows of bottles next to the men, complete with torn pieces of fabric poking from their necks.

Her parents were sitting opposite snoozing in each other's arms. She was happy enough just to watch them breathing, until she noticed the guns in their hands.

When she stole herself away and peered around the overturned chairs, she saw how much the foyer had changed since their arrival. The Discovery

Station was gone. The microscopes had disappeared, the souvenir kiosk gutted of its memorabilia. Even the print on the wall behind the reception desk had been taken down and added to the pile of ruins.

She weaved in between the barricades, the sound of her footsteps reverberating through the silence. The dead were not moaning anymore. When she reached the front entrance, she couldn't see their faces – only their hands. They were slapping lazily on the glass, as if they'd lost their will to feed. She leaned in, holding her favourite bunny toy upside down by one of its legs.

The darkness masking the dead seemed to possess a kind of substance – black swirling sand, engulfing almost everything it came into contact with. One hand pressed against the glass and stayed there, its fingers spread out evenly, its sullied palm white, bloodless. Emily felt compelled to reach out to it, placing her hand on the pane too. She matched the spread of its fingers so hers overlaid it.

The rest of the hands continued to claw at the glass, but their movements were getting slower. Time began to freeze, prolonging Emily's connection with the creature. She half-closed her hand, only her fingertips and the base of her palm still making contact with it. The hand on the other side mimicked her gesture. Then it withdrew into the black sandstorm, as did the rest.

Emily shuffled right up to the entrance so her nose was touching, desperate to catch a glimpse of something out there. The hands did return, but this time they sprang violently out of the gloom, punching holes in the glass and grabbing at her clothing. She screamed and tried to wriggle away, pushing back on the doorframe. Before she could straighten her arms and lock her elbows, a hand burst through and grasped her hair from the front. Her resistance hopeless, she was dragged through the centre of the rupture. The shattered shards sliced her skin open, peeling it from the muscle as she entered the black to be devoured.

♆

Emily lurched forward, teetering on the edge of the sofa. The first thing she saw when she opened her eyes was her father standing over her. 'The monsters!' She struggled against Vincent, unable to differentiate between his grasp and the dead's.

'Emily, listen to me. It was just a nightmare. Just a dream.' Vincent found it difficult to get hold of her properly because her skin was slick with sweat.

'But the monsters,' she repeated, wild-eyed and panting.

'You're not there anymore. You're back here with us.'

Her father's words soothed her, and his embrace suddenly didn't feel so alien. She stopped flailing and her breathing slowed down. But when she looked at him again, hoping for further reassurance, there was none to be found. She had been dreaming, but something was still wrong.

'Emily, the monsters. They are coming. They're breaking through,' he said. 'I need you to come with me now.' He lifted her up and headed back to the others.

Salty, Kristin and Raine were already aiming their guns behind the last line of cover. The glass on one side of the entrance had a long crack down its centre. The horde outside were whipping themselves into a frenzy, realising it was about to give way.

Vincent planted Emily on the staircase and stared into her eyes. 'Stay here – whatever happens. Daddy won't allow any of them to get up here.'

Emily hugged her bunny toy, still spaced out by her dream. She just nodded and Vincent joined Kristin at the back end of the barricade.

'She OK?' Kristin said as he drew his revolver.

'As long as she does as I told her and stays put,' he said.

One half of the broken pane shattered. The other half shortly followed, and the dead started to stumble through.

'Remember, don't open fire until they reach the last line of display panels,' Raine said, directing her instructions to the Grahams. 'I don't care if you have to press the barrel to their heads, as long as you take them down.'

Vincent squinted into the darkness. The silhouetted bodies of the dead were swaying as they approached the first barricade, constructed from the display carousels. 'I can't see a goddamn thing,' he said.

'Things are gonna get brighter real soon. Isn't that right, Ethan?' Raine called.

'Yeah, I think so.' Ethan fumbled with the bottles, couriering them from the bar to their vantage point.

'Don't think – just do.'

One of the creatures managed to get its shirt snagged on a metal prong and started trying to tug itself free, eventually ending up on its backside. At least thirty more were already inside, swarming through the first row of the barricade. Another toppled face forward over a bookshelf. Its neck snapped as it landed. When it rose, its head was now set against its left shoulder and its dislocated jaw hung down to its chest.

Ethan flicked the top open on the Zippo lighter and rolled his thumb across the flint wheel. He brought the fresh flame to the wick, tossing the bottle into the foyer. It sailed over the furniture and display stands with a fluttered whisper, smashing against the second row of bookshelves. The fire spilled out of the broken glass, and snaked through the alcohol now coating the shelf and the side of the wall.

The hungry flames were reflected in the pits of Raine's eyes. She eased down on the assault rifle's trigger and the weapon roared with a controlled burst. One of the dead took a hit in the shoulder and spun around like a top; a second caught a shot to the head and stayed down. She let loose with three more volleys and two more creatures fell.

Ethan launched another bottle. This time it landed perfectly by the entrance to the movie theatre, casting a sheet of flame and setting three of them alight.

The creatures had already started to congregate down the centre of the foyer, getting in each other's way and making them an easier target. Raine fired off two further controlled bursts into the crowd, and several of them dropped.

'Ethan.' She pointed to the area she'd just targeted as Ethan lit his next cocktail. In mid-throw, Salty let loose with the first blast of his shotgun, causing the young man to toss the bottle too high. It struck the ceiling close by and ignited a section of the tiles above.

'Shit,' Ethan said.

'Forget it.' Raine turned her head from the butt of her rifle to look at him. 'Next one.'

The burning began to take, clinging to the flammable parts of the barricades. Plumes of thick smoke, full of chemicals, drifted towards their outpost.

Raine noticed that some of the dead near the movie theatre had survived the flames and were halfway through the foyer. A few more were stumbling along on the opposite side.

'Kristin, Vincent. Either side. Deal with them.' She pointed to the creatures currently flanking them and the couple responded.

Vincent ducked under Salty's shotgun and took up a position on the right, and Kristin supported Ethan on the left side. Vincent got off his first shot once the dead moved from behind a display screen. He missed his intended target by a good two feet and the bullet embedded itself into the wall next to the theatre entrance. He opened out his stance and steadied himself, exhaling slowly before squeezing the trigger. The second shot struck the creature in its chest, and it staggered back from the impact, knocking over a corpse that was walking behind it.

Kristin fared much better than her husband, ending the march of two creatures with just four rounds. Ethan tossed yet another cocktail over her head. The bottle scored a direct hit, smashing over a creature dressed in army fatigues. Its body was consumed and it fell to its knees.

Pausing to release the spent magazine of her rifle and jam in the next one, Raine heard another pane of glass give way at the front of the building. This allowed twice as many dead to flood in. The flickering flames from the cocktails caught the grotesque forms of their approaching enemy within its stroboscope, darkness alternating with the grim reality of their predicament.

'There's too many of them,' Kristin said.

Raine noticed the panic in her eyes and moved over to grab hold of her shirt. 'Just keep it together and hold the line. You won't hit a thing unless you breathe.' She shoved her back to her station and Kristin did as she was told, taking aim at the closest marauder.

Meanwhile, Salty was blasting away at an oncoming group. He saw that one of the bookshelves nearby was starting to collapse from the damage caused by the flames. A group of three shamblers on Vincent's side were just about to pass it. Salty climbed up over the stacked tables and chairs separating them from the carnage.

Before he could make it to the bookcase, he came face to face with a female creature, freshly turned, that must have weighed at least 280 pounds. Its greasy strands of black hair hung down over its face, allowing it to chew on the split ends. Salty pumped the twelve gauge and pulled the trigger. The blast hit the monster flush in the face. Its features disintegrated and the bullet propelled its brains from the back of its head.

He then rushed over to kick the bookshelf. It toppled after two attempts and crushed the dead in range of it. The embers from the burning wood dispersed into the air and covered him. He screamed as they singed his face and he turned away from the cloud of smoke that followed. Coughing and spluttering, he tried to make his way back to the outpost. An emaciated hand reached out from the black smog. It was about to close its fingers around his neck when a shot rang out and a round entered the creature's forehead.

Salty spun around to see its body fall. Vincent leaned over the barricade less than ten feet away, his pistol raised. 'You're welcome,' Vincent said.

'Jake! Get your ass back here,' Raine shouted, scowling in his direction.

Vincent helped him over the barricades and he ran to Raine.

'Help me concentrate the fire here. See if we can thin out the numbers through the centre,' she said.

They both let rip with their weapons, blasting holes in the near-skeletal forms in their way, slicing through them. The bodies, some still burning, piled up, forming a new obstacle for the remaining dead to traverse. Some of them stumbled and fell on the uneven ground.

Two more creatures made it past the burning entrance to the movie theatre. Vincent held his nerve and waited until they were almost upon him before pulling the trigger. The first one caught a bullet to the face, but when he lined up the second, the trigger clicked and nothing happened. He tried again – same result. The six chambers of his gun were empty. The creature lunged at him and grabbed the shoulders of his shirt. Vincent pulled back to try to free himself, and the animated corpse toppled over the furniture, landing on top of him.

Salty and Raine weren't that far away, but they were too busy opening up on the approaching horde to notice his plight. He was nose to nose with it, desperately trying to hold it at bay. The sides of its head had been stripped down to the skull after its squeeze through the broken glass of the front entrance. Shredded pieces of flesh hung from it like old shoe leather. Its receding lips exposed its teeth and they snapped at him, half an inch from his face.

Emily watched in horror from the stairs as the monster attacked her father.

Ethan launched another cocktail through the air and watched it explode into the crowd. He paused to mop the sweat from his brow and heard Emily's screams over the gunfire. He turned to see her and realised what was causing her such distress. He knew he couldn't abandon his post, so he put his hand on Salty's hatchet.

'Vincent!'

Vincent managed to turn his head towards the shout and Ethan slid the hatchet across the floor to him. He put enough into it so that the tool came to rest just within reach of Vincent, who grabbed the handle. From his position on the floor, he was too restricted to swing properly and the blade bounced off the creature's skull. He gritted his teeth and swung again, opening the gunshot graze on his arm. This time it made a more powerful connection, but it still wasn't sufficient enough to break through the bone.

The strength in Vincent's other arm, which was what was keeping the creature from sinking its teeth into his cheek, began to wane.

'Argh, no!' In desperation, he shoved the head of the hatchet into the rotter's mouth. It bit down on the metal as if it was expecting to gain some sustenance from it. When it didn't, it hankered for Vincent's flesh with renewed vigour, tearing a hole in the breast pocket of his shirt.

Vincent's cries were cut short by a gun blast at close range. Brain matter splashed over his face and the creature lost its grip, dropping like a dead weight onto his chest. The ringing in his ears from the shot intensified, as someone dragged the corpse away and helped him back onto his feet. He was greeted by the relieved face of his wife.

'Are you OK? Were you bitten?'

'No, no. I'm OK,' he said.

There was no time to say anything more. Kristin left him to return to her post, where the creatures were piling up.

The dreaded sound of a click from her rifle told Raine that her penultimate clip had run dry. As she jammed in her last, she took in another lungful of the fumes from all the small fires around the foyer. To her right, Salty loaded the three remaining shells into his shotgun. Ahead of them, they'd thinned out the crowds of marauders and several more were wandering away, burning. Nevertheless, there were still too many for them to make a run for the entrance. Soon the fires would be enough on their own to prevent them from doing so.

'Fall back,' Raine shouted. She retreated to the staircase and sprayed the group of twenty or so creatures that were about to reach the alcove.

The others followed her. Vincent scooped Emily up in his arms. Ethan went up next, taking a cocktail with him. Salty and Kristin were the last to leave their posts, Salty only removing himself once he'd fired his final two shells. They made sure to collect the backpacks filled with supplies.

The front line of the horde broke through the alcove and bottle-necked to the foot of the stairs.

Raine stepped down and kicked the first one that tried to climb up after them. 'Throw it,' she said to Ethan.

He tossed it underarm to the bottom. The flames rose to block the staircase and cover their escape. The foyer had been laid to waste, overrun and infested with the smell of charred, necrotic flesh.

They headed to the top of the stairs and ran along the second floor corridor. Raine pushed her way to the front again and snatched on the chain above them to bring down the ladders that led to the skylight in the ceiling. 'You first,' she urged Vincent.

'You'll have to help me, sweetheart. Can you do that?' Vincent said, placing Emily on the first rung of the ladder. She nodded, still holding onto her bunny rabbit for dear life. He shadowed her on the way up by using the frame on either side. He reached the top, and one firm shove caused the skylight to open with a pop.

Kristin went next. While she was trying to climb through, she felt resistance on the straps of her backpack; part of it had become snagged on the frame of the skylight.

'Get out of it. I'll grab it on my way,' Salty said.

Kristin pulled her arms free of the pack and let Salty unhook it after he'd followed her.

Raine made sure that everyone else went first. She stood at the foot of the ladder. She couldn't see through the rising smoke, but she sure as hell could hear the moans getting louder. Some of the dead had already reached the top of the stairs.

The night had turned cold, and it felt even colder from their elevated position on the roof. Raine closed the skylight and silenced the moans and the crackle of flames from below. The others had set themselves and their packs down, and were now trying to clear their lungs of the fumes they'd inhaled.

The mineral-felt crunched beneath her boots as Raine wandered to the front of the roof. They had left their torches downstairs, but the emergency floods outside kept the complex lit. She hoped to see that the ground around the building was relatively clear, having assumed most of the dead would now be inside the foyer of the visitor centre. But what greeted her when she peered over the edge was exactly the opposite. The horde had managed to fill the visitor centre to bursting and there were still at least six rows outside, standing shoulder to shoulder. She narrowed her eyes at the sight of them and went to take a look at the other side of the building. They were completely surrounded. Only the fenced-off parking lot remained free of the rotten infestation.

The multitude of moans and shuffling feet soon brought the others over to the edge of the roof, where Raine was standing.

Kristin gasped and turned away, ushering Emily back to the middle next to the skylight.

'Where did they all come from?' Ethan said.

'Maybe they were close, hidden by the forest, and the gunfire attracted them,' Raine said.

'Who gives a shit? The only thing that matters is they're here, and we're fucked,' Salty said.

'Just shut up,' Raine replied.

Salty grimaced at her, a faded trace of blood soaked through his head bandage. 'How many rounds you got left in that thing?' He gestured to her rifle and then held up his shotgun. 'Wanna know how many I got? It's as dry as the taco on one of those creatures down there.'

'I don't want to hear this shit now. We need to think of a way of getting down to the parking lot, and fast. If they tear down the fence and get amongst those cars, there's no way we're driving outta here. We have to move,' Raine said.

Vincent pushed their raised voices to the back of his mind; he'd seen something on the right hand side of the roof. Just behind the ventilation unit, he had noticed the ends of a ladder poking out. He went over to inspect it more closely, and found that it was doubled up on a sliding frame, so the ladder could extend to twice its current length. A toolbox sat next to it. Someone must have been doing some maintenance just before the outbreak started, and then left in a hurry. Vincent then traced the length of a cable running from the vent unit and down the east wall.

'Well, your plan to hold them off worked out real nice, didn't it? Things are gonna get real toasty now you put Twilight up to settin' fires.'

Raine squared up to Salty, flexing her muscular shoulders as a physical invitation. 'Remember out on the road when you told me to shape up? It's about time you started listening to your own advice. You've been going into a slow meltdown ever since those idiots blew up the fence. This place was good – I get it. But it's gone now. It's gone, Jake, and that's what we need to be – gone.'

Salty's eyes flickered and he took a half-step back. Her words had obviously rung true with him, but he wasn't about to back down. 'And what made you Queen Bee all of a sudden? Killin' those men give ya the taste for it again?'

Raine returned with the same stone cold stare. 'You keep on pushing, I'm gonna push back,' she said.

'I must say, this is a really constructive way to spend our time,' Ethan said.

'No one asked you, Twilight,' Salty said.

'I have an idea?' The comment interrupted their confrontation and they all turned towards Vincent. 'We may be able to get across to the parking lot without having to fight our way through.'

On this occasion, Kristin stayed with Emily to comfort her. It was Vincent's plan after all, but despite that, she wanted to; she felt that she needed to. She wrapped her little girl in her arms and pulled her jacket around her shivering body as she watched Raine and the three men rip the cable from the ties that secured it to the roof.

They made sure the wire was long enough to reach the edge before tying it off on one end of the extended ladder, making the cable taut around the base of the skylight.

Vincent also came up with the idea of knotting a section of wire to a central rung of the ladder, so that when they lowered it down over the gap to the top of the parking lot's fence, it wouldn't fall too quickly and bounce off.

Once they had it in place, Salty double-checked the cable around the skylight to make certain it wouldn't pull free when there was weight on the ladder.

Vincent gazed at the metal frame, noticing how much it sloped on the way to its destination, on account of the height differential between the roof and the fence. It was far from ideal – it was treacherous in fact, but it was the best chance they had. 'Until someone can get across and hold the other end, it could shift and slide right off the edge,' he said.

The group fell silent and took a long look at what they were about to traverse, the ravenous horde of dead trying to claw at them from the ground.

'OK then,' Ethan said. 'I'll be your canary down the mine.'

'You sure?' Raine said, realising that any colour in his already pale complexion had just washed away in the first breath after he'd spoken.

'Not really, no. I'm shit-scared of heights and my sense of balance has never been great, but aside from Emily, I'm the lightest one here – and I know you're all too polite to say it, but I'm also the most expendable.'

Raine glanced to Salty, expecting a sarcastic remark from his mouth.

'What?' he said. 'Kid's steppin' up. All power to him.'

Ethan bent to pick up one of the backpacks.

'Forget about those,' Vincent said. 'Just concentrate on getting yourself across in one piece.'

Before Ethan shuffled to the edge, Raine grabbed him by the arm and locked eyes with him. 'Try not to look down.'

Ethan blew out nervously. 'Yes. Thank you, Miller – excellent advice.'

'Just saying',' Raine replied.

The slope on the ladder was reasonably sharp, but from Ethan's vantage point, it looked close to vertical. He did his best to block out the moaning below. As he stood on the edge, it intensified, the primitive sound of the horde's renewed excitement resonating. He acted upon Raine's suggestion and didn't look down.

'You have a better chance of keeping your balance if you climb feet-first,' Vincent said.

The idea gave Ethan some brief but welcome relief. It suddenly didn't seem so bad now he was putting his back to his destination and slowly edging down to the first few rungs.

They all watched and held their breath. Kristin and Emily both stood up. They didn't join the others close to the edge; they could see fine from where they were.

Ethan couldn't figure out whether it was the cool night breeze, his anxiety or a combination of both, but he started to shake so much that the frame of the ladder rattled every time he moved. The noise seemed to rile the horde even more. One of them was so preoccupied with looking up at him that it walked straight into the wall of the visitor centre and smashed its nose in the process.

'Try to ignore them,' Vincent said.

Ethan peered down through a gap in the ladder to the waves of foul flesh and gnashing teeth. 'I see a bed of feathered pillows.' No sooner had he cracked an ironic smile than the end of the ladder resting against the pole at the top of the fence shifted to the right.

He froze, digging his nails into the metal and curling his toes around the side rails. He made the mistake of looking down again. The creatures were opening and closing their mouths like guppy fish, as if they were waiting for him to fall. A solitary bead of cold sweat ran along the outline of the vein pulsing in his forehead.

'Balance your weight,' Vincent said.

'I feel pretty balanced,' Ethan said. Once the shock had subsided, he edged his way along once more. Each step back was more tentative than the last, but eventually he made it to the other side and remained at the top of the fence, holding on with one hand and securing the end of the ladder with the other. He drew his feet in as soon as the creatures pushed against the wire mesh, clamping their bony fingers around it.

The rest of the group felt it was safe to breathe normally again. Vincent walked over to his family and held out his hand to Emily.

'No', Emily moaned, clinging tighter to her mother. 'I don't want to.'

'You have to, sweetie,' Kristin said. 'It's the only way out of here.'

'I can't do what Ethan did. I'll fall.'

Vincent knelt down beside her. 'You'll be with me. You can't fall. I won't let you.'

'No.' She began to cry and hid her face in Kristin's shirt.

Vincent turned to Raine and Salty. 'You go. I need to talk to my daughter.'

Salty proceeded to shove the empty shotgun as far down into one of the backpacks as he could, pulling the zip around its stock. 'Hold that end steady,' he shouted to Ethan.

'OK, I'm ready. Go for it,' Ethan replied.

Salty made his parallel descent and Raine watched, her sweaty hands clutching at the thighs of her pants.

'Emily, please look at me.' Vincent forced her out of Kristin's arms so she had to face him. 'We can't stay here. We don't have enough food to last us any longer than a week, and in the daytime, there's no cover from the sun.'

'But the monsters can't get me up here,' she said.

'You're right. They can't, but we can't survive here. As soon as the monsters break through the fence down there, we'll never have any chance to leave, and the building is burning.'

Emily screwed up her button nose and frowned. She glanced over to Salty, who was halfway across, having no apparent problems.

'You remember how Daddy would always give you piggy-back rides when you were little?' Kristin said. 'You put your arms around his neck and your feet around his tummy and there's no way you can fall, even if he's running. Remember when he'd run with you?'

'If I cling on really tight?' Emily said.

'Yes – If you cling on really tight.'

'And we won't be running,' Vincent said. 'We'll take it as steady as you want to.'

Salty reached the top of the fence and handed his backpack to Ethan. 'You get your ass down there and warm up the cars.'

Ethan put the bag on his back and dropped onto the asphalt of the parking lot.

Salty locked one of his wiry arms around the end rung of the ladder. 'OK, next one.'

Raine walked over to the Grahams, but stopped before she got to them. She knelt down and placed the flat of her palm on the mineral-felt.

'What is it?' Kristin said.

'We need to hurry,' Raine said.

'You go,' Vincent said.

Kristin looked at him, and then at Emily, shivering in his arms.

'It's OK. We'll be right behind you, won't we, Em?'

'Yeah,' Emily replied, though she sounded unconvinced.

Raine offered her hand to help Kristin up and passed her one of the three remaining backpacks.

Before he reached the vehicles, Ethan gazed at the creatures on the other side. They pushed against the fence and chewed at the wire mesh, trying to get at him. Their sickly eyes, discoloured by burst veins, held him there, mesmerised.

'Hey, asshole. You gonna get those cars started or what?' Salty shouted.

Ethan flinched, broke away and jogged to the opposite end of the lot, where the cars were parked.

When Kristin made it across, Salty insisted that he stayed where he was, so she jumped into the lot and watched for the rest of her family.

Raine followed shortly after, carrying the last two bags and her rifle. She clamped her feet around the outside rail and virtually slid down to the fence. 'Take these.' She gave her things to Salty. 'Check on Ethan. I'll wait for Graham.'

Salty did as she'd asked and threw their supplies into the back of the pickup. Ethan had already started the sedan and flipped on its headlights.

Vincent double-checked that the cable holding their end of the ladder was secure, then he approached the edge. Emily was on his back, her arms wrapped around his neck. 'OK, honey. I'm going to turn around and climb backwards. Just hold on tight to me and use your feet, OK?'

'OK.' Emily hid behind her father's shoulder as soon as he began to climb down. He could see the horde stumbling around below them. Their numbers had increased during the wait for their turn to cross.

Kristin bit down on the nails of her three middle fingers, seemingly oblivious to the creatures trying to squeeze their faces through the small diamond-shaped holes between the mesh.

At the halfway point, Vincent paused to take a breath, struggling to get a proper grip on the now-greasy rungs of the ladder. 'This is like being on one of those big climbing frames at the Lost Valley Adventure Park in Maine. Do you remember?'

'I'm scared,' Emily moaned.

'We're almost there.' Vincent looked between his legs and saw Kristin standing at the fence. 'Mommy's safe. She's down in the parking lot waiting for us.'

'The monsters can't get in?'

'No. They can't get past the fence. It's safe, and we're going to get in the cars and drive far away from this place. To somewhere where the monsters can't find us.'

Raine shuffled further up the pole and reached out with her free hand to grab the leg of Vincent's pants.

A ferocious rumble from within the visitor centre was immediately followed by an explosion, which blew out the glass on the ground floor. The creatures standing opposite were either knocked to the floor or thrown into the gate.

The force of the blast caused Vincent to lose his balance. He twisted his body to the right, and Emily squealed, her hands slipping from around his neck. She bounced off the ladder's outer rail and fell into the gap between the parking lot and building.

Vincent launched himself from the side and caught her by her forearm. Emily stopped screaming for a moment, until she realised her dad had caught her, then she continued, kicking her little legs as if attempting to swim back up to him.

'I've got you. Don't struggle. Don't struggle,' Vincent said.

Raine sprang into action and grabbed onto Vincent's jeans, locking her muscular arm around the frame of the ladder to prevent it from slipping any further.

The dead who were still on their feet crowded into a huddle at the spot where Emily was dangling. Teased by her flailing legs, they reached up to them, licking their lips at the prospect.

'Vincent, don't lose her!' Kristin screamed and clutched the mesh, powerless to help.

Salty and Ethan exited the vehicles so they could see what was happening.

'Give me a count and then pull her up. I got you,' Raine said, bracing herself for the strain.

'I'm gonna pull you up after three, Emily. Try to get your legs up onto the ladder.'

Emily was too terrified to listen to what he was saying and just kicked her legs even harder. Her screams intensified when one of the creatures managed to catch hold of her left shoe.

'One, two, three.' Vincent employed every ounce of energy he had left, pulling her up with one arm and dragging her back onto the frame. Once he'd regained his balance, he passed his tearful daughter over to Raine, who gently lowered her into the arms of Kristin, who was still in the parking lot.

Kristin wanted to comfort her, but she had to make sure that Raine and Vincent got down from the fence safely.

Raine noticed that one section of the mesh close to them was damaged; strands of it had already snapped away from the fence pole. 'This side is going to give. Let's move.'

Ethan and Salty got back behind the wheel and the remaining group members ran across the lot.

Vincent felt the tug on his hand from Emily and saw that she was limping. 'Is it your ankle?' he said, assuming she'd twisted something during the fall.

'My leg,' she sobbed.

He spun her around and checked her legs. On her left, a small circle of blood had soaked through the material of her sky blue jogging pants. He rolled it up to reveal a bite mark on her calf. It wasn't deep, but the creature's teeth had broken the skin.

'Daddy.' Emily rubbed the tears from her eyes, gazing toward her father for reassurance.

He lifted her into his arms and ran for the car. 'I've got you,' he whispered in her ear, trying to keep his own emotions at bay. 'I've got you. I've got you. I've got you.'

Raine steadied her aim on the roof of the pickup and then released a burst of fire, taking down the creatures in front of the gate. Then she fired again, blowing off the lock.

Both vehicles set off. The pickup went first. Salty put his foot on the gas and smashed open the gates, knocking down the dead that remained in their way.

Out in the grounds of the preserve, they were able to avoid the crowds. They doubled-back to get onto the access road, and followed it to the west side of the perimeter, exiting the facility through the hole the intruders had made. Most of the herd had already entered, so the road was relatively clear.

Their false sanctuary was now behind them. They entered the shadow of the forest, with only the headlights of their vehicles to battle against the darkness.

A Road Less Travelled

Darla slid on her side through the milkweed of the embankment. Her baggy pants rode up around her matchstick legs and collected at her knees.

When she hit the bottom and rolled onto the Christopher Columbus Highway, the blanket containing her belongings, which she had been holding in one hand, tumbled over the top of her and struck her on the head. She staggered to her feet, still smarting from the knock she'd sustained from a can of beans inside the blanket.

Before she could get herself together, O.B. came plunging down the slope, and she was forced to leap out of the way. He continued to accelerate, falling onto the road and squashing his backpack beneath him.

'You better not have spilt the last of the water,' Darla said, catching her breath.

O.B. winced as he felt the stiffness in his shoulder. 'That looked like a really bad fall, O.B. You sure you haven't hurt yourself there?' he sniped.

'Whatever. Just check the bag,' Darla said.

He stood up and dusted himself down, pulling the bag from his back and unzipping it. 'Well, it's not spilt as much as it is crushed.' He lifted the bottle, revealing it was now nothing more than a flat, dripping piece of plastic.

'This may come as a shock to you, kid, but not all of us like the taste of our own piss.'

'Did you see what happened up there?' Wide-eyed, O.B. jabbed his finger towards the steep embankment he'd just unceremoniously navigated.

'Yeah, I saw. A fat ass who doesn't know when to watch his fuckin' step.'

Darla suddenly doubled over, clutching her stomach.

'What's the matter?' O.B. said, moving close to her.

She shrugged him off and took a couple of awkward steps away from him, still bending over in pain.

'Its withdrawal, isn't it?' O.B. said.

'Don't worry about it. Just do what we came down here to do. We don't have time to screw around. Seeing as you destroyed the last of the water, we better get lucky this time.'

O.B. gazed at the rows of abandoned vehicles stretched out along the highway. An image of his mother's Station Wagon flashed through his mind – the creatures as they swarmed it, the jets of blood that had sprayed the windows.

'Hey, Oswald. Snap out of it,' Darla said. She'd partially recovered from her discomfort and was standing a little straighter. 'Let's just get it done. It'll be dark soon, and we still gotta find shelter.'

O.B.'s nightmarish recollections made him shiver. He tried to focus on the cars to put it out of his mind. He felt a twinge in his right knee, which he had locked out in the fall, and he stopped to rest against the first vehicle he came to. The surface of its bodywork was sticky. The layers of grime began to cling to his jeans. The vehicles had been sitting idle for months, so it was hard to see through their windows.

He gave the passenger side's door handle a tug and it reluctantly peeled away from its frame. To his relief, the interior was empty – no corpses, no blood. O.B. rummaged around but found nothing.

'What the hell is that shit?' Darla croaked. She looked up at the side of the white stone overpass. Someone had spray-painted a strange set of red symbols close to the centre of it.

O.B. shrugged and carried on searching. He came upon an SUV. Again, its windows were coated in dirt, but even so, he could see there were people inside. He could make out the shape of their heads. They weren't moving, so he felt safe in the knowledge they hadn't reanimated.

Cupping his hand over his mouth and nose, he snatched open the door. He was right to guard against the smell. It drifted out onto the road like a cloud of death. Even with his hand in front of his mouth, the mortal stench was enough to cause him to gag and step back. That was as much as he wanted to do with it, but he knew Darla would be on his case if he passed up such a large vehicle.

He lifted his Vandals shirt to use as a mask and approached a second time. Once he'd ducked inside, he immediately wished he'd incurred Darla's wrath instead. There were four bodies in total: a male and female in the front seat and two children of opposite sex in the back. Being sealed for so long had partially preserved them. The couple held hands across the gear lever, their rigid fingers interlocked; both were slumped forward. O.B. noticed blood stains along the woman's hairline, tainting her blonde hair, and a revolver in the man's other hand.

He then turned his attention to the back seat, holding his breath, determined to only capture a glance of the kids. Instead, he found himself lingering on them a little too long. Their heads were tilted back, making it easier to see the entry wounds in their foreheads.

O.B. poked his head out of the SUV and slammed his back against its flank. Hyperventilating, he did his best to hold down the vomit rising in his throat.

'Whatcha got in there?' Darla headed to him, her interest piqued by his distress. She looked inside the SUV and rolled her eyes. 'Just dead bodies, kid.'

'It's not the bodies. It's what they say – about how they died,' O.B. said.

Without hesitation, Darla prised the revolver from the man's necrotic grip. 'Better get used to it. The longer you live now, the more of it you're gonna see.'

O.B. managed to catch his breath and wiped the traces of the dead smell from his nose. 'I don't see the world the way you do. I get it; I do: the kind of life you've had – the things that happened to you before all this. I'm just not built that way.'

A sickening snap followed, as Darla freed the gun from the fingers of its previous owner. She moved away from the SUV with a look of satisfaction. 'Then maybe you'll taste better to them than I will,' she said.

O.B. turned his big head to the road.

Darla noticed the wounded look on his face and sighed. She reached around to the back of her pants and pulled out the Colt she'd found in Posen. 'Hey!' She handed the gun to him.

'No thank you,' O.B. said.

'Take it, kid. It ain't loaded anyway – just for show.'

O.B. lifted his head. 'You said it had as many bullets in it as when you found it.'

'That's right. It was empty from the start. Now, come on. Take it. It's for the living.'

Before O.B. had closed his fingers around the pistol's plastic grip, the sound of a voice made them jump out of their skins.

'Raising your voices on a long stretch of highway with no cover? Not what I'd call smart.'

Darla aimed their only loaded gun wildly around her, frantically scouring the sides of the road for danger, until her eyes came to rest on the speaker. A young boy, no older than fourteen, sat crossed-legged on the roof of a Camaro. The kid was black and sported the kind of hi-top fade haircut that anyone in the late '80s would have been proud of. His body was swamped by a brown duster jacket, at least two sizes too large for him. Its lapels were pinned with a myriad of buttons.

'Did someone shrink the sheriff? What hole did you crawl out of?' Darla said.

The boy smirked. 'Been here the whole time. You were just too busy with your two o'clock drama show to notice. My moms used to watch those all the time when I was little. Rotted her brain, I figure.'

'We got ourselves a smart ass, right here,' Darla said, pulling back the hammer on the revolver.

'There's no need for that. I'm smart enough not to get involved in the affairs of others. I ain't gonna give you any trouble.'

'Why don't you start by tellin' us who you are?' Darla refused to lower her weapon, despite his admission.

'I'm your eyes and ears, baby doll.' He gestured to the overpass and the symbol spray painted on the side of it.

O.B. tried to decipher what it meant. It was hard because it appeared to be various letters that overlaid each other. After a few seconds, he was able to separate them to form a word. 'Kaos?'

'That's Mr. Kaos to you, homie.' Kaos twisted his body slightly, and O.B. spied the red cap of a paint can sticking out from the inside pocket of his jacket.

'What's the point in taggin' if you're the only one?' O.B. said.

"Cause my tags ain't claimin' nothin'. All this circus belongs to them now – the others. I leave my marks as warnings, for numb nuts like your good selves.'

'Warnings of what?'

'Of not to go that way. Where you two headin' anyhow?'

'That way.' Darla pointed her gun towards the overpass.

'See, I wouldn't do that,' Kaos said.

'Why not?' O.B. asked.

'You really should keep up with what I'm tellin' ya. Might save your skin someday.'

'We're just scavenging for supplies. Then we're heading for the coast.' As soon as O.B. had finished his sentence, he received a firm kick to the shin and a scowl from Darla.

Kaos smiled again. 'Good luck to you is all I'll say on that.'

'Good. 'Cause you've said about as much as I can stand.' Darla picked up her belongings and set off on the road.

O.B. lingered for a moment, fascinated by the strange boy and his cryptic omens. 'Why don't you come with us?'

'Think I'll give that one a rain check,' Kaos said.

'You wanna be alone?'

'I do pretty well at it. Been doin' it for a long time before we had a change in management.'

'Well, be seeing you then,' O.B. said. He waved and followed after his companion to check the cars directly beneath the overpass.

Kaos saluted to him. 'You never know. The world got a whole lot smaller,' he said.

Episode Eight

Frailty

Chapter 1

The 5 a.m. petrichor rose from the forest surrounding the road and drifted through the crack in the passenger window of the pickup truck. Raine closed her eyes as she drank it in and listened to the song sparrows chirping their morning chorus.

They'd been driving for over half an hour and not seen one member of the new species that had repopulated the earth. Any moans or rotting stenches from nearby were masked by the serene shield of Wayne National Forest. The skies were clear above them, save a few traces of cloud vapour, scorched orange by the breaking dawn.

The events of the previous night had been so traumatic that they now seemed like they had taken place over a period of several days. Raine didn't want to think about that graveyard they'd escaped from for another second. However perfect they may have wanted it to be, it was gone – lost. And there could be no return. The only thing left to focus on was the road ahead. At least for the time being, it looked free of danger.

A short flash reflecting from the side mirror caught her attention. The morning was still dull enough to see the headlights of the Sedan behind them. 'He's signalling to us. He must want to stop,' she said.

Salty chewed at the inside of his mouth as he tried to concentrate on the winding stretches of open road. 'We're too exposed. We should keep movin'.'

The headlights flickered again – this time the flashes were more prolonged, more forceful.

Raine frowned. The calming sensation from the drive disappeared. 'Something's not right. Pull over.'

'If it's just Twilight wanting to take a piss, I'm gonna leave his ass behind,' Salty said.

'Just stop the truck.'

Salty deliberately performed the stop without care, slamming on his brakes so hard that the pickup turned and entered a skid. The sedan was also forced to brake sharply to avoid ploughing into the back of them.

⋏

Ethan fell back in his seat and slapped both hands on the wheel. 'Shit me, Salty.' He turned to the back seat and checked on the Grahams. 'Everyone OK?'

Vincent nodded, holding Emily's head against his lap. Emily gritted her teeth, cold sweat clinging to the skin of her forehead, as Kristin tightened the bandage around her leg. The married couple's eyes met and they shared a grim look. 'Do you want to come?' Vincent said.

'Of course I do,' Kristin replied.

'I'll keep an eye on her,' Ethan said.

'Thank you.' Kristin had said it before Vincent could, so he refrained from saying anything.

'Where are you going?' Emily said. She tried to pretend the bite wasn't there by looking anywhere but down towards her feet.

'Just outside to talk to the others. You'll be fine with Ethan. We'll only be a few steps away. You'll be able to see us from here,' Vincent said. He moved over so he could place her head on the back seat. Kristin did the same at the other end and exited the car.

'Daddy!' Emily said, lifting her head. 'I did what you told me to, didn't I?'

'Yes, sweetheart. You did everything I said.'

Her eyes glazed over and her bottom lip started to quiver. 'So why did this happen to me?'

'I...' Terror and utter despair clawed at the inside of Vincent's throat, sucking the life out of him. 'I don't know.' He forced a smile, jumped out, and shut the door behind him.

He and Kristin met in the centre of the road, brushing shoulders as they walked to the pickup where Raine and Salty waited.

'What's the problem?' Salty called.

Dumbstruck, Vincent attempted to blurt it out, though he could still scarcely believe it. 'It's our... our...'

'Emily was bitten when we were escaping.' It didn't exactly roll off the tongue for Kristin either, but she could say it. She'd tied off the wound. She'd seen the uneven teeth marks imprinted on her daughter's calf. She'd witnessed the blood soaking through the layers of dressing. It could not have been more real to her.

'Oh, fuck me.' Salty immediately stood on tip toes and peered into the windshield of the sedan.

'How? When?' Raine said.

'When she slipped on the ladder,' Kristin said.

'Should have told us right then,' Salty said.

'I didn't know until we got to the cars, and we had to escape that hell, remember?' Kristin said, raising her voice. 'What would you have done, Jake? Suggested we leave her behind?'

'You think I'm that much of an asshole, huh? We might have been able to do somethin' for her if we'd taken her to the medical bay.'

'With those things swarming around? Did you see how many of them we were up against? We'd never have gotten out alive. Any of us.'

'She's right,' Raine said.

'Can't we still do something for her now?' You wouldn't have guessed it from how he asked the question, but Vincent already knew the answer.

'It's been almost an hour already,' Salty said.

'The bite didn't go that deep. It barely broke the skin,' Vincent said.

'But it did break the skin, Vincent.' Kristin reached out to him, but he pulled clear of her.

'We have to amputate right now and take our chances,' he said. He tried to steady himself, blinking frantically.

Salty took a breath and prodded at the bandage around his head to scratch near the bruise he had sustained. 'I don't advise that.'

'You don't advise that?'

'That's right. Look, Graham, I'm real sorry about your kid. I ain't the most congenial guy you'll ever meet, but I sure as hell didn't want anything to happen to her.'

'Then help us.'

'To hack off your daughter's leg in the middle of the road? Even if she was a healthy adult, and we had access to a medical area – even then. We've got nothin' – at least nothin' that'll do any good.'

Vincent's eyes flared, desperately searching his mind for a solution. 'The morphine shots you took from the soldier,' he said.

'We still have them. I brought them in from the truck when we arrived,' Raine said.

'So we give her a shot, and then what?' Salty said. 'There are no antibiotics, no way of cauterising the wound without setting her on fire. Who's gonna put her through that shit? You? 'Cause I certainly ain't.'

Vincent's sweat and tears flowed along the stress lines of his face. He paced halfway towards the dipped headlights of the sedan and back again.

Kristin caressed his palm with her fingertips, if only to break him from his despair for a moment of lucidity. 'He's right, Vincent. She couldn't survive it – not out here. By the time we found somewhere, the infection would have taken over her. Maybe we should just make the best of the time we have left.'

He fixed a glare on his wife. His eyes reflected back a man she didn't recognise – one full of anger and resentment. Then the red curtain pulled back and the sadness took hold of him again. 'I'll go wait in the car,' he said.

'Vincent.'

He ignored her, wandered to the car in a daze, and got into the back seat.

'I'm sorry,' Raine said.

Kristin sniffed and drew the back of her hand across her nose. 'Let's focus on where we're going so we've at least got somewhere to hold up tonight.'

'The coast is over five hundred miles away. Travellin' cross-country to avoid the cities will almost double the time it'll take. That's before we even account for the roads bein' blocked,' Salty said.

'We aren't too far from Paden City. The nearest bridge across the river is north of here, up in New Martinsville,' Raine said.

'We could check out the byway – see if it's passable,' Salty said.

'We'll follow you.' Kristin avoided making eye contact and headed over to the sedan.

Raine began to chase after her. 'Kristin?'

'Just get us to the coast. Let me worry about my daughter,' she replied.

And so they moved on, in the direction Salty and Raine had suggested. The byway looked clear enough, aside from a few wrecked vehicles. They followed it for about 30 miles. Eventually, they pulled over and ate some of the food rescued from the visitor centre. It had been a long day. As they took their cold sustenance from a can, they could barely sit up straight. All except Raine. She remained wired and alert, sweeping the edge of the embankment outside with her rifle.

Emily didn't feel much like eating, but Vincent and Kristin managed to coax her to have some chocolate to help keep up her blood sugar. It wasn't much, and it would never be enough – they just hoped it would give them an extra few minutes with her when it came down to it.

Vincent wouldn't look at Kristin. At first, this upset her, but then all she wanted was for him to see how pissed off she was with him.

After they'd finished their unsatisfactory meal, Raine waved a stiff arm in their direction and pointed to the car, indicating she'd heard something moving around in the trees below.

Beyond the deep cyan sheen of the Ohio River, the now-dead city of Paden exuded an overpowering stillness. The industrial park, textile mill and numerous churches lay destitute, apart from the occasional distant figure staggering aimlessly through the streets. Ethan noticed several bodies floating face-down in the water. Whatever the place used to be had been erased forever. Paden had new residents – swarms of flies, come to feed on the decaying flesh that littered every block.

'She's getting warmer.' Vincent placed a hand on Emily's forehead while she slept.

Kristin delved into the backpack between her feet. She retrieved a piece of cloth and a bottle of water, then poured some of the water out to soak the rag. 'Here.'

Vincent took the cloth and pressed it against Emily's clammy skin. As soon as the cool water made contact with her, Emily was roused from her sleep. She groaned, then swallowed hard, frowning as the thick saliva went down. 'My throat's sore,' she murmured.

Vincent beckoned to Kristin to give him the bottle. 'Here. Take a sip.' He tipped it gently so little drops of fluid ran between her lips. 'And another.' He lifted it higher the second time, enabling her to take a proper mouthful.

She didn't wince after her next swallow, giving her a minute or so to drift off to sleep again in her father's arms.

Vincent and Kristin glanced at each other, neither of them even pretending to be cordial – they were heavy-eyed and pale. 'Next time we stop, we should change her dressing,' Kristin said.

'Good idea,' Vincent said.

Kristin realised that the sound of the engine had been reduced to a low growl and the outside world was now passing by the window a little more slowly. She leaned between the two front seats to see that the pickup was already coming to a halt. 'What is it?'

'Something... up ahead,' Ethan said.

As they edged further around the bend in the road, the popped hood of a car emerged from behind the trees. The vehicle was positioned across the road, blocking both lanes.

'Trouble?' Vincent said.

'Maybe,' Ethan said, squinting through the dirty windshield.

Raine and Salty got out of the pickup and proceeded to cautiously inspect this new obstacle. Ethan opened his door, immediately drawing Raine's attention.

'You're fine where you are, Ethan. Stay in the car,' she said. She approached the side of the vehicle and scanned the interior, then she leaned through the window and released the parking brake. 'Are you gonna help me move this thing?'

Salty walked around to the back and crouched down to get some leverage. Raine grabbed the wheel and the frame of the door with her other hand. Just as they began to push, someone burst from the trees behind them.

It was Darla, her eyes wide and bloodshot, brandishing her pistol.

Raine heard her first and tried to pull her rifle from her shoulder.

'I wouldn't if I were you,' Darla said, stepping much closer to her so she couldn't miss.

Salty didn't look down to his belt, but he could visualise his hatchet hanging from it.

'O.B., you got him?'

O.B. responded to Darla by showing himself. He held the revolver with a limp wrist, reluctant to actually point the weapon in Salty's direction. 'What are you doing?' he said.

'I'm savin' us, like I always do. So just keep your mouth shut, fat ass, and make sure the redneck doesn't get the jump on me.' Darla was still wearing her baggy pants and beanie, but she'd now acquired a red hoodie. A dark smudge stained its front. 'There's no need for anyone to be collecting holes today. We just want food.'

The door to the sedan creaked open and Ethan ducked his head out again.

'What did I tell you?' Raine said.

Ethan got back inside.

She then turned to look at Darla and Darla was taken aback by how the woman's eyes burnt into her. 'We have a sick child in the other car.'

'Sick?' Darla said. 'She get bit?'

Raine kept her mouth shut.

'Hey, did you hear what I said? Is she bit or not?' Darla stepped even closer, until the pistol's barrel almost touched her head.

'Yeah. She's bit.'

'Then I guess she won't be needin' any of the supplies you got. Let's have that rifle for starters. Slowly now... '

Raine unhooked it from her shoulder, making a small loop in the strap with her fingers. In the process of turning, she tightened the loop around Darla's wrist, yanked her arm towards her, and headbutted the unsuspecting ambusher on the mouth. In the struggle, the pistol went off and the bullet struck the road, ricocheting into a nearby tree.

Darla dropped the gun and fell on her ass, blood streaming from a split in the centre of her bottom lip.

In the time it took for Raine to neutralise the threat, Salty whipped the hatchet from his belt and strode towards their other attacker.

O.B. placed his gun on the ground immediately and held up his hands. 'Please, I didn't want any part in this. It's not even loaded.'

Salty stopped himself from taking a swing at his large head and instead stooped to collect the weapon.

Raine stood over Darla grasping the assault rifle. Darla was too busy wiping the blood from her mouth to pay much attention. She grimaced and gazed into the red mess that had pooled in her palm. 'You knocked one of my fuckin' teeth out.'

'By the look of those teeth, I did you a favour.'

'Ain't you the humanitarian?'

'Coming from someone who was willing to steal from a dying girl, I'll take that as a compliment. What hole did you two crawl out of?' Raine said.

'Stick it up your ass, you black bitch,' Darla replied.

'We've been down in Coolville for the past couple of days, hiding in some guy's basement,' O.B. said, much to his companion's disgust. 'Turned out to be a psycho, so we got out of there. We haven't eaten since.' The admission caused the hefty teen to feel light-headed. He steadied himself and then sat on the road in case he passed out.

Raine examined every inch of the boy, and then turned back to Darla and her blood-stained scowl. 'Ethan, bring one of the packs up here,' she called.

Salty watched curiously as Ethan brought the bag to her. Ethan took a good look at the two would-be-bandits. He seemed at ease with their presence.

'How's Emily doing?' Raine said, unzipping the bag.

'As expected,' Ethan said.

Raine pulled two cookies from their wrapper and threw one to each of their captives. 'Eat. Then move that car out of our way.'

'And after that?' O.B. said.

'You're coming with us. You can ride in the back of the truck.' She stepped forward, virtually on top of Darla, her muscular shadow looming over her. 'If I even smell suspicious on you, I'll knock the rest of those shitty teeth out.'

Salty frowned and walked over to the gun Darla had dropped. He gathered it up and gave it to Ethan. 'If the hag moves, put one in her head.'

'Right.' Ethan failed to hide his discomfort, but he took a firm grip on the gun and trained it on Darla.

Salty wasted no time in pulling Raine to the side of the road so he could talk to her in private. 'Have you completely lost your shit?'

'I'm not offering this up for debate. They're coming with us,' Raine said.

'What the hell for? I'm not sure whether you were paying attention, but Ren and Stimpy just tried to rob us.'

'We need the numbers.'

'We've been doing pretty well with what we've got,' he said.

'The Grahams are preoccupied with their daughter, and they'll be even more so when it comes to the end. Half of you is still back at that nature facility. Ethan has his uses, but he's no fighter. We need the numbers.'

'More people mean more mouths to feed.'

'If the supplies we have don't last us to the coast, it means we're never gonna get there,' Raine said.

'And if the coast's a bunch of horseshit, what then?'

'Then we think of something else.'

Chapter 2

They continued on the byway and crossed the New Martinsville Bridge, telling themselves that going to the coast wasn't just some vain attempt to delay the inevitable. What they would become if they were to fail haunted them with every mile on the clock. They needed only to glance out of the window to see their fate lying at the side of the road in pieces, reaching for them as they passed by, or wandering alone in the deep woods of West Virginia.

They hadn't travelled far on the Dolin Road before coming across another obstacle. The accident must have taken place some time ago and involved four cars. One of them had caught fire and was completely burnt out, the driver frozen to the wheel, covered in ash. The second vehicle had half-eaten remains, now infested with flies, hanging from its windows. The other two cars were empty.

Everyone got out to clear the blockage – except Vincent, who stayed with Emily. Even Darla and O.B. lent a hand, under Salty's watchful eyes.

Two of the cars were easy to shift and roll down the embankment, but the others were altogether a different challenge. The impact of their collision had been so severe, they were locked in place through their mangled bodywork and both front tyres on one of them had blown out.

In the end, they were impossible to separate, and the group were forced to flip the cars onto their side to create enough space to drive through.

Once they were a few miles from Morgan Town, Raine went to scout ahead, seeing how dangerous it would be to search for supplies and bed down for the night. She returned empty-handed and bearing bad news. She couldn't even get close to the city. The outskirts were teeming with some of its 30,000 infected residents. The place was nothing more than a feeding ground – no place for a few strung out survivors and a sick child.

After a further hour of searching, they discovered a small cavern in the forest, about 40 feet off the ground. They took the sedan and pickup off-road and used branches to hide them from anyone who could possibly pass by during the night.

They tried to make it as habitable as possible. Vincent and Kristin fashioned a bed with the blankets they had for Emily. Salty started a small fire close to the cavern's entrance.

⋏

Salty sniggered as he watched Darla pull off one of her basketball shoes. She'd clearly stolen them from a broken shop window or a corpse. They were emblazoned with bright neon colours – the kind an NBA pro player would wear.

His smirk soon faded when her dirty socks released their stale odour into the tight confines of their hiding place.

O.B. recoiled at the smell too, but judging by the look on his face, it wasn't the first time he'd had to tolerate it.

'Is it really necessary to take those off?' Salty said. 'It smells like we're spending the night in the crack of someone's ass.'

'Hurts like a bitch to walk on these corns,' Darla said. 'And by the looks of the fuel gauge on that pickup, we're gonna be doin' a lot of walkin' real soon if we don't find any more gas... I'm just gettin' prepared.' She removed one of her socks and curled her toes, revealing circles of hard, irritated skin on the ball of her foot.

Much to Salty's disgust, she began to peck at them with her grimy fingernails. He shook his head and held his nose. 'Christ. How did you live like that before?'

'You mean people always lookin' at me like I was a piece of shit on their shoe?'

'I was thinkin' more about never havin' to shower unless it rained.'

'You get used to it. You get used to a lot of things,' she said.

'I'll never get used to that stink. Hurry up with that and put your shoes back on.' Salty sat hunched over on a rock, holding his hatchet and Darla's gun loosely in his hands.

Darla barely acknowledged his comment and continued to pick at the pale yellow skin.

'What happened to your head?' O.B. said, staring at his bandage.

'We ran into some people who were better at stealin' shit than you two are,' Salty said.

'Were?' Darla said.

Salty sat up so he could look her in the eye. 'That's right.'

O.B. took a gulp. 'Y'know, we could just leave. You can even keep the guns.'

'You ain't goin' anywhere, Stimpy,' Salty said.

'He's right,' Darla said, much to O.B.'s surprise. 'We'd be better off hanging with these folks for a while. Obviously know how to handle themselves.' She gazed over to the Grahams nursing their shivering child on a collection of blankets, using a knitted sweater as a pillow for her. 'Although that's gonna be a problem sooner rather than later.'

'Well, it ain't your problem,' Salty said.

'If she starts gettin' a taste for blood, it will be.'

Darla's words sent a shudder through him, one that rattled the revolver in his hand. 'Don't talk about the kid. Don't even look at her.'

'Fine, but I'm sleepin' with one eye open tonight.' Darla finally left her feet alone and pulled on her socks.

'You do that,' Salty said. He watched Emily shake in the corner, her parents at her side, scrutinising her every breath like physicians.

'Is there anything else I can get you, sweetheart?' Vincent said.

'My legs hurt,' Emily whispered.

'Both of them?'

'Yes. They hurt more when I move, but I can't stop shaking. My head hurts too.'

'When you say hurt, you mean they ache?'

'Yes.' Emily gazed up with her big eyes. Her complexion had dulled. Her once-rosy, bubblegum cheeks were white-washed. Vincent knew he would never see the colour return to them.

'Here.' Kristin nudged him and showed him the bottle of pills in her hand. 'The meds Adam gave to us. There's some left over. They should lower her fever a little.'

He glanced at the bottle. After what happened with Adam – what he'd revealed himself to be – he instinctively worried that they contained some kind of poison or sedative to subdue a child, but he knew it was irrational and took the pills from her.

'They'll make you feel better, Emily,' Kristin said with a smile. As soon as they'd settled in the cave, she'd washed and redressed her daughter's wound, noticing that the skin around the bite had started to develop a purple hue, and the veins close to it were more pronounced.

She grabbed a bottle of water and moved up next to Vincent.

'I can manage,' he said.

'Let me help you.'

'I can manage.' He snatched the bottle of water away from her.

Kristin recoiled in shock as Vincent closed in, forming a protective shield around Emily's bed. 'Here, take these.' He placed a hand behind her head to raise her up, popping one of the tablets onto her discoloured tongue. He then put the water bottle to her lips. 'Good. Now one more.' He gave her the second pill and tipped the bottle higher. 'Take a big drink so they go right down to your tummy.'

Emily gulped hard. He then lowered her head back onto the makeshift pillow and ran his hand through her hair. 'Once they start to work, you won't shake so much.'

'I hope so, daddy.'

Raine stood up, her backside numbed by the cold, hard floor. She'd been watching the family unit fragment further before her eyes. It was not her place to get involved. Instead, she moved away from them, out of the cave entrance to where Ethan was sitting, overlooking Morgan Town. In the failing light, the city was nothing more than a dull outline against the surrounding landscape. Every now and again, there were pockets of movement, but it wasn't life. Nothing could survive down there.

It was easy for Ethan to hear her approach. He didn't turn around. He sat with his hood up and his knees tucked into his chest. It reminded Raine of the time she'd first noticed him, back at the refugee camp. She shuddered as the breeze hit her, hugging herself and rubbing her arms. 'It's getting colder. Why don't you go warm yourself by the fire for a while? It's about time for my shift anyway,' she said.

'I'm fine here, thank you,' Ethan said.

'You look it. Go inside, get some food in your belly, and sleep if you can. We're probably gonna have to fight to put gas in those vehicles.'

Ethan chuckled and then frowned, deep in thought. 'If I didn't know any better, Miller, I'd say you are more at ease with our situation than you were back at the preserve.'

Raine shrugged. 'I don't like being surrounded by fences, no matter how much land there is in between.'

'You fascinate me.'

'The feeling's mutual,' Raine said.

'I guess that's the reason we're not shuffling around in the dark like the goons down there.' Ethan again looked towards Morgan Town, the moving shadows in the streets.

'I don't know about that. The cards could have fallen differently for us,' Raine said.

'What do you make of our new friends?' Ethan said.

Raine sat down beside him and glanced back to the flickering flames just inside the cavern. 'The kid's harmless enough. The woman's a tweaker, but she's street-smart, and that's a valuable skill set right now. If we get her onside, she could be helpful. You get any impressions from them with that thing you do?'

Ethan shook his head and removed his hood. 'Not gotten close enough yet. You'll be the first to know if I pick anything up.'

Now his face was exposed to the moonlight, Raine saw how pale he looked. The dark patches beneath his eyes hollowed him out. 'You should really get some sleep. You look like a Halloween costume.'

'I always look like a Halloween costume. Why do you think Salty calls me Twilight every five minutes?'

'Because he's an asshole. Now do as I tell you and get your ass inside.'

He smiled and turned towards the entrance. Raine noticed his smile fade and a shadow of dread descend over his face. 'What?' she said.

'What do you think?'

'Emily?'

'I can't just sit there and watch her...'

'There was nothing any of us could have done, Ethan.'

'Still doesn't make it feel any better. Seeing them together, as a family, it made things that little bit more bearable, y'know?'

'Yeah,' Raine said. 'I know. Do you think they'll tell her what's going to happen?'

'Sometimes ignorance is better,' Ethan said.

She stared at him. 'No, it's never better,' she said with piercing conviction.

'You're wrong, Miller.'

'It's better that she knows,' Raine said.

Ethan leaned forward so he could run his hands through his greasy locks of hair. When he brought his head up again, his eyes contained a greater clarity, even through his fatigue. 'Salty did a pretty good job of telling that story about the Thompson case, but there's a part he missed out. There's no way he could have known. It wasn't in any of the newspapers or TV reports. Not even the police knew.

'The boy – Kenny. He wasn't dead when his parents committed him to the water. The Thompsons listened for a heartbeat, and they firmly believed their son was gone. His pulse was extremely low, but he was still alive. As deceitful as they were, they would have called the police if they'd realised.'

Raine could sense the pain oozing from him like sweat through his pores.

'Before he drowned, Kenny regained consciousness.'

'Why didn't you tell anyone?'

'Because there was no proof without the body. No way the accusation would have stood up in court, not even with my track record.'

'What about the boy's story? Didn't it deserve to be told?'

'No. It certainly did not,' Ethan said.

'Why?'

'Because when I got the impression, I felt everything. I can still taste the minerals – feel the lake water filling his lungs as he slipped away in the dark and the cold.'

Raine felt a chill race through her. It was like she was there, floundering in the water.

'What good would it have done to have people share that pain? The Thompsons were responsible and they were weak, but would tormenting them with the revelation that their son suffered change a goddamn thing? Would it bring him back?'

'No,' Raine said.

'No. It was between me and Kenny... you too now.' Ethan pulled his hood back over his head to hide his tears. 'Like I said, sometimes ignorance is better.'

Raine had nothing to come back with. All she could do was gaze down to the city below, at the shapes staggering through the night.

Chapter 3

The neon sign of the video arcade was out, just like every light at the truck-stop and the rest of Westminster. The pumps of the oval gas station were battered and scratched. They looked like someone had attempted to break into them.

The diner at the other corner of the truck-stop had been ransacked for supplies, its windows smashed, but the five rows of trucks in the parking bays were relatively untouched. Each long hauler was filled with the usual modern conveniences that allowed their drivers to spend weeks on the road.

Salty and Kristin silently weaved between the vehicles of the third row. They crouched as low as they could while still being able to jog. Both carried large gas cans. Salty held a rubber tube in his other hand, his hatchet and walkie talkie swinging from his belt. Kristin aimed her Beretta between the gaps in the parking bay, at every turn expecting to come face to face with an enemy.

Salty stopped next to a truck with a red cabin, and extended his arm to signal to Kristin. He grabbed his walkie and whispered into it. 'Anything?'

'*Nothing*,' Raine came back.

He lowered the walkie and looked at Kristin. 'OK, last one. Let's get this done.'

Kristin covered him, checking in front and behind, as he popped the truck's fuel cap and inserted the rubber tube. He sucked on it until the foul gas flooded his mouth and placed the tube into the neck of the can he was holding. He spat the offending substance onto the asphalt and grimaced as its spicy taste hit the back of his throat. 'Don't get trigger-happy,' he said. 'If you see one, I'll take care of it.'

He'd filled half of the can before he realised that Kristin hadn't responded to him. She looked northeast, no further than the towering bulk of the next vehicle. 'Do you hear that?' she said.

'Hear what?' Salty could only hear the sound of the fuel splashing around inside the drum. He removed the piece of tubing and set the can down.

It was like static on the road at first, and then it got louder, heading their way. There was no other movement in the area, and they could feel the slight tremor under their feet. Then the collective sound became more defined – the shambling walk of the dead, the dragging of trailing limbs, the gentle sway of their monotonous journey.

Salty grabbed Kristin by the arm and dragged her under the red truck. They shuffled to the middle, huddled together, tucking their legs close to their bodies.

Kristin held her breath as the walkers were almost on top of them. She stared at the two gas cans they'd left behind and wondered if they would still be able to get away with them.

The smell hit their nostrils before the herd arrived. They covered their mouths, trying not to gag. When the rotting procession passed by, it blotted out the light that had crept beneath the truck. The feet of some of the creatures were twisted like tree roots, only attached by strips of muscle and splintered bone. One of the dead fell to the ground right in front of them and was trampled as it attempted to get up again. Salty reached for his hatchet in case it noticed them, but it never did. By the time twenty or so of its brood had walked over it, its body was too crushed to get up.

Kristin covered her ears to block out the moans. However unbearable it may have seemed, they had no choice but to lie still and wait it out.

⁂

Raine peered over the trailer to the pickup and watched the dead horde stagger through the truck-stop, across the highway and around the motel on the other side. Everyone else was hiding next to her, except for Vincent and Emily, who were lying on the back seat of the sedan.

Wrapped in a blanket, the once-vibrant young girl tensed every muscle in her body. She twitched at the distant sound of groaning. Their numbers were so great that even as the first roamers were reaching the motel, the tail end was still passing through the truck-stop.

'Are you going to call them?' Ethan whispered.

'It's still too risky. We haven't heard any shots. That's a good sign. We sit and wait a while longer,' Raine said.

'Why do they act like that? Like they know where they're goin'?' O.B. said.

'Maybe they do,' Darla replied.

'Don't know about that, but I do know where they'll end up if they don't change course,' Raine said.

'Same place as us,' Darla said.

'Then we better hurry up and get there,' Ethan said. He glanced over to the sedan and the sick little girl under the blanket.

No one else said another word until the putrid parade had gone beyond the motel and into the forest. Raine stood up first, directing her cold stare at the rows of trucks.

'Shouldn't we go and look for them?' Ethan said.

'We wait.'

'Where are they? Where's my wife?' Vincent said, hanging out of the back door.

'She's coming,' Raine said. The stress lines in her forehead melted away, lifted by the sight of a man and a woman running from the opposite end of the service station, each carrying a can of gasoline.

Vincent emptied his lungs in relief and slumped into the car seat, barely able to raise his head.

'Is Mommy safe?' The voice that came out of Emily instantly chilled him and made his stomach flip over. It was pronged. She was there, but something else was there too, speaking in tandem. Something deep and alien to his ears. Not even a human pitch or tone – like an old cassette tape at half speed. 'I'm thirsty. Could I please have some more water?' She was too feverish to notice it herself, but the sound projected to ask her second question confirmed that he hadn't imagined it. This thing. Whatever this curse might be, it was taking her over.

Won't be long now, he thought.

Chapter 4

Emily slept against her mother, a damp section of torn shirt draped over her forehead. It was the first time she'd dozed off since they had left the byway. When she entered the car, Kristin had heard the chilling way her voice was distorted. So had Ethan.

Vincent noticed his wife shuffle uncomfortably in her seat. 'You OK?' he said softly.

'I'm fine.' Kristin looked away, preoccupied by her thoughts. 'Do you remember when we first brought her home from the hospital? It took us so long to get her to sleep. It didn't matter how much feeling we lost in our arms. We didn't dare move a muscle in case we woke her again.'

Vincent smiled. 'I remember.' He reached over the seat and did his best to massage the top of her arm, the one that Emily was pressed up against. 'Kris, I...'

'You don't have to say it.'

Emily began to stir. Vincent withdrew his hand, but it was too late. Her eyelids flickered and opened. She turned and frowned at Kristin. 'Mommy, I don't feel...' Her sentence was interrupted as she lurched forward and started to heave.

'Stop the car!' Kristin started opening the door before Ethan could pump the brake.

The couple jumped out of the still-moving vehicle and carried their daughter to the side of the road. Ethan immediately got on the walkie to alert the pickup in front of them.

Emily retched, and a stream of red bile projected from her mouth and splashed onto the concrete. The tail of drool from her violent purge hung from her bottom lip and reached down to the pool of blood and mucus.

The Grahams supported her from each side as she fell to her knees, clutching her stomach. 'It hurts! It hurts!' She cried out, her voice fracturing between plaintiveness and the sinister overtones of her biological intruder. 'Make it stop! Make it stop!'

'Vincent.' Kristin looked to her husband in desperation, but he was just as helpless.

As they gazed at each other, Vincent felt the sharp pain of something cutting into the flesh of his right hand. Emily had emerged from her weakened state and latched onto him, biting down between his fingers and thumb.

Instinct caused him to pull away, but Emily was determined to hold on, opening his skin with her teeth and sucking on his blood like a baby feeding from its mother's breast. When he met her eyes, he was surprised to see it was still his little girl staring back at him. Her eyes were bloodshot, her skin a dull grey, but part of her remained.

With each slurp, her eyelids grew heavier and her body more relaxed in his arms. He sensed that if he could withstand the pain, he would be able to nurse her to sleep.

Kristin wrapped her arm around Emily's neck, yanking her back violently and forcing her to release her vice-like grip.

Vincent fell onto the road, cradling his wound. Emily gasped and then proceeded to lick the excess blood from around her lips. She didn't struggle or double-up in pain anymore. She was passive.

Ethan approached from the sedan, confused as to what he'd just witnessed. 'Is she?'

'No, but Vincent's hurt,' Kristin said.

The others arrived at a sprint from the pickup to see Ethan helping Vincent to his feet and the trail of blood leading to Emily. 'She bite him?' Darla said.

'He'll be safe enough,' Salty said calmly. 'The infection don't spread unless they bite you after they're dead – after they've turned. What happened ain't no magic wand, Graham. It'll just ease her hunger, help her rest, but when she wakes up, she'll want more. They always want more.'

Kristin noticed that Emily had already fallen asleep in her embrace.

Conscious that everyone's eyes were now on him after his remarks, Salty grunted and placed his hands on his hips. 'Best get back on the road. Sittin' out here with one of us bleedin' is like presenting those bastards with a buffet cart. You can treat his wound on the move.'

He was right, of course: there was no time for an inquisition. They helped Emily and Vincent into the car, and Kristin bandaged his hand while they drove on.

Chapter 5

They took the 40 and crossed the Susquehanna River, passing through Aikin. The roads into Delaware City were blocked by makeshift military compounds and armoured vehicles. Those soldiers not completely devoured by the dead littered the streets. The reanimated ones had been partially eaten and therefore were unable to walk. Most of them rolled around trying to get somewhere, only to be set upon by birds. Their flaking skin made easy pickings. The outskirts of the city seemed totally deserted, but the familiar hum of activity coming from its centre was clearly audible.

Raine directed the group away from the sounds. She wouldn't even allow Salty to search for fuel and supplies. They were running on half a tank of gas and had plenty of food to last the rest of the journey. So they headed further north, sticking to the back roads, following the river into Delaware Bay.

As Salty had mentioned, Emily remained at ease and dozed between her parents.

Eventually, they discovered a small fishing village called Bower. Raine and Ethan scouted ahead and found that it was abandoned, most likely because its residents had escaped by sea when the evacuation first started. They brought the vehicles in and drove through the windy streets to the rocks overlooking the beach.

Raine saw O.B., Darla and Ethan scrambling up the rocks with too much enthusiasm. 'Wouldn't get excited. We'll be lucky if we find a small row boat along the shoreline,' she said. 'Our best shot is to build a signal fire.'

'And what makes you think it'll make a ship come inland? Right now, they'll be protecting themselves against being boarded and taken over, and I wouldn't blame them. There's no way I'd risk it,' Salty said.

'I'd just settle for some ammunition right now.' Raine inhaled the sea air, hoping the hit of freshness would compensate for her lack of sleep. What she got instead was an intense smell of ash, carried on the breeze. When most of the group reached the edge of the rocks, she'd already guessed why they had nothing to say.

They stood in awe of the burnt-out carcasses bobbing on the waves. Hundreds of ships, not just in the bay, but further out to sea. From clipper ships to ocean liners – nothing more than charred ghosts slowly sinking into the depths.

'They couldn't do this,' Ethan said. 'They couldn't.'

'They could and they did,' Darla replied. 'I knew it was a mistake comin' here. Fuckin' retarded.'

O.B. shook his head, unable to process the mass destruction, the number of lives that must have been condemned by fire and water. 'Why?'

'Maybe they thought they could contain the outbreak in Europe. Chances are, there were people with bites on board,' Raine said as she stepped to the edge.

'You sound like you approve,' Ethan said.

'It's a smart move if you're thinking about containment,' Raine said.

'So what's the bigger picture for us, besides drivin' around and around until we're up our own ass?' Darla said.

'There's a few houses down there.' O.B. pointed to a group of five houses on stilts above the beach.

'They were built to withstand high tide, but if a herd finds its way on to the beach, they could tear those houses to shreds,' Raine said.

'We can't relocate tonight. The kid don't have much time left. It'd be insane to deal with that situation on the road,' Salty said.

'I don't disagree with any of that.'

'So what then?'

'We need somewhere a little sturdier.' Raine examined the landscape along the shore, eventually focussing on a small lighthouse situated where the sands ended and the reef began. 'That's the place. We'll have a vantage point to see if we have company on its way.' She turned to O.B. 'You can come with me. We'll scope it out. Make sure there are no surprises.'

'Me? Why me?' O.B. said.

'You look like you could use a walk.'

'I'll tag along,' Darla said.

'No, you won't. You'll stay here with the others.' After cutting the woman off, Raine leaned in to whisper in Salty's ear. 'Watch the Grahams. I don't want it getting out of hand.'

'I won't let it come to that,' Salty said.

As Raine made her way down to the beach armed with her assault rifle, O.B. looked back tentatively to the group.

'You'll be safe with her.' Salty whipped his trusty hatchet from his belt and offered it to the frightened teen. 'Take it. I know you don't know the first thing to do with it, but it'll make you feel better.'

Darla nodded to indicate it was OK, and O.B. turned and followed Raine's path through the rocks.

'I'll go tell Vincent and Kristin what the plan is.' Ethan slipped away to the car and left Salty to keep a watchful eye over Darla. His pointed nose twitched as he observed her expression.

'For someone who's been actin' like the kid is just dead weight, you sure as shit seem awful concerned about him all of a sudden.'

Darla shrugged and her face soured like she'd caught wind of a bad smell. 'I wanna hurry this up is all. Standing out in the open with our pants down like this ain't how I've survived this long.'

'Whatever you say,' Salty said.

'Hey, I ain't the one keepin' secrets about the enemy. How did you know that daddy of the year over there wouldn't get infected?'

Salty raised his eyebrows until they disappeared behind his head bandage. 'Think I'd share that with you? Maybe you've forgotten you tried to rob us.'

'I can see Miller ain't no charity worker. The only reason we ain't dead already is cause she wants us to pitch in and be part of this group. If there's somethin' you got that can help us against those things...'

'It can't help shit,' Salty spat.

'Even so, it can't hurt none.'

'It's personal.'

'It happen to family?'

Salty moved nearer to the edge, watching the two distant figures enter the keeper's house next to the light tower. 'When the infection took hold, I headed to my ex-wife's house in Chesterfield. Every road was fuckin' chaos. By the time I got to her, she was bit. One of the neighbours did it. She was sick. I'd got sliced by this guy tryin' to jack my car and she went for the wound. That's how I know. And that's how I know it won't do that little girl any good.'

▲

Ethan shifted his weight from foot to foot as Kristin emerged from the sedan and walked over to him. She looked strained. Her blonde hair had lost its body and gloss from back at the refugee camp. Even in those cramped, makeshift conditions, she still retained a certain glamour, a glamour that had no doubt worked to her advantage in the courtroom when the world used to be more complicated. She had been sharp and clean then, but no more. The constant struggle to survive and having had to watch over her daughter deteriorate before her eyes had taken its toll. The once-attractive and confident woman was a shell of her former self. She looked her age. The lines of her face seemed to cut deeper than before, and dragged her cheeks to the corners of her mouth. 'What is it?' she asked, hushed and unintentionally agitated.

Ethan rolled open the fabric case he was holding. 'Miller asked me to give this to you when the time came.' Five morphine pens were secured inside of it by small loops of material.

Kristin glanced down and hesitated. 'I... I haven't spoken to Vincent about it yet.'

'Would you like me to hold onto them for you?'

'No. That's OK.' She snatched them from his hands before she could change her mind.

'Kristin, you know we're all here for you – both of you.'

Her eyes flickered and glazed over. 'There's three of us.'

'Of course. I meant...'

'I know what you meant. I have to get back.'

'Sure,' Ethan said.

She rolled up the case he'd given to her and returned to the car. She noticed Vincent was hunched over, virtually standing up in the back seat. Rather than call to him, she moved around to the open door. Her husband was holding up a knife dripping with blood and Kristin's heart leapt, wondering what he had done in her brief absence.

A closer inspection revealed Emily had latched onto the open wound he'd sliced into the palm of his other hand. She was now able to feed more deeply than before, drawing more blood from him.

Emily became aware of her mother's presence before Vincent. The whites of her eyes were blighted by a tapestry of veins that extended to her neck and chest, the dressing on her bite was hanging open, obviously unwrapped by her father.

'Vincent, what have you done?' she said, almost choking on her tears.

He turned around, his eyes dull with guilt and degradation. 'Her bite – it's getting worse.' He was right: the area of Emily's skin around the puncture wounds had turned a dark purple colour and the flesh was visibly throbbing in time with her weakened pulse.

'I know, but what you're doing isn't going to make her better. Did you listen to what Jake said on the road, or did you just hear what you wanted to hear?' Kristin said.

He laughed ironically, trying to temper the sting of Emily's feeding. 'Since when did you accept everything that uneducated redneck says as the authority on infection? I can feel her getting stronger with every drop she drinks.'

Emily paid no attention to their argument. She just continued to feed, taking bigger gulps until she started to gag and released her grip on Vincent's hand. Then she lay back in his arms, blood rolling from her cheeks onto the leather seat, her low, wheezing breath softening as she drifted off to sleep.

It was only then, gazing at her daughter, so helpless, so transformed by her illness, that Kristin broke and started to cry. 'She isn't getting stronger. She's dying, Vincent.'

Vincent turned his back on her to deflect the truth in her words. 'And what would you have me do? Even if it keeps her going for a little longer, isn't that worth something? Hell, you know my beliefs. This is it as far as I'm concerned; there's no ever after. Every minute is precious.'

'Not like this. With her in pain. Becoming something else.' Kristin thought about opening the case and showing him a much better solution to their anguish, but she decided it was the wrong moment. 'Go get yourself cleaned up. Salty has a kit in the pickup.'

Still running his bandaged hand through Emily's hair, he paused for thought.

'Go – before it gets infected. I'll watch over her.'

Eventually, he got up from the backseat, cradling his new, self-inflicted wound and walked to the other vehicle.

Kristin climbed inside the sedan, wiping her cheeks dry. She lifted Emily's head onto her lap and the little girl opened her eyes. 'Mommy?' The demonic voice was still present, but in her whispered, drowsy tones, it was subdued somehow. Either that or Kristin had gotten used to hearing it.

'I'm right here, baby.'

'Were you and Daddy fighting about something?'

'No. It was just something silly. You know how we can be sometimes.'

'I remember. Then you make friends again and you laugh about it, right?'

'That's exactly right.' Kristin leaned forward to kiss the top of her head.

'Those times when we were back at the house with Tugger, they seem so long ago,' Emily said. Her chronic wheeze seemed to be getting worse with every breath, stirring an ominous rattle from her chest.

'Like a lifetime away, but nothing can ever take those memories from us... nothing.'

'I love you, Mommy.'

Kristin had to compose herself so she didn't blub during her reply. 'I love you too. Now close your eyes and go back to sleep.' Before Kristin could rest her own head on the seat, Ethan appeared at the open door.

'Sorry to interrupt. Miller just got on the radio. She says the house is clear. She's going to check out the light tower, but she's sending the kid back with something to help us with carrying Emily down there.'

'I'll get her ready,' Kristin said.

⁂

From their vantage point on the rocks, they saw O.B. returning, large objects under his arm. When he reached the edge of the sand, he stopped to catch his breath. Salty had to climb down to help him. The items he'd been struggling to carry were two wooden poles and a waterproof sheet that had been used as a makeshift windbreak.

Salty realised why Raine had sent him back with it. They slid the poles through each side of the sheet and gently lowered Emily into the middle of it. With no place to hide their vehicles this time, they left them where they were and hoped no one would come by.

Vincent took up one end of the stretcher they'd made, and Salty grabbed the other. Kristin stayed by Emily's side all the way to the beach, both to comfort her and to try to keep her as still as possible. The painkillers were pretty useless now, and she cried out whenever they tilted the stretcher as they stepped over the rocks.

Approaching their shelter for the night, they saw that the light tower was built onto the reef. It was difficult to distinguish between the end of the reef and the beginning of man-made construction. The tower itself only rose a little over ten feet above the keeper's house, from which it was separated by an iron walkway. The stone foundations of the house were rife with saltwater corrosion, indicating where the tides had crashed in to surround the reef. It offered a chance for the kind of isolated existence that all survivors craved in the new world.

Now they were much nearer the shore, the winds swirled around them, rattling the railings of the walkway. Ethan stopped to gaze up to the top of the tower, which was encased by storm glass panels. The long spike of the lightning rod and grounding system were connected to the cupola roof. He stared for so long that all of the rest of the group passed him and entered the house. The realisation that he was on his own sent a shiver through him.

The interior of the house was quaint. The walls were rendered and painted grey. There was a grandfather clock in the corner, the sofas were upholstered with a floral pattern reminiscent of the 1970s, and old pedal-powered sewing machine sat on a table near the window. A smell came from the toilet, just as in most places now. Raine had already checked it and discovered that it was backed up and overflowed with water.

They set Emily down in the bedroom, still lying on the makeshift stretcher. Vincent and Kristin watched her through the open door while everyone else gathered in the living quarters.

'Do you think we should fortify this place?' Salty said.

'The tide will be coming in soon. That'll protect us from any unwanted visitors. We'll take shifts up in the tower so we can see any company on its way ahead of time,' Raine said.

'I don't like the idea of our rides out there – exposed.'

'If you wanna go sleep in the pickup tonight, knock yourself out,' Raine replied. 'We'll fix something to eat, then someone can take the first shift in the tower while the rest of us get some sleep.' She noticed that Darla was standing with her arms folded, looking at the others in disbelief. 'What's on your mind?'

'I don't know 'bout the rest of you, but I'm pretty far from OK 'bout that.' Darla pointed towards the bedroom door.

'Excuse me?' Kristin said.

'Hey, lady. I'm real sorry about your kid and all. It's a terrible shame, but I ain't gettin' any sleep knowin' what could happen during the night. I mean, she's in another room, but she's less than five feet away from us and there's no locks on the doors.'

'No one's forcing you to stay here,' Vincent said.

'I ain't the one that got bit. Look at her. She's practically one of 'em already.'

Vincent's eyes flared and he threw himself at Darla. Kristin and Ethan grabbed hold of him before he could attack her.

'She's just a little girl, you heartless bitch!' he screamed, still trying to get to her.

Salty put himself in the way and held up his scarred hands. 'I think you should take a timeout.'

'Did you hear what she said?'

'I did. I'm not excusing the way she said it, but she does kind of have a point,' Salty replied.

Out of shock, Vincent stopped struggling and turned his anger on the man in front of him. 'I can't believe this. So you and her are best buddies now? United in your condemnation of the outsider? For one second, I'd started thinking I had you wrong, but you're just like all the others when it comes to it, aren't you, Jake? Southerners stick together when there's dead weight to cut loose.'

'Come on, Graham. He's thinking about the safety of the group. We have to discuss this,' Raine said.

Vincent shook his head. 'You too, huh?'

She replied to his question with her usual cold stare.

It was more than enough for Vincent and he shrugged Kristin and Ethan away. 'Fine. I get it. I'm taking my daughter outside, and I'm not coming back.'

'Vincent, please,' Raine said.

'No, no. It's a mild evening, and we have plenty of blankets. Besides, I'm not too keen on the company I'm keeping right now. At least this way you won't have to take matters into your own hands.'

'We never said...'

'You never said it, but you thought it. I can see it in your eyes.' He gave Darla, Salty and Raine one last look of disgust and headed into the bedroom.

'I'm going too,' Kristin said. Before Raine could speak, she cut her off. 'Really, it's fine. It's for the best.'

Raine nodded and Kristin proceeded to help Vincent lift Emily from the bed in her stretcher and carry her outside.

'I'd prefer it if you kept your mouth shut from now on,' Raine said.

'All I did was say out loud what everyone was thinkin',' Darla said.

'Well, don't.' Raine turned to O.B. 'Do you think you could fix something to eat out of those bags?' She gestured to the packs rescued from the preserve. 'Don't go overboard. It's got to last.'

'Sure,' he said, immediately getting to work.

'I'm gonna take first watch in the tower. You OK holding things down here?'

'Do you have to ask?' Salty said.

'Yeah, I have to ask.'

He passed her a walkie and one of the throws from the floral patterned chair. 'Two hours and we switch over.'

'Ethan.' Raine got close enough to the young man to whisper her message. 'Watch the Grahams for me. Give them space, but keep an eye on Emily's condition, and on Vincent – especially on Vincent.'

'I can't say as I feel comfortable about it, but I'll do it,' he said.

'Good. Anything happens, anything at all, you call me.'

Chapter 6

Vincent and Kristin managed to wedge the poles between the jagged rocks of the reef so the stretcher was suspended off the ground with Emily in it. Even with blankets piled on top of her, she continued to shiver and sweat.

'I can smell the sea,' Emily said in her split voice. She started to cough, and blood coated her tongue and her bottom lip.

'Hush now. It's better if you don't speak.' Kristin wiped the blood from her mouth with a napkin.

'We decided we didn't want to be with the others anymore,' Vincent said. 'We wanted it to just be us as a family. Like it used to be.' He watched the waves crash against the beach below. 'The others can go straight to hell.'

Kristin screwed up the bloodied napkin and clenched it in her fist. 'They were right about one thing.'

'What?'

'It's almost taken over her. It will happen soon, and I don't think we should let her suffer any longer.' Kristin removed the fabric case tucked in her jeans and allowed it to fall open in front of him. 'She can just drift off to sleep.'

Vincent gazed at the small delivery units filled with morphine and broke down. He wept uncontrollably, so much that he shook. Kristin embraced him from behind and they cried together. 'Oh God, Kristin. I don't want her to feel anymore. I just can't bring myself to...'

'Look at her,' she said.

Through his tears, he could make out something that vaguely resembled his child. The infection had almost consumed her. Her breath was laboured, her eyes blood-red, her pupils dilated, her skin adamacious, gums swollen purple. No amount of denial could protect him from the reality of Emily's condition. He reached out to trace his fingers over each of the five remaining morphine pens. 'It's a shame there aren't enough for all of us. How many bullets do you have left?'

Kristin loosened her hold on him and turned him around to face her. 'Vincent, I... I don't want that. I want to carry on. If we die, her memory dies with us. We have to survive.'

Vincent nodded, as if he'd expected that reply. 'I've been contemplating it ever since she was bitten.'

'I was here. I was always with you. Why didn't you confide in me?'

'It's OK. Forget I even said it,' he said.

'How do you expect me to do that? I want to understand, so I can help you get through it.'

'To understand, you'd have to be me, and you're definitely not me, Kristin.'

She sensed the harsh undertone to his voice and understood what he really meant. She took her hands from him completely and stepped away. 'I see now,' she said. 'That's been it, hasn't it? Ever since she got infected – before that. I can't possibly fathom your sense of loss because I'm incapable of loving her like you do?'

As Kristin walked away, he snatched at her wrist and squeezed to the point where it hurt her. 'Please. I'm sorry, Kris. I don't know where I am anymore.' He dropped to his knees and pressed his head against her stomach.

She hesitated before pushing her fingers through his grey-flecked hair. 'We can get through this. We'll help each other, but we have to put that to one side for now and think about what's best for Emily.'

'I know. I know.'

'I'll do it,' she said.

Vincent stopped crying and looked up at her. 'I can't let you...'

'It's ok. I'll do it.'

Vincent thought for a moment. He dried his eyes and stood up. 'I want to help.'

'Then do what you do best.' She caressed his damp cheek. 'Talk to her. Make her feel safe.'

They were so caught up in their emotions they didn't notice Ethan approaching with two plates of food until he was right on top of them.

'I thought you might like something to eat,' he said. On each plate were some ringlets of cured pineapple, a piece of bread they had taken from the freezer at the visitor centre restaurant, and slices of canned pork. 'I turned the meat down, so you get extra.' Ethan stopped smiling when he saw how much distress they were in and the open case of morphine.

'We're OK, thank you, Ethan,' Kristin said. 'Just need some privacy.'

Ethan nodded repeatedly. 'Of course. I'll get out of your way.' He glanced over to Emily before he made his way back up the steps to the house. 'I'm so sorry.' He plodded along the walkway, taking the plates with him.

Darkness was near and the stars were beginning to show themselves in the cloudless sky, their light masked only by the persistent smog from the previous mass burning of vessels on the water. The ashen ghosts floated aimlessly. Vincent felt like one of the ships, burnt out and broken – lost.

'Are you ready?' Kristin waited patiently for his answer. He moved back to Emily's side and held her hand. It felt so cold, even through his bandages. No matter how much he rubbed and put pressure on it, the blood wouldn't flow.

'Would you like me to tell you one of my stories?' he said.

The little girl opened her eyes and looked around, as if she'd forgotten where she was. 'A story outside?'

'Yes – under the stars.'

'I don't know. I'm really tired,' Emily said.

'Don't worry. You'll like this one. It's about a girl about your age,' Vincent said.

'OK.'

'OK, here goes.' He beckoned Kristin closer and she joined them. 'In another time, in a faraway place, there was a town called Glow. A powerful magic ruled over everyone who lived there, in that they were at the mercy of the weather. When the sun shone, their hearts were filled to the brim with life and joy, but when the rain came, a great shadow of sadness overwhelmed them.

'The only person in Glow who was not subject to this strange spell was a little girl. She was always happy – always saw the good in people, rain or shine. Some of the town's folk said she was surrounded by an invisible light. Even when the weather turned the grimmest of grim, just being in her presence made everyone feel better.'

Emily coughed, hacking up some blood, which spilled onto her bottom lip and dribbled down her chin. Vincent paused to wipe it away. Once she'd finished spitting it out into the napkin, she settled back into the stretcher with a tired wheeze.

'Things stayed the same in Glow Town for a long time. Some days were bad, and others were good. Then one day, snow began to fall. It had snowed there before, but never this deep; never had the weather been this cold. It snowed for days, and days soon turned to weeks.

'The girl could not bear to see everyone so sad. They struggled to get out of bed in the morning, to kiss their children as they sent them off to school, and they couldn't muster the energy to care for their neighbours. So the girl decided she wasn't going to stand for it or see her beloved town fall into ruin. She started to visit the residents more often. She spread her light around with her presence and helped to thaw their icy hearts. Of course, they were all grateful to her for it, but the whole experience began to wear her down as the snow kept on falling.

'Weeks became months. The girl gave up more and more of her time to visit each household twice a day. Still the snows did not cease. In fact, it only seemed to get heavier. The girl never slept after that. All she could do was keep on walking from door to door, taking food and shelter while giving people the benefit of her warmth.

'The residents would beg her to slow down and take some rest. Most of them were very worried about her, but she didn't listen. She could see how vital it was for Glow Town's survival.'

Hands shaking, Kristin pulled one of the morphine pens from the case and tightened it in her grip. She struggled to even look at her daughter.

'All of a sudden, her visits stopped. Although they knew their sadness would soon consume them utterly, the townsfolk were relieved that the girl was finally getting some rest. But they were wrong.' Vincent's voice began to break. He pushed on through in order to finish the tale, fading into a whisper. 'The residents searched everywhere and eventually found her lying in the street. They tried to wake her, but they couldn't. She was sleeping an endless sleep. Everyone wept for her and wondered what would happen to Glow Town now it had lost its light. Then they noticed that the snow around her body had melted. It stopped falling shortly after. Soon, all the snow started to thaw until there was nothing left of it. The sun came out and it shone brighter than ever.

'Glow Town lost its eternal sadness and everything was right again with the world.' He smiled at Emily, tears freeing themselves from his eyelids. 'The little girl had saved them all. Although they missed her every day, they told stories about her, passing them down to future generations to make sure she would never be forgotten, and that they would always carry her light inside of them.'

'Is that the end?' Emily murmured, keeping her eyes closed.

'Yes, that's the end.'

'I really liked it. The little girl was really brave, wasn't she?'

'Yes, she was,' he said.

Emily's breathing slowed and her parents heard the fresh blood and mucus gurgling in her throat.

'Am I going to die too, Daddy?'

Vincent looked away and squeezed her hand as Kristin held the first morphine pen over her daughter's leg. 'Everything dies, sweetheart,' he said.

Kristin pushed down and injected the shot into Emily's thigh. There was no jolt from the shock of it; any sensation within her muscles had long since deserted her. Kristin dropped the pen and removed the second one. Once she'd administered it, she checked Emily's chest and she didn't appear to be breathing anymore. Nevertheless, she still took up a third pen and injected it into the same leg.

Vincent leaned over to kiss Emily's cold, discoloured forehead. 'Goodnight, baby.' The Grahams embraced around the stretcher.

⚚

Ethan had been peering through a crack in the door of the keeper's house, observing their grief from afar. He'd seen enough by that point and closed it, turning to face Salty, O.B. and Darla, a single tear rolling down his cheek. 'It's done,' he said.

Chapter 7

Dusk settled over the reef, painting every rock grey. From the bottom of the walkway, the keeper's house looked as though it was in soft focus.

Kristin sat next to her husband, the stretcher still supporting Emily's body. The blankets had been drawn up to cover her face. She'd lost all concept of time, and the outpouring of grief had left them both silent and emotionally numb. Vincent stared into space, refusing to let go of his daughter's hand.

Ethan watched them from the end of the walkway, shifting awkwardly, hands in the pockets of his hoodie.

Kristin heard the door to the house creak open, and Raine emerged holding a bottle in one hand and a gas lantern in the other. She walked down to Ethan and whispered something to him. Then she headed over the rocks towards them. She gestured to Kristin by shaking the bottle out in front of her.

Vincent didn't move. He hadn't even noticed that Raine was close by. All he did was stare into the shadows of the reef and the crashing swell of the waves, rolling in his hands the bloody napkin which had been used to wipe Emily's mouth.

Kristin had to steady herself when she got up, at least until her head stopped spinning. She stood in front of Vincent and gently squeezed his shoulder. 'I won't be long. Will you be OK?'

He didn't answer or look up. Knowing it was futile to try again, she went to meet Raine. Raine offered the water to her as she approached. Kristin shook her head.

'It's not a request. Drink it.'

Kristin snatched the bottle and took a swig. 'I thought you were up in the tower.'

'It's Salty's shift,' Raine said. 'Take the water back to your husband. He needs it just as much as you.'

'I can't promise anything.'

'I know it's probably the last thing you want to do right now, but you should eat something.'

'You're right. It is.'

'We'll be hitting the road at sun-up, and you both need something inside you for the journey.'

'Whatever you say.' Kristin turned to leave.

'Hey! I can do... what needs to be done. I'll be gentle with her – make it clean.'

Kristin thought about her grim proposal for a moment. 'I'll have to ask Vincent.'

'Kris, whatever you decide, we can't wait much longer. The tide's coming in and...'

'I know.'

'Take this.' Raine passed her the gas lantern and watched her wander back to where Vincent was keeping vigil over their daughter.

Kristin held the bottle up to Vincent's face. 'Just take a sip.'

He gazed through the clear plastic like he gazed through everything else.

Kristin soon gave up and sat down beside him. 'Raine offered to take care of Emily. I was thinking we could let the waves take her afterwards. She used to love the sea.'

'No,' Vincent said, suddenly lucid again. 'No one else will touch her. No one.'

She looked into his eyes. They were burning with determination. 'OK, we'll do it together.'

'No, Kris. You've done enough. It's something I need to do on my own. I have to be the one. I know how.' He reached around to touch the handle of the knife on his belt. 'I'll do it down by the water. I'll call for you when it's done and we'll let her go together.'

Kristin leaned over to kiss him. Their embrace was short. Vincent grabbed the lantern to light his way to the water's edge. He lifted Emily's body from the stretcher and cradled her, like he was nursing her to sleep. He navigated his way down the reef until he disappeared behind the rocks.

A few minutes went by and Kristin began to catch a chill from the rising winds. She gathered up the blankets from the stretcher and wrapped them around her. They had Emily's scent all over them. It comforted her to press the fabric to her nose – and to take it in. Within days, the smell would be gone and nothing would bring it back. In that moment, she noticed something else within it and snatched the blanket away from her face. The aroma was sullen – a signature of decayed flesh.

The footsteps on the walkway belonged to Ethan. He'd returned, carrying the same plates of food as before. 'I covered them with cling film to keep everything fresh. I believe you call it Saran Wrap.'

'That's the name of a brand. Just set it down over there,' she said.

'I'm so sorry about what happened. We'll all miss her very much,' Ethan said.

Kristin glanced over to the beach and the dark outlines of what used to be civilization. 'This is no place for little girls anymore.'

'I'm here for you, you and Vincent – whatever that's worth.'

'It's the only thing that's worth something now. Maybe it always was,' Kristin said.

Ethan smiled, and then noticed Vincent stumbling over the reef to get to them.

Kristin prepared herself to follow him back so they could finally lay their daughter to rest. The first thing she noticed was that he wasn't carrying the gas lantern. When the moonlight cast its gaze upon him, she knew something was very wrong. Blood soaked the front of his shirt – so much blood. The source of the red flood was an untidy bite wound pulsing in Vincent's neck. The flesh hung open like an unhinged door. 'I'm so sorry, Kristin,' he gargled. 'I couldn't do it.'

From the rocks behind him, she saw another figure. Its arms were flailing about as it tried to keep its balance, moaning and growling with every maniacal step. It wore a dirty ribbon in its hair; it had bubblegum cheeks and the ravenous eyes of a monster.

'Oh, Jesus Christ!' Ethan released both plates and they shattered as they hit the ground. 'Miller!' he screamed, taking off up the walkway towards the keeper's house. 'Miller!'

'I tried, but I couldn't... do it.' Teary-eyed, Vincent struggled forwards, trying to reach his wife, choking on his own blood, some of which was spilling from his mouth.

Kristin's face was cold, a blank slate.

'I'm sorry, Kristin. I'm—'

But before he could say another word, she drew her Beretta and put a bullet between his eyes. There was just enough time before he collapsed at her feet to witness the shock on his face. Without hesitation, she turned on what used to be her daughter. The first shot struck the creature's shoulder, almost spinning it around in a circle, but it re-adjusted and continued to plod towards her. The second had the desired effect, blowing out the back of its head on exit, halting the monster's march.

Ethan burst from the house, leading Raine, Darla and O.B. in a sprint down the walkway. By the time they got to her, she'd turned to face them, no hint of emotion in her expression.

Raine pushed her way to the front and saw what was left of Kristin's family strewn upon the reef. 'Kristin?'

Kristin responded by lifting her weapon, pressing the barrel into her own temple.

'Kristin, wait!' Raine held her hands high in the air and Ethan averted his gaze.

Before Raine could get any closer, she pulled the trigger.

You can find news of upcoming titles by T.W. Malpass and sign up to the mailing list via
www.facebook.com/T.W.Malpass
Or
https://www.facebook.com/EverythingDiesSeries
Join him on Twitter: @TW_Malpass

About the Author

Although T.W. Malpass is well-read, he would consider himself more a student of film than of literature. He regularly attends London's Film 4 Frightfest film festival. Like one of his favourite authors, Clive Barker, he believes that fantasy-horror is the neglected offspring of the genre and feels there is a great wealth of originality and talent to be found there.

After completing his Fallen Gods series, Malpass continues to explore other sub-genres of horror, including his recent flirt with satire and social commentary in the novella Cherry Licks.

He believes that one of the biggest tragedies in modern fiction is the lack of strong female characters. Malpass does not subscribe to the idea that a strong female in fantasy has to jump around doing martial arts in a tight costume. His female characters distinguish themselves by the choices they make. He hopes that his characters offer something a little different for both female and male readers.

Malpass occasionally writes freelance articles and movie reviews and continues to live in his hometown of Stoke-on-Trent in the UK. He would like to write at least 20 novels before he becomes worm food.

Printed in Great Britain
by Amazon